Glimpses of Reality

To Marcy

May your reality be
filled with happiness.

Karla Baker
march 2008

Glimpses of Reality

A Collection of Stories

Karla Baker

iUniverse, Inc.
New York Lincoln Shanghai

Glimpses of Reality

iUniverse books may be ordered through booksellers or by contacting:

iUniverse
2021 Pine Lake Road, Suite 100
Lincoln, NE 68512
www.iuniverse.com
1-800-Authors (1-800-288-4677)

This is a work of fiction. All of the characters, names, incidents, organizations, and dialogue in this novel are either the products of the author's imagination or are used fictitiously.

ISBN-13: 978-0-595-42180-0 (pbk)
ISBN-13: 978-0-595-86518-5 (ebk)
ISBN-10: 0-595-42180-6 (pbk)
ISBN-10: 0-595-86518-6 (ebk)

Printed in the United States of America

In memory of my father, Karl A. Baker, Sr.,
a true individual with a zest for life.

"Oh, what a tangled web we weave, when first we practice to deceive."

SIR WALTER SCOTT

Contents

Introduction

Seeing the world through cultural prisms, we pursue success in conventional ways, hoping that happiness and fulfillment will automatically result. Culture colors our world and frames our experiences. It is a shared way of living that is passed on from one generation to the next, one in which we find ourselves and create meaning for our own lives. Once internalized, cultural messages shape our consciousness and determine what we think, what we value, and what we do. Just as a colored lens distorts other colors on the spectrum, our cultural lenses show us the things we expect to see and obscure those we do not expect. Without a perspective by which to interpret and sense our way in the world, we would be immobilized.

Our sense of who we are comes, in large part, from our early interactions with significant people in our lives and from the culture. From childhood on, we all receive cultural messages about gender roles, attractiveness, and success. We are told how to walk, dress, converse, sit, and eat, and a host of other behaviors. Cultural stereotypes and media images are so embedded in our consciousness that we think of them as normal.

Growing up, our lives were governed by parents, teachers, and clergy. "Don't pick your nose." "Sit up straight." "Brush your hair." "Be polite." "Study harder." "Don't sin." We were rewarded for good behavior and reprimanded for behaving poorly. Peers taunted us for losing a race or failing a test, and rejected us for being poor or unattractive. Situation comedies like *Leave it to Beaver*, *The Brady Bunch*, and *The Cosby Show* offered ideal depictions of American life. All of these experiences provided a framework for acceptable ways of living. In time we learned what is worthwhile or useless, good or bad, beautiful or ugly, valuable or valueless. We rarely questioned widely accepted beliefs; we tended to believe what the people around us believed.

These cultural messages become a voice in our heads that praises or punishes us to the extent that we measure up to its standards. Our reliance on the culture for identity and self-worth keeps us constantly preoccupied with how well we are doing. Aiming for perfection in all things, we are perpetually disappointed. Still, like actors in a play that has been written by others, we anxiously strive to conform to our societal roles and expectations to avoid being box office flops.

The weaving of fantasy and reality takes place through a plethora of media images that pervade every aspect of our lives. We are bound by stereotypes, consumer values, and celebrity lifestyles. Television sitcoms, theatres, magazines, and commercials are filled with images of happy people living the *good life*—yachting in Southern France, driving luxury cars, vacationing in Tahiti, and residing in luxurious mansions. Happiness is for sale everywhere. These aesthetically engaging and deeply satisfying images are hardwired into our brains. Savvy marketers have convinced us that this opulent life is the perfect life. So we find ourselves working like machines or hoping to strike it big so that we can bask in the *good life* with the boatloads of money that go with it.

The American Dream is the hallmark of the *good life*—upward mobility, material success, and the pursuit of happiness. It is celebrated along with matrimony, parenthood, and attractiveness. Certainly, this philosophy of opportunity inspires extraordinary achievement by pushing us beyond our limits, but dreaming about success and realizing success are distinctly different.

Reality sets in and we find that working hard and playing by the rules no longer guarantee our success. And by conflating results (monetary mostly) with character, those who are unable to achieve the *good life* are soon jettisoned failures. "We just didn't work hard enough." In fact, the concept of "good enough" appears so out of range for most things that it is tantamount to failure. We are rarely "rich enough," "attractive enough," "smart enough," or "successful enough."

With success being vital to Americans' self-worth (we expect to achieve), any form of failure is demoralizing. And failure, like death, deprives us of happiness and hope. There is something inside each of us that causes us to think less of ourselves when we fail. Observing others who have achieved the dream makes failure all the more devastating. If we have not earned a million dollars, landed the dream job, found the perfect mate, or sculpted the perfect body, we assume that we have somehow fouled up because other people have *made it*.

Possibly our expectations have outstripped our capabilities, or reality for that matter. Yet, despite a great variance in shared experiences, millions of people continue to buy these messages and to believe passionately in the American Dream. We are no longer capable of seeing the flaws in its logic. With so many trusting wholeheartedly in the lofty expectations promised by the dream, it is no wonder that anxiety, workaholism, and depression are on the rise. Most of us seem to have forgotten that the dream (for some) is a cognitive illusion and not a statistical reality. Nonetheless, sound reasoning yields to our illusions.

Real life unfolds quite differently. Every day there are stories of romantic loss, layoffs, and personal misfortune, which suggest that the concept of "failure" is a central and ubiquitous part of the human journey. Gleaming hope and bitter disappointment exist together.

I began writing this book after the realities of my life made it impossible for me to continue to believe in cultural myths; leaving me devoid of dreams for my future. Had I not been steeped in feelings of confusion, anger, and inadequacy, I would not have needed to search for answers or to write this book. Moreover, I would not have understood the plights of others or have been motivated to share what I had learned.

Since childhood, I have been intrigued by people's lives, circumstances, and personalities. It is from my observations and conversations with friends, colleagues, and strangers that I was inspired to write a broad range of fictional narratives—some comical, a few tragic, but most all too human. Clearly failure in America has many faces. These stories are about personal lives complicated by job loss, rearing children, weight gain, the pursuit of wealth, fear, aging, failed romances, and cosmetic surgery. The portrayals are not of ideal lives crafted from perfect Hollywood scripts, but of ordinary lives influenced by cultural scripts.

Most of the characters in this book have overcome obstacles and achieved a measure of personal success. Some are married; others are single. A few have children. Most have pursued higher education. They are in their twenties, thirties, forties, and fifties—a wide range of ages. Some are coping with life's challenges, while others are struggling with their vices of choice.

Where possible I have added quips for humor. My hope is that these vivid stories will offer a way to cut through the tangled web of delusions and expectations that snag us. You may even find your story echoed on these pages or be able to relate to some of the characters mentioned. May you find this book enlightening and enjoyable.

In Pursuit of Happiness

"Happiness is the meaning and the purpose of life," declared Aristotle centuries ago. Yet there are approximately 20 million—roughly nine and a half percent of the United States' population—adult depression sufferers in this country.[1] This statistic represents a glaring paradox in a country that was founded on the principles of life, liberty, and the pursuit of happiness. To some extent, cultural and social expectations have us all in a bind.

It seems we are always looking for happiness, the spark that allows us to feel completely alive, and we envy those who seem to be happy when we are not. Life satisfaction, we believe, is ephemeral—just over the horizon—and merely a matter of getting thinner, younger, more attractive, having a baby, making a million dollars, getting hitched or divorced, buying a house or a bigger house, relocating, or landing a dream job. Conventional wisdom tells us that happiness is a byproduct of achieving the American Dream, of being rich, powerful, and good-looking.

Like most people, I believed that happiness was the result of my dreams matching my reality, a dream fashioned by the glitzy veneer of the American Dream. Seduced by the allure of money and success, I earned a master of business administration degree (MBA) and entered the workplace with the hope of becoming a corporate leader. I had pictured a phenomenal career, an electrifying social life, a grand house in the suburbs, and all of the trappings of the Dream. But the reality of my life was quite different. The job was not fulfilling, Mr. Right was MIA (Missing in Action), and other elements were missing from my American Dream—a dream that was fading fast. After ten years, I settled for a paycheck—damn the career and personal fulfillment! Despite hard work and careful planning, I had failed to achieve my life's goals. Where was the top-ranked, glamorous job that I was supposed to have after my MBA? Disappointments and criticisms were eroding the once-idealized perception of my being. In retrospect, it seems rather shallow.

Depression crept up on me in tiny increments, like a leaky ceiling that slowly dissolves the plaster, leaving you unaware until a piece of the ceiling falls. For months I walked around immersed in a dark, smothering haze. Days passed without notice. I was bored out of my mind and could not seem to get any relief. My depression created a kind of nullity where all emotions were muted except fear and anxiety, which operated in overdrive. Anxious and irra-

---

[1] Robins L.N., Regier D.A. (Eds.) *Psychiatric Disorders in America: The Epidemiologic Catchment Area Study, 1990.* New York: The Free Press.

tional thoughts interfered with my ability to cope. I would wish for sunshine, but if the sun did shine I would think, *What difference does it make?* It appeared that things would never change for the better. My life was inexplicably joyless. Instead of living fully, I was a spectator in the game of life.

Our culture is so saturated in feeling good that my walking around with a solemn face invited cheering from the cheerleading squad: "Life is not so bad," "Look on the bright side," or "Put on a happy face." Hiding behind a veneer of contentment, my world shrank. I lost interest in socializing, shopping, decorating, and other things that once sparked my fancy. Invitations to attend social events were tossed and I found comfort in my home, alone.

In our "be happy" culture, where truth is presumed to embrace negativity and cynicism, no one discusses this mystifying malady. So I did not bother to talk about my condition. Moreover, I was living the kind of life that some people believed was enviable in some ways, which made it more difficult to readily admit what I was experiencing. I knew that I was in bad shape when my mother told me candidly, "If you don't change your thinking, you're going to end up in a straightjacket locked away in the nearest asylum just like Jamie Ellen." (Miss Ellen was an eighty-year-old, bitter, prune-faced woman who, unable to bounce back from disappointments, suffered a mental breakdown. She walked around the city in a horrid black coat fastened so tightly at the neckline that people wondered how she could catch her breath.) My mother has zero tolerance for self-pity; she is a find-a-solution person. I resisted seeking professional help and decided to try to work my way through it.

The following day I purchased a stack of journals. Soon after, at every free moment, I recorded my feelings and beliefs little by little. I recorded beliefs about my job: "If I work harder, I will succeed," "I should move up the corporate ladder," and "I should be rich." The belief about my beau was that "My boyfriend should make me happy." Beliefs about life in general included "I should not have to suffer," and "Life should always go my way." I was so caught up in the myths about life, love, and success that some aspects of reality were nearly alien to me. It was soon apparent that most of these *shoulds* were irrational and demanded change. As I started to hear my own voice, it was soon plain that my view of success, life goals, and my career pursuits were simply cookie-cutter versions of the *good life.*

After months of retreating, blaming, and cycling through bouts of sadness, I was getting back on track. I generally pride myself on my reasoning ability, so I was doubly frustrated by my inability to pull myself out of the slump overnight. I decided to face life. I soon realized that my distress would not be relieved with plaudits, trite clichés, or facile solutions, but only with my own choices and resilience.

Making new choices, even though I felt that fate had dealt me a terrible blow, helped to enlarge my perception of the world and myself. I had a greater sense of awareness; everything was clearer now. My life was heading in a new direction. True wisdom seems to be a byproduct of unpleasant experiences. Once we learn new lessons, we are less likely to cause our own suffering in the future. If we are lucky, we can share a portion of what we have learned with others so that they too may see themselves and their lives with renewed appreciation.

Acknowledgements

I am elated to have a finished product. Let me begin by offering gratitude to my parents for their unconditional love and support, and for seeing the best in me. I am delighted to thank my editors, Dr. Keflyn Reed and Gertrude T. Small. Several of my friends were my soundboards during the writing of this book, and I am grateful to them all: Ernestine Wilkins, William Pierce, Janice Marks, Tony Lee, Marcy Clark, R. L. Phillips, Renee Sharp, Keith Phillips, Susan Alston, and Prince Charming. I also offer my gratitude to my family and friends who have enriched my life and encouraged me to continue writing when my motivation was running low: Gertrude N. Baker; George Nettles, Sr.; Lola Nettles; Dr. Andre' Smith; Robert Nettles; Julian Nettles; Dominica Bryant; Dawn Raspberry; George Alexander; Kara Bryant; Larry Bowie; Vernon Hart; Lennie Smith; Kathleen Smith; Rev. Marshall Nettles; Abraham Nettles; Jerrell Nettles; Nicole Henderson; Bianca Evans; TaJuana Mitchell; Dr. Bette McGee; Patricia Barrett; Barbara Brown; Richard Hughes; Chris Outlaw; Joyce Lewis-Barrett, Esq.; J. H. Hart; and Clifford Merchant—and to those I have not mentioned but who I hold close to my heart. All of these people deserve my profound thanks.

To Kim Melichar, Brenda Kluck, and the editors at iUniverse for believing in the project and moving it forward, I extend warm thanks. My thanks go also to Kathrine Rend for a stunning cover and for helping to shape this book in its final form.

Lastly I would like to thank the people who told me their stories of love, loss, beauty, aging, layoffs, divorce, dieting, and success for their invaluable contributions, which helped to bring the richness of life to these pages. Thank you.

1 Success

Money, Ambition & the Lure of Success

JANUARY 1995

We have produced a culture in which work is our primary source of identity. Scores of people practically kill themselves by focusing all of their energy in one facet of their lives—work—and still they are rarely satisfied. Yeah, I am referring to the culturally celebrated and glorified workaholism that secretly claims the joy of scores of people each day. In workplaces throughout the country, employees are tested on their capacity to handle stress and demands, and pressures from employers mount to see if they "can take it." Absenteeism is penalized, assumed to be a symptom of a lack of commitment. Heart attack victims are pitied, mental breakdown sufferers are dismissed, and those who do not move up the ranks are written off as corporate failures.

Gavin Miraldi lived in a city jammed with racing workaholics where it was customary to brag about endless workdays the way cocaine addicts would not dare brag about their addictions. Work was a place where people fell asleep with their laptops and cell phones. Fresh out of college and ready to make my mark on the world, I met Gavin at Catauga Power Company (CPC). CPC was located in Catauga County, Tennessee, a conservative town in the heart of the Bible Belt, nestled between the Appalachian Mountains and the Cumberland Plateau. The scenic ridges and lush valleys in this region were breathtaking. Once a polluted manufacturing hub, Catauga had undergone a tidal-wave transformation and was now a thriving metropolis.

Like most new hires, I wanted to blend into the corporate world by adhering to the company's unspoken dress code. I did not want to look like an American tourist in Paris. Dressed in traditional corporate attire—navy suit, crisp white shirt, and navy pumps—I was introduced to Gavin, who was one of the company's most celebrated employees.

For a time, Gavin was a valuable associate for me, offering professional feedback and encouraging me to take on high-profile assignments. As a newcomer working for a leader in the industry with a solid management team, I was destined to be a successful corporate warrior. I was challenged, given responsibility, and delegated interesting work. My evaluations were quite good.

Gavin was in his mid-forties with an olive complexion and dark hair. Decked in Armani suits, with that *Forbes* cover quality, he was the consummate corporate executive. Gavin fulfilled the stereotype of what the company believed an executive should look and act like. He had mastered the art of self-promotion. Equipped with a dynamic personality and impeccable social graces, his career took off without a hitch. Gavin thrived in the competitive rat race that was a source of misery for many.

When I met Gavin, he had been working in corporate America for nearly twenty years. A graduate of Ohio State University, he had worked in the energy industry for fifteen years and had been with the company for five. Idolized by many of the minions in the lower ranks, like me, Gavin had risen to the top ranks in the company. We all wanted the salary, power, and praise that hard work and good fortune had bestowed on Gavin. What was not apparent to most of us was that his life was one-dimensional; he had a singular fixation: success.

Gavin was employed with Catauga Power Company as a senior vice president of fuels and had received several commendations for his exceptional work. Within three years of joining the company, Gavin's staff was responsible for a $175 million highly leveraged, non-recourse financing of a 300-megawatt, gas-fired, combined cycle project. The project went over without a hitch. "When I received my award, my boss told me that they'd never had an employee quite like me before. It's great to be praised. I was flying high!" an elated Gavin recalled. With each success, Gavin's pride inflated like a balloon at a Macy's Thanksgiving Day parade.

As part of his function, Gavin played an active role in establishing policies and rules for new competitive markets, and provided oversight in plant operations, fuel management, and environmental and regulatory compliance. For a while, everything went well and Gavin saw a solid future and confidently believed the company's mantra that it employed only "the top of the line."

Life for Gavin was one of seemingly endless workdays, disappearing vacations, and excessively long hours, and he was fast approaching burnout level. He had climbed the ladder of success by working long hours and taking on extra projects, often sacrificing time with family. "I head to the office around seven a.m. and I'm usually there until eight p.m. On most days, my assistant picks up my lunch and leaves it on my desk. The guys complain that I don't play golf much anymore or meet them for drinks after work. 'You've ditched us for your job!' they tell me. I just don't have much time for leisure anymore. My family calls me 'estranged.' Last year, I managed to squeeze in a week for vacation."

Because most of his self-evaluation was based on achieving, Gavin had nearly worked himself to death to be successful. "My annual salary, plus bonuses, is now over $400,000. It feels good to believe that you're indispensable in an otherwise bleak job market." The thrill of hard work was so gratifying that he hardly noticed that he spent more time at work than at home and he'd missed his daughter's preschool recital, his son's baseball games, and a series of other momentous events.

After Gavin was hired as a senior vice president, he immediately set his sights on being promoted to chief executive officer. "That position offers more latitude, huge bonuses, and a tremendous amount of power," related Gavin. To ensure his success, he frequently worked on multiple projects when he could have easily delegated them to another staff member. True to form, he was hailed the "Lone Ranger."

What Gavin did not know was that he was a candidate for the most insidious and tragic kind of exhaustion due to intense pressures for achievement and rigid self-demands. The bottom started to fall out as Gavin took on more job responsibilities than he could handle over the long haul, and the quality of his work started to slip. More, his intense desire to succeed combined with the family sacrifices put a strain on his marriage, which only compounded his troubles.

Gavin had invited me and another newcomer to observe a preliminary presentation for the Executive Committee. This was a small group, so we met in Gavin's office. The walls in his office were covered with motivational posters and a few framed photographs of Buckeyes' sports stars. An orange ceramic football bearing the Tennessee Volunteers' logo was strategically placed near the rest of his Buckeyes' paraphernalia. He was, after all, steeped in Vols' territory. After the review meeting, we talked during a coffee break.

"How's work, Kay?" Gavin asked.

"Going well," I replied.

"Good," he said.

"Everything okay with you?" I asked.

Visibly irritated, Gavin told me, "Kay, home is hardly pleasant. No one in my house gives a damn about how my day went, and I don't bother offering details."

"Sometimes we slip," I said.

"You said it," Gavin replied, his voice rising with annoyance. "My family thinks I'm an automatic teller with legs."

"Oh, it's a dad thing."

"Yeah, we're the lucky ones," he snapped. "Take my wife; she's never really understood my need for achievement. Her goals were accomplished when she married and had children."

That last remark conjured up stereotypes. "Okay," I said.

"Hell, what does she care as long as the paychecks keep rolling in?" he said, his features sharpening.

"I'm sure she cares."

"The kids are always bickering," Gavin continued.

With a wide grin, I said, "Sounds like total excitement."

Gavin wasn't amused. "They have X-Boxes, plasma TVs, and iPods, thanks to me," Gavin said.

"I bet."

"But nothing I do is enough for them." It seemed that Gavin was expecting love and admiration in return for his gifts. He had gotten neither. Sometimes it is hard to tell if our gifts are demanding or loving.

"Gratitude will come later," I said.

"Sure," he said. "No wonder I've lost my enthusiasm for life."

"Oh, that happens to best of us."

But Gavin's career was his life. "I get rave reviews at work; it's quite fulfilling. I feel complete there. But nothing at home."

Leaning towards me to ensure that he had my full attention, Gavin said, "I am at the peak of my game with a house in the suburbs, a wife, kids, a great salary, and a status job. I have all of the trappings seen in *The Family Circle* magazine."

"You're a poster boy for the American Dream," I said, smiling.

"To some extent," he said, looking directly at me.

"I'd say."

"Working hard and rearing a family fosters the illusion that all is well with the world," he continued. "My wife and I sometimes feel that we've made it based on what we've accumulated."

But obviously a slice was missing from their happiness pie. I finished off my cup of coffee while Gavin wrapped up the conversation.

"Life," I said.

"This is the way it goes," Gavin sighed.

After nearly two hours of sitting, I stood up, excused myself, and walked back to my cubicle.

Ambition had lengthened Gavin's workweek and tampered with his home life. Over time Gavin's misery faded into the scenery, unnoticed like the static in an old TV. He actually believed that his life could not be any better than this. Gavin's quandary had a familiar ring to it. I had heard similar accounts from couples who were living in homes worthy of HGTV and sleeping like mannequins, cold and stiff, in luxurious bedrooms, uninterested in touching each other.

After working at a frenetic pace since joining the company's management ranks nearly five years ago, Gavin's productivity had started to decline. Moreover, he had failed to streamline his division. Those in charge noticed that he was no longer cutting costs, and his division was affecting the company's ability to react quickly to changes in the industry. Catauga Power Company had a major reorganization and the new power lords named their choices for key management positions. Gavin was ousted. According to Gavin's superiors, his management philosophy was "too aggressive" and he expected too much; and he was itching to do it all himself. Although they recognized his intelligence, articulate speech, and ambition, they still considered Gavin inflexible and too cocksure. Good companies need proper management to grow. They were looking for someone with confidence tempered by humility—someone more team-oriented who knew how to delegate, not some maniacal corporate climber.

The day Gavin got his walking papers, we chatted for a few minutes in the corridor. Gavin was a casualty of corporate war (restructuring) and he reacted bitterly, blaming his boss and staff. Although he tried to be optimistic, he was overwhelmed with resentment and felt discarded and used. "At my level, the company spits men out left and right," he said. Falling from the corporate sky was a real shock for Gavin. "This is the first time that I've experienced failure. The jackasses gave me a month to wrap up my biggest projects and offered me six weeks of severance pay for my time," Gavin snarled. His unfinished projects were reassigned or ditched.

Perhaps Gavin could have handled all of this better if he had not sacrificed everything to be a success. But that was not the case, so he was doubly riled and he openly denigrated his boss and his staff. Gavin had always believed that exceptional work, willing conformity, and wholehearted loyalty tied him to the organization. Maybe he did belong to the company, but only in a tenuous way. "At the end of the day, my exceptional work performance proved of no significance to the company," he said, emptied of his near-manic ambition. Gavin's feelings of worth and professional competency were entirely eroded by the incident. He now wanted revenge that was harsh and swift. "These son-of-a-bitches will pay for wrongfully terminating me!" Gavin yelled while leaving the building.

Intense pressures placed on him to be the breadwinner compounded Gavin's problems. "It's easy to get a feeling of importance from being a big moneymaker with a top ranked company. And I did. It was proof that I had what it takes." But Gavin could not see that his compulsive drive to be successful was destroying him. That fabulous cocktail of money, acclaim, and opportunity can be addictive. "It was hard to break free," he told me.

We live in a society that makes men feel ashamed for not being millionaires who wear well-tailored suits and drive expensive cars. Men may not need to be young or attractive to have worth, particularly if they have swapped youth and attractiveness for wealth and power. Still, that doesn't let them off the hook. Far too often men work themselves to the verge of collapse to prove to themselves, and others, that they can live up to some monolithic potential. Understandably, men in the workplace who are totally devoid of ambition don't last too long. It seemed as though Gavin had been driven by his ambitions and fears. He hoped to avoid being a failure.

On the brink of marital collapse and unable to face the snide remarks about being zapped, Gavin distanced himself from his friends and family. His wife was panic-stricken about his job loss and could not talk to him without yelling and crying. "Mortgage! Tuition! What are we supposed to do now?" yelled his wife. But he did not hear it, because he had mentally checked out. For months Gavin endured sleepless nights, headaches, and bouts of depression, fearing that he would be blackballed in the industry. After all, he had been a manager and he clearly understood the impact of back door conversations that could make or break an employee or keep him from moving up the ranks.

Better Angle of Vision

Several months after the firing incident, I saw Gavin at Circuit City and some of his anger had subsided. Now that Gavin was no longer spinning, he had changed his outlook and managed to find some humor in his misfortune. "I was wearing thin, trying to climb the ephemeral ladder of success. But after being stripped of my position as vice president, I had to learn to be okay with who I am instead of my rank."

Gavin regained his confidence and accelerated his job search efforts. With his impressive credentials, it didn't take very long for him to land a new job with a smaller company.

"My new position is less demanding and pays a competitive salary," Gavin informed me.

"Sounds like you hit the jackpot this time," I said.

"It sure looks like it," Gavin said happily. "I'm a better person now."

"That's great."

"Before the firing, I had a permanent restlessness. I wore a thin skin and was always defensive. I walked fast, talked fast, and processed a thousand tasks in my mind in a second," he said, proud of his incredible abilities.

"You worked like a machine."

"Hell yeah," he laughed. "I was so into my job that I would be thinking about projects while I was making love to my wife."

"Oh boy!"

"My whole being was wrapped up in work."

Gavin, like me, had been wired to get a measure of self-worth, within the company, from his salary, position, and performance reviews. Work was a safe place to hide his true feelings. It was similar to how alcoholics drink and compulsives clean to hide their feelings. But Gavin had seen the light, which toned down his edginess.

"I feel better since I took off my Superman cape," Gavin told me. "I've realigned my priorities and I no longer have to prove anything to have worth."

Constantly proving one's worth takes a great deal of effort. When we believe that we are valued and liked for what we produce, we can never produce enough. Things were also improving at home.

"I actually have a much better quality of life and can spend more time with my family," Gavin said happily. "Feels like my wife and I are on a second honeymoon," he continued, clearly pleased with the way things turned out.

"I'm sure they're all glad to see more of you."

Gavin was well on the road to recreating the American Dream; for him it was no longer solely about money.

"Although a comfortable standard of living will always be attractive, maintaining a reasonable standard of living while doing work that I enjoy is far more exciting," he told me.

Further, he now had the time to coach his son's team once a month and volunteer for community-sponsored charitable events.

"I get more enjoyment out of each day now than I did when I was working myself to a pulp. I'm happier than I've been in a while," he added.

"Glad to hear it," I said. "I'll see you around."

"You bet," he said. "Keep those lights on!"

We laughed and then walked in opposite directions.

Gavin was back on track. His career and love life were in harmony; life had a sweet timbre and a proper fit, and he was no longer chasing the dollar. Driving home from work, I started to think about how Gavin's near obsession with his career had tipped his overall life success in the opposite direction. Reflecting on Gavin's life taught me something else: Although workaholism is considered an admirable trait in our culture, it has the potential to doom us to frustration and failure. Gaining competencies is excellent, but idealistic pursuits are the villain. While Gavin was pursuing the coveted CEO position, hoping that his life would eventually rise out of the doldrums, it did not. The rush of glory from our achievements rarely stays with us for long; it is quickly replaced by the need to accomplish more.

The value of work cannot be minimized. Work makes us feel useful, needed, and productive. It also gives structure to our days, providing us with an income and a way of demonstrating our competence. At a point in my life, I had a near-neurotic need to excel, but later I began to see the light. Workaholics are revered and put on a pedestal for the amount of work that they do. Many people applaud themselves for being workaholics, and others envy them for working so hard. Work can have an anesthetizing effect on negative emotions, but at the end of the day all of the fears and insecurities that we have been trying to escape remain.

Opportunity Costs

MARCH 1996

Madison Olsen suffered with good judgment but bad timing. Not long after graduating from college, she went to work for one of the giants in the energy industry, which, at its pinnacle, crashed, leaving thousands without jobs, savings, and pension plans. But there was more to Madison's life. "I can't find an eligible man anywhere," she'd said. Madison had been dating unsuccessfully, with a few disastrous attempts at love since college, and now worried about making time to meet the right guy. Recently, she had turned to Internet dating and matchmaking services in hopes of meeting the perfect chap. When all else fails there is always high-tech coquetry, though hardly a novel approach to matrimony. Madison longed for romantic evenings and sexual intimacy. Sure, she complained like hell that the men were nothing like their profiles, but she continued her quest nonetheless.

By now, I had been working in the energy market for several years and was employed as an energy trader, which is where I met Madison. Madison, intelligent and ambitious, was part of the go-getter culture that did not have time for leisure. Her job was her life. She sacrificed leisure, skipped time with family, passed on dinner invitations, and postponed romance and having children—in pursuit of the *good life*. But her salary was impressive.

Madison, in her early thirties, was a stunning brunette with a tall, model-like frame. She was charming and followed professional protocol: tailored

11

business suits, couture of course, an ear length bob, and minimal makeup. Material success had become the end-all of life and Madison knew that motto well. She was an energy trader who worked in an intense environment surrounded by a bevy of young men and women, most under forty, who were striving to hit it big and cash out. In a few years, they could retire and really live the *good life*. During my tour of Mega X's trading floor, Madison told me, excitement rising in her voice, "Mega X teaches that money is the only objective measure of human worth. And we've all memorized that ethos."

After graduating from the University of Texas at Austin, and doing a stint with Reliable, Madison landed a job with Mega X as an energy trader. For a while, everything went well. Madison was flying high, earning more than $180,000 a year and quite proud of her success. "Deregulation opened the doors to landfall profits and caused the trading of electricity to explode," Madison said.

Mega X evolved into an environment where employees trampled the opposition using a combination of ruthless drive, deception, and sheer brute force. But Madison was hardnosed enough to survive in this "take no prisoners" business world. She simply shelved those aspects of her job that did not contribute to the bottom line.

Madison's day started at six a.m. with her screen crammed with weather forecasts, real-time price feeds, and position updates. Armed with data influencing energy supply and demand, Madison started buying electricity, betting that a heat wave or cold snap would materialize and drive market prices upward. If the market moved as Madison predicted, she earned a few thousand for the company. Her success hinged on how fast and accurately traders could interpret the information. Split decisions could reap huge profits or cause the company to lose millions.

The bulk of the people on the trading floor worked hectic twelve-hour days with minimal breaks, forgoing holidays and weekends. In this environment of high stakes and high profits, most people burn out in five to ten years. But the money is so good that no one sweats working nights, not taking a vacation, or missing time with loved ones. "I have friends at work who are quite nice," Madison remarked. "But off days are a real bore. I can't wait to return to work," she continued.

She did not have any close friends near, but working made her feel complete. And Madison was doing a great job at work. However, beneath the laughter and personal triumph was a feeling of emptiness, a painful sense of aloneness that was growing more acute with each passing day. If other aspects of Madison's private life were more satisfying, she probably would have been happier.

Still, life was rocking along for the most part, until her company landed in the center of a national scandal. Suddenly her picture-perfect world started to crumble. Madison was losing her position and subsequently her house, status, and sense of self-worth. Vitality soon gave way to frailty. Madison and I attended a PowerMarketing meeting together just when things were really falling apart. Dressed in a black Donna Karan suit and Prada shoes, she was at the meeting to network and maybe land a new job.

Before the fallout, Madison was headed straight for the top. Max Brighton, the Senior Vice President of Power Trading and Risk Management, recruited her based on a recommendation from the CFO of one of their subsidiaries, Reliable Energy. The American Dream was in reach, and Madison was living the life. She had purchased a Lexus convertible and a house in an exclusive complex in the I'On Village near Charleston, South Carolina. Madison was also a regular at the upscale trendy clubs and restaurants in the city, thanks in part to her expense account. Mesmerized by seductive advertising and the glitter of shopping malls, she filled her shopping bags with a slew of couture pieces and designer handbags, and a few pairs of Manolo Blahniks to polish the look. "I hate being one of those fashionably inferior people," she'd said, with a gleam in her eyes.

One step from really making it, and everything was going up in smoke for Madison. Her corporate gold cards and four-figure bar tabs would soon be gone. Most Mega X employees were painfully aware that outside of their company their title was devalued. There were only a few places in the industry where traders could make this kind of cash.

Though everyone in the industry was affected by that shake-up, most were able to land new gigs with other companies despite the glut in the energy market. But Madison's confidence was evaporating and she was sweating her future. "In a few weeks, I'll be out on my ass. Flat. Busted. And my company stocks are worth nothing," she moaned. Madison was starting to go downhill. She stayed out late and drank as much as she could afford. No longer one of the brat pack, Madison wanted to die. "My glory years and all hopes for a dream career have ended," she lamented.

Madison bottomed out for a few months, but then she realized that her life was not over. When I last talked to her, she was back in the game. The past few months had been a nice vacation from the pandemonium and offered her some time to reflect.

"Kay, I graduated from UT at Austin believing that the world worked for me," Madison said.

"I think all recent graduates have that feeling," I said.

"Part of my motivation for getting an MBA and working like a maniac was to impress my peers—all graduates of top schools like Wharton, Kellogg, and Tuck," said Madison. "I wanted to prove that I belonged."

"That's normal."

Madison had great trading skills and knowledge of competitive electricity markets, so she parlayed those talents into an energy-consulting firm that catered to large utilities.

"The company is still new, and I do miss the nice salary I had with Mega X," said Madison.

"The money will come."

"As my own manager, I feel incredibly free to be myself."

"You're one lucky chick."

Madison had found her niche and was thriving in a much calmer, yet equally challenging work setting. Prior to attending graduate school, I wanted to be an interior designer; but I needed financial stability and didn't think that I could earn a living decorating. I knew the jobs were in business at the time that I graduated. So I earned a degree in statistics and later went back for an MBA. Sometimes life comes full circle. Being able to love what you get in life and to make the best of it is where real satisfaction lies. But it seems that few people get that opportunity. Most of us are working to live.

A Closer Look

Madison was smart but always felt the urge to aim higher, to outdo the competition. And that meant more money too. Though she had been a National Merit Scholar and had attended a top-ranked university, in her opinion, she was minimally successful. Madison always expected more from herself. That she was single and attracting all of the wrong guys did not help matters, and she blamed herself for her dilemma. Madison's business had been operating for nearly six months and she was soliciting work with Catauga Power Company. After giving a brief presentation on market dynamics and hedging to CPC's senior traders, Madison was given a tour of the complex. In keeping with business etiquette, the division hosted a small reception after the tour. I attended the reception. Once we'd filled our plates with hors d'oeuvres, Madison and I grabbed two seats in the row of chairs along the wall.

With a bad case of the "No Wedding Bell Blues," Madison was swimming in a pool of agony and self-doubt. Those who were close to her considered her an unmarriageable woman who had squandered her youth by being too ambitious, too strong willed, and too picky. Madison felt doomed as she lamented her circumstance. "For a while I wondered if there was something hideously wrong with me," she said with wry bemusement.

"That thought has crossed my mind a few times," I told Madison, "but I've concluded that I'm okay," I said with satisfaction, folding my arms.

I knew that feeling of questioning one's worth well. I had noticed the stares, particularly at weddings, from people who, after learning that I had crossed the twenty-something threshold unmarried, averted their eyes and conjured up personal theories of what could possibly be wrong with me. Surely there was some valid reason for my status. Their stares translated into "What did she do to drive the men away?"

All of Madison's sisters were married in their early twenties. Madison did not have all of the checkmarks needed to complete the "success package." And she was not making much progress. "I was competing with my siblings, and their marriages made me feel inadequate, like a failure," she recalled. Before now, Madison had always considered herself the leader of the pack. Though she wanted to marry a guy so that her family and friends would be sick with envy, she had overlooked several obstacles that kept her from pulling off that feat. Madison had not been focused on marriage until recently. And she failed to consider that she had entered the workforce right out of college and had jumped all over the globe chasing the dollar. She had also worked grueling hours, and she was meeting guys who were not marriage material, all of which steered her away from paired happiness.

Though Madison romanticized about being a stay-at-home mom, her reality was quite different. As Madison's life came into view, she knew that a life with no family, no intimacy, and no close connection to others was no kind of life at all. She needed balance.

"Sometimes I feel that I'll never find the love of my life or have children," Madison said downheartedly.

"I haven't met my knight in shining armor either," I said.

"Maybe the supply of eligible men is shrinking."

"Sure seems that way."

With the media portraying single women as weepy neurotics who are hysterically tracking down a spouse or frigid workaholics who have chosen high-profile careers over matrimonial bliss, it is no wonder that most women try to avoid the infamy. Bachelors are envied and single women are pitied. *Where is the justice?* I thought, throwing my arms in the air.

It seems that far too few women are willing to challenge the perception that all single women are miserable and desperately seeking husbands. Maybe it's pointless; their voices would likely be muted under the deluge of messages promoted by movies, books, and magazines on how single women need to stop being picky, selfish, or unsightly, and find a mate fast. It is quite bizarre that an entire industry is being built on exploiting women's anxieties.

In the absence of love, Madison worked. "Working those grueling hours at Mega X and raking in the cash made me feel valued and accepted," Madison said.

"I bet."

"I didn't have a family, but I had a great job," she said evenly. "And the perks were good too."

"That's a good thing."

"But the contentment was always fleeing."

Somehow raking in the dough did not make her feel good for long. Periods of exhilaration after a success were quickly deflated by a desire to climb further up the ladder.

"Call it ambition," I said.

"In part," Madison said, "but slowing down and seeing your life as it is can be scary."

Madison thought that she needed to be a tremendous financial success to feel whole. But the competition has ended now, and getting to know herself has been its own reward even if it was not reflected in her career or salary. Sometimes we burst our own bubble by raising the bar and believing we need more money and another promotion in order to be happy. Madison's life is more balanced now. "I have friends, read great novels, practice yoga, write poetry, host dinner parties, and do all sorts of interesting things," she said with glee. "I'm finally learning to appreciate the pleasures of ordinary life," she said with a new sense of confidence.

Madison glanced at her watch. "I have a plane to catch."

"What time?" I asked.

"In an hour," she responded. "Gotta run."

"Okay," I said. "Have a safe flight."

"I'll call you," she said as she walked out of the conference room.

Often we pour all of our energies into our jobs to compensate for not having a life away from work. Maybe our family relationships are tense, our romantic life is vanishing, or our social life is the pits. Work is a safe haven where we feel needed and accepted. We become so fixated on our jobs that the only emotion that we experience is the pleasure of having completed a task. There is nothing like the quick ego-building aspects of a job well done. Plus, working hard is far less menacing than tuning in to needs that have been muted out. In the meantime our needs for genuine self-esteem, intimacy, and close friendships remain unmet. Reflecting on the ordeals of Madison and Gavin, it was becoming clearer to me that we all have needs that cannot be met entirely by our careers. Sometimes people don't need more money to feel better, they just need a life.

Now I could see that there were two ways to respond to life's challenges: face them or escape them. Both Madison and Gavin had chosen the escape route initially and worked to numb their discomfort. But they later rebounded and created for themselves a life that was perhaps more suitable for them than the frayed narratives of their former lives. Plainly, exaggerated ambition can exceed the results it obtains. This pursuit of an unachievable goal may yield little satisfaction other than the pursuit itself.

Bright Lights Fade

DECEMBER 2002

Ellis Sasser drifted into drugs to avoid working through his painful emotions. It was a splendid way to divorce himself from reality, which was not where he wanted to be. Before long, partying and having fun escalated to a compulsive drug use to meet his emotional and spiritual needs. And it was this gritty drive to escape that lay at the core of his addiction.

I'd met Ellis at the Sun Festival in south Florida in 1992. Ellis was good-looking, tall, broad-shouldered, and muscular, with a smug demeanor. With a macho swagger, he had a habit of grabbing his crotch as if he were making sure that his manhood was still in check. As one of the performers at an event that was sponsored by my old company, Cell Tech, Ellis was part of an industry that reveled in excess and he was soon caught up in the mix, out-snorting and out-drinking his peers. Fame creates insecurity faster than it fills voids with money and adoration.

Ellis flaunted his drug habits and other antics. "One night I was so stoned, I blacked out in an alley and woke up in a pool of vomit," he'd told me once.

After a few months on the music scene, Ellis was lauded as one of the year's biggest newcomers and pop sensations. His first release was filled with chart-toppers. Success, for him, was like a veritable elixir that made him feel good enough. Ellis was swept into a fantasy world of money, fine cars, groupies, and star-studded parties that temporarily hid his personal issues. But his pop started to fizzle out when his second release received a lackluster radio response and failed to ignite sales, entering the charts at number twenty. Music critics lambasted his CD calling it an "outright flop." With music sales faltering, company executives at SoniDisc canned him. When the concerts ended and the acclaim and adulation died, Ellis' reality check bounced and his world collapsed.

Shortly after this incident, I'd booked a flight to Miami for a weekend getaway. I ran into Ellis while hanging out with friends at Sundays on the Bay, an amazing seafood restaurant in Key Biscayne with the best reggae music in Miami. As soon as we stepped through the bamboo doors, I spotted Ellis near the bar and walked over to meet him. Flashing a big grin, he gave me a hug. I introduced Ellis to the crew shortly before a handsome waiter escorted all of us to a long communal table near the water. The waiter, speaking with a faint British accent, took our drink orders and quickly returned with a round of frozen mango margaritas. Ellis and I caught up on things between reggae performances as the sun set over the bustling marina.

"What's up?" I asked Ellis.

"Not much," he replied, his voice trailing off a bit. "What's up with you?"

"Still working for CPC," I said, "and trying to carve out a bit of excitement on weekends."

We both laughed.

"Kay," Ellis continued, his mood shifting, "I've been screwed again by those cut-throat bastards in the industry."

"Things were going so well," I said. "I'm sorry to hear that."

"Yeah, me too," he said. "Damn, I miss the crowds, the vibrations from my guitar, and all of the excitement of being on stage."

"There are other labels."

"Not for me, Kay," he said, as anger flared up. "Shit, I've blown it. Everything is ruined!"

While raging, Ellis was unaware that he was reliving not only the pain of his sacking but also the recent split with his girlfriend and a multitude of other losses and rejections. He had failed too many times and now felt completely helpless.

"As soon as the bright lights dimmed and the shopping sprees ended, that gold-digging bitch left me high and dry. Everyone wants to fucking use me!" he continued, his heart pounding against his chest.

Most of the villains in Ellis' stories about his life's disappointments were women—girlfriends as a rule. For weeks following his being dropped from the label, convinced that he was seizing the moment and living life to the fullest, he woke up every morning and snorted coke and drank gin until he passed out. Ellis was creating an artificial sense of happiness when his life was in shambles. "When I'm high, I feel confident, invincible, and perfect," he said.

Ellis' world had been ripped open and all of his flaws were exposed. His carefully constructed presentation as a moneymaking macho man—one who suppressed his feelings—was being destroyed. As the rungs on Ellis' ladder of opportunity weakened, so did his feelings of worth. He started to hate himself for not being enough. "Tons of people are blowing up in the industry, doing their thing, and I'm not doing shit. I don't give a damn anymore," he said, his voice full of defeat. "I have no life, no self," Ellis concluded.

Pleasure Highs

Ellis was ashamed of his failures and weaknesses. Without fame and wealth, he felt like a nobody. "It's a scary thing to have once been a big name and to then have nothing," he admitted. Plagued by feelings of worthlessness, negative self-evaluations convinced Ellis that he was not good at anything or important to anyone. It was impossible for him to see his opportunities in this state of mind. His suffering was multiplied by the feeling that he had exhausted all of his options; it was slowly killing him.

Holding tightly to the belief that other people controlled his life, Ellis abdicated his personal power, giving up the throne. Each self-inflicted assault was like medieval bloodletting, slowly draining the courage out of his body.

"Those assholes robbed me of my self-esteem," Ellis raged. "Now, I'm dealing with depression and addiction."

"That's not good," I said.

"I was hooked before I knew it. I mean, we were all driven insomniacs with shot nerves," Ellis recalled, his tone anxious and chatty. "One night my friends offered me some coke and after the first hit I was hooked. Now I crave it … can't get enough," he confessed.

"Ever consider going to a treatment facility?"

Peering at me through glassy, bloodshot eyes, resembling a lizard on weed, he shot back, "They don't work."

"Okay," I said. My last remarks nearly sent him into orbit.

"I'm trying to save myself," he said through cracked lips.

"I wish you the best," I said, trying not to feel sad for Ellis; he was having a really rough time.

"Everybody has used me," he said with his voice deepening and slowing. "It's hard."

"I'm sure."

"I'm okay right now," he said. "But every day is a struggle."

I nodded and didn't say a word.

"You have no idea what it's like because you're not an addict," Ellis continued, his voice filled with grief.

"You're right, I don't."

Cocaine entered his Garden of Eden like a serpent providing Ellis with quick lifts and a feeling that he was good enough. For a time he was free and happy. But his drug-induced orgasm was quickly replaced with fear and rage. When he returned to his normal life from time to time, he was weighed down with self-reproach and heightened addiction. Unable to cope, his cycle continued, and he was indulging in the next pleasure to temper the pain of excess. Ellis' urge towards excess was fueled by a reckless effort to fill the deep holes in his soul formed by loss, emptiness, and shame. The more he smothered his feelings, the more he needed drugs to numb his pain and to avoid *the crash*.

The drugs had already taken a toll on Ellis' body. He had lost so much weight that his muscles sagged and his frame protruded through his sallow skin. Old scars covered his hands. With sunken eyes and a gaunt face, Ellis looked like death eating a cracker. Ellis' good looks were a distant memory. His folks lived in fear of getting a phone call from the county morgue.

When the Party's Over

Although some party people get lucky and never experience the horrors of addiction, Ellis did not. Now he was trapped in a cycle of tragedy. After a night of bingeing, Ellis shuddered uncontrollably and clasped his hands to keep them from shaking. His thoughts were scattered and he wanted to die.

"When I get high, sometimes I feel like shit the next day. My body aches, my stomach burns, and my eyes feel like they're going to pop of out my skull," he confided.

"I don't know how you stand it," I said.

"Nothing makes me feel as good as the drugs. I've never felt anything like it," he said with his eyes averted from me.

We talked on and off, during intermission, about his life and his busted career. The concert ended after midnight and we all left the club together. It took a few minutes for the valet to drive the cars around to the entrance.

"Nice meeting you all," Ellis said as his car arrived.

"Same here," my friends said in unison.

"Kay, send a word up to the Big Guy upstairs for me," Ellis said as we hugged good-bye.

"I will," I said.

Ellis got in his car and drove away. Minutes later, the valet delivered our car. We tipped the valet and headed to the city where Art Deco buildings were accented by bright neon lights, and palm trees lined the streets. Despite Ellis' news, it had still been a fun night.

Ellis was living in that hidden seam of street drugs from where some people never come back. When Ellis came down and crashed into the earth, his pain was always there. He was not aware that without his escape mechanisms he was just another human being who was filled with fear and a spiritual yearning. Pleasure is simply another way to drown out underlying fears. Much like feeling in love, pleasure engulfs the senses in a beneficial way. Our problems disappear and we feel joyful, relaxed, and free. But too much pleasure comes with a high price: it numbs not only pain and fear, but also the mind, spirit, and ultimately life.

Vivid Sight

Ellis had fallen short of his goals, just as I had. Instead of honing his skills or finding a new agent, he rationalized his firing by levying fault and totally withdrawing from the rat race. Had he been more concerned with becoming a better musician as opposed to creating an image in the industry, perhaps his loss would not have been so excruciating. Nonetheless, Ellis had failed in a nation that worships success, and by equating his failure with his identity and not an outcome, his identity was smashed.

Ellis suffered with a kind of magical thinking that told him that he could avoid the unpalatable truths in his life by blotting them out. But Ellis was overloading his brain's pleasure centers and depleting his feel-good transmitters, prohibiting further pleasurable sensations. Clearly, Ellis' attempts to stave off his reality had failed, as reality has a way of sticking to us, like Amazon leeches, hard to dislodge and revealing itself in pain, anxiety, and depression.

It was clear after seeing Ellis that he was sinking in a sea of helplessness. Unaware, his own catastrophic thinking was undermining his ability to cope. Fragile feelings of worth interfered with his ability to see himself realistically and to take responsibility for his own mistakes and deficiencies. Ellis desperately needed to shift his focus away from his problems to his opportunities. With the proper resources, beliefs, and coping skills, he would likely overcome his addiction and live a productive life.

Until Ellis decides to accept responsibility for his problems and his life, and to use his intellect to manage his emotions, he will likely continue to accept his fate. On the other hand, if Ellis hones his coping skills—his ability to handle life's irritations and disappointments—he could succeed as an artist or a partner or anything. As his capacity to solve problems increases, he will probably regain his courage. He has a chance—and he needs to take it. One day maybe Ellis will stop resenting life just because some of its outcomes have been painful.

There are no celebrations or plaudits for taking responsibility for one's own life. But the personal rewards are enormous. Having a sense of power is one of the ways out of addiction. Courage is that unseen force that enables us to endure life and to feel okay even when life gets hard. With courage, life is not so intimidating and we feel that we can handle whatever it offers. Sure, other people can affect us, but with courage they cannot control or destroy us.

Our feel-good society tells us that we should banish unpleasant feelings like sadness, anxiety, and depression, which tell us that something is out of balance. But if we dampen our emotions, we may never improve our condition. Bad feelings can sometimes spur us to overcome helplessness. A great many of our accomplishments involved some small failures, something we had to overcome (e.g., a skill or personality deficit). When we circumvent feelings of failure, we make it more difficult to achieve a sense of mastery. We also forfeit the opportunity to gain strength from our life experiences. Now, when I am tempted to run from my problems, I think about Ellis and others like him, and I hang on and keep trying.

Widening the Lenses

A largely held American fallacy is that there is a quick-fix solution to every problem. When pain arises—job loss, divorce, death of a loved one, or abuse— we habitually reach for a palliative relief, which is most often temporary. We tend to plaster over loss, stress, pain, and anxiety with shopping, alcohol, sex, drugs, or overeating. Although most of us are aware of the potentially harmful effects of unbridled sensual pleasures, we still indulge in them to varying degrees. We all love to celebrate happy occasions: holidays, birthdays, weddings, and promotions. Happy people will toast in the New Year with a glass of champagne or celebrate the completion of a taxing project with a cold beer. Libations can make us feel carefree and alive. But unhappy people often keep the party going and overindulge purely for pleasure's sake.

Ellis expected a powder to magically remove his sadness; it did not. If one is depressed because of events like job loss, financial pressures, body image distortions, or divorce, drugs will not make those problems fade away. Sometimes we cause our own suffering and life requires that we shift our perspective and make positive alternative choices.

Time is needed to sort through the muck and mire of life's experiences and to come to terms with less favorable attributes and painful thoughts that are interfering with our happiness. Moreover, we have to realize that life may not be as we would like it to be. But we can do ourselves a favor and try to live our best lives in our current circumstances with what we have been given. There is no blaming others or playing the victim role; we simply must take responsibility for our feelings, which may well be one of the greatest achievements in our lives.

Living on the Fringes

Though our quest for fame and fortune has produced impressive results, economic mostly, in many ways it has created an opposite effect. Connecting with people has never been more of a challenge than it is today. The incidence of loneliness has reached pandemic proportions. A startling number of people today find themselves isolated and bereft of close friendships, thirsting for a sense of belonging. Indeed, the pleasure of good company is a rare experience for many.

The transient nature of our society has ushered in a new kind of life. We now live in a world of unlimited mobility and countless opportunities for education, employment, entertainment, and lifestyles. We order food to be delivered to our homes, we shop online, we rent movies, we work at home, we e-mail, text-message, and we fax, all while diminishing the number of meaningful face-to-face interactions between and among us. More, we don't make eye contact and we rarely know our neighbors' first names. These new trends, combined with our fiercely ingrained individualistic attitude and our need for expediency in every area of our lives, leave us abysmally alone. We are usually relying on our diversions of choice, our therapists, our spiritual advisors, or ourselves to handle the challenges of daily living. This partly explains why Internet chat rooms, dating services, and other chancy means of curing loneliness are booming.

Where Do I Belong?

Where do I belong? It's one of those age-old questions that we all ask at some point in our lives. Our lives revolve around frequent interruptions and relocations, which happen whenever we graduate, or get a job, or get a better job, or our company slashes staff, or we relocate to a new city.

Our frenzied search for wealth appears to have eclipsed the importance of close interpersonal relationships. Fed on the myth that our individual success makes life worthwhile, we pursue our professional goals, leaving our support systems behind except via travel or telephone. Life becomes a matter of sowing our career oats, strengthening our romantic ties, and building our own lives. Our friends are preoccupied with their lives and establishing their own identities. New friendships are made and forsaken in a short time. Close ties are lost. Everything is expendable. We pack up and move so often that we are leery of forming deep attachments in the communities we inhabit, so our new associations are often artificial and tenuous. These are a few of the prices we pay for upward mobility. This was my life.

Living in Catauga, I was feeling like a total outsider who did not fit into the conversation, much like a new spouse at a family reunion. It is difficult to get a sense of belonging in a place where natives are embraced and outsiders are seen as trespassers. Coincidentally, many of my friends, also transplants from New York, Virginia, Florida and other distant lands, had a similar feeling. After talking with them and others about my condition, I realized that what I was experiencing was simply part of a cultural malaise. Although we all chatter about close friendships with other people, our desire to keep our private lives separate from others seems to rule our choices.

I was just one of many who, for a time, felt a profound sense of alienation and isolation. Since it is culturally humiliating to admit that one is lonely, I did not bother. In this culture where sizzling romances and happy families rule, such a confession can evoke a cringe followed by pity and downright repulsion, as if it were a contagious disease. So I decided to learn how to conquer loneliness on my own. For starters, I dated like a mad woman, volunteered for every imaginable community service project, and hosted small dinner parties on weekends. Then that got old, so I tried to reconnect with my friends from college (all of whom were living miles away from Catauga) with moderate success. Needless to say, I spent quite a few empty weekends imagining that I was in Jamaica at the Sumfest or dancing in the streets in Miami at Calle Ocho or attending a fabulous A-list party. For a time, it seemed that everyone was having more fun than I was—until I talked with Shelby.

Chasing the Dollar

In a culture of unbridled individualism and competition, we now define ourselves based on our individual achievements and not our relationships. Competing for rewards and popularity, we see people as obstacles or enemies, which exacerbates our loneliness.

Mason and Shelby Winslet were included in the staggering number of Americans who moved in 1998. It was that classic tale of the leading spouse chasing a career dream wrapped up in the excitement of yet another move up the corporate ladder. Shelby trailed behind, leaving her career, friends, and 401(k) retirement plan. Few people seem to work at any one job long enough to build a steady career or retirement savings.

I'd met Shelby, an eye-catching blonde with soft features, at my first job in New Jersey and we'd kept in contact over the years. After moving from place to place, Shelby had the unbearable feeling of being alone, left out, and unplugged. Shelby was in Catauga for a business seminar, and we met for dinner at the classy St. Jean's Restaurant—a fabulously restored former hotel lobby with bright yellow walls and marble counters. The hostess escorted us to a table for two. Literally seconds later, a waiter appeared and we placed our orders: an entrée of sliced Kobe beef with roasted potatoes for Shelby, and grilled lamb chops with asparagus for me. After confirming our orders, the waiter walked away.

Looking up from the menu, Shelby said, "I'm living in the land of soccer moms and SUVs."

"Welcome to the club," I said with a sense of resignation.

"It's a helluva shock to my system!" This bit of information was followed by a roaring laugh, and then she continued, "I don't want my mother's life—not yet."

Shelby and Mason had recently relocated to Mesa, Arizona. On the advice of friends, they had moved into a family-oriented community, which was not the wisest move for a cosmopolitan couple with no children. These world travelers enjoyed such cultural amenities as the symphony, theater, and art museums. Soccer games and backyard cookouts were not exactly their cup of tea. But Mason had adjusted. He had easily settled into his job; he played racquetball and had drinks with his colleagues outside of work. On the other hand, Shelby was wishing that she had a pair of ruby slippers to magically transport her back home.

"Kay, we've lived in five cities in nine years," Shelby said.

"Wow, that's quite a bit," I said.

"My husband moves around for the sake of adventure and hefty paychecks," Shelby said, her doe-like eyes wide.

"We all want the big bucks."

"Yeah," Shelby sighed, "and what a trade off."

One waiter removed the salad plates just as another one arrived with our entrées and two bottles of sparkling mineral water.

Every time Shelby and Mason relocated, she left behind another job and another set of friends only to go where no one knew her, to start all over again. She needed someone other than Mason to confide in, someone she could relate to. That was just the personal side. I've skipped around a bit too, so I know what it is like to keep starting over again. Though relocating can be frustrating, it can also be quite rewarding.

"You're gaining new skills, which boost your resume," I said.

"I guess," Shelby said.

At work, Shelby had a new set of bosses who had no idea about her capabilities. She had to work twice as hard to prove herself, and Shelby wanted to make a good impression. It didn't stop there; Shelby was also earning less leave, had less flexibility, and had less job enjoyment.

"Changing jobs can be draining sometimes, and quite lonely," Shelby muttered. "You feel sort of isolated in a new city."

"So what's a girl to do? Shop?"

"Works for me," she chuckled. "Sure beats worrying about my new job, financial losses, and severed friendships."

"I agree."

In some ways shopping has become a substitute for human relationships. It is as if we hope to gain a sense of identity, purpose, and joy from buying things. But I could not afford that hobby for long. I was forced to find a cheaper way to entertain myself. Perhaps the biggest knock down for Shelby was that she had no identity.

"For someone like me who has always been independent and self-reliant, this kind of life is a real challenge," she explained. "Now I have to rely on Mason for practically everything."

In the meantime, Mason was living it up. He had kept most of his friends because he worked for the same company, just in a new location. Though Shelby was working with people of similar age, she nonetheless felt wretchedly isolated.

"Despite my best efforts to shape my personality to fit more comfortably with my staff, I am failing miserably," Shelby said. "No one understands me."

This feeling was compounded by the sight of others who seemed perfectly at ease in the office. Some were making friends and forming cliques, while Shelby was merely tolerated on the margins.

"It makes me wonder if there's something wrong with me," she said with angst.

"I understand, Shelby."

Shelby looked skeptical. "Really?"

"Yeah," I answered. "There could be something incredibly right about you."

"Never thought about that," she responded, dabbing the corner of her mouth with her napkin.

"Maybe your background, values, interests, intelligence, experiences, ambitions, or a host of other things are considerably different from your colleagues," I continued.

"You're right; we simply don't relate to each other," Shelby said.

I said with confidence, "It takes strength to be yourself, even if you don't fit in."

"You're not kidding." Then she bellowed, "Oh, Auntie Em, take me back to Kansas! I wanna go home ... I wanna go home."

"I wanna go home!" I echoed in consolation. "Let's click our heels three times."

We both laughed.

The waiter cleared the plates away and we paid our tabs and departed the restaurant. I drove Shelby to the Reeve House, a lovely hotel located on Broad Street, just a few blocks away from the restaurant. We pulled in front of the hotel.

As Shelby opened the car door Shelby said, "Thanks for the lift."

"Sure, no problem," I said.

"Let's keep in touch."

"That would be great," I agreed.

Shelby waved and then disappeared through the sliding glass doors.

It was difficult for Shelby to absorb that at a point in her life she had lived an active life where she met new people daily, circulating with new clients and employees. It was also hard for me to believe that several years ago I had a fun and exciting life. I attended Broadway shows, football games, professional mixers, concerts in the park, dinner parties, and the like. This was just par for the course, I concluded. It's a new day in Old Town. Perhaps constantly aching about living away from family and friends, when the rewards of one's career seem hardly worth the sacrifice, is a signal that one may need to move closer to family. Life is about balancing demands and making choices. We must all decide what we need at our core level and then make provisions to get it.

Feeling Disconnected

While solitude is often desirable, none of us wants to experience the distressing ache of feeling disconnected and lonely. We all yearn for the physical closeness of others and of being in the company of people with whom we have common interests. Connecting is essential to our happiness. Sure, hearing a voice on the other end of the telephone is better than not, and an encouraging e-mail is better than no communication at all. Personal relationships that are binding and close give meaning to our lives because they show that even if the world is indifferent to us, we matter to someone.

Nowadays, many of us are seldom afforded the opportunity to socialize in familiar surroundings; changing our situation may require developing a new circle of friends. That could mean reaching out to others first instead of waiting for them to talk to us or invite us over for pizza or a movie. Talking to people in the lobby or saying hello to people we pass on the staircase is also a way to connect when we are new to a city.

In my experience, one of the best ways to break out of the loneliness trap is to try to understand others. Seems strange, but it works. It may also help us to understand ourselves a bit better. Showing a genuine interest in other people's lives and an appreciation for them as individuals feels good because it helps us to connect with others. But Shelby was not feeling at her professional or social peak, which made engaging in social activities more difficult. That had a familiar ring to it. We often allow our thinking to close us off from potentially rewarding friendships with others. But life is much happier when lived in the company of other people.

Clearer Lenses

A new view of loneliness was emerging for me. Since high school, I have lived in eight cities, and in most of them I did not know a single soul prior to relocating. Each time I relocated, I was a little jittery, but things improved rather quickly. Within weeks, I would meet new friends and join in the festivities and delights the cities had to offer. It was exciting to see new places and to meet new people; I loved the experience. It takes courage to interact with strangers and to maneuver through cities by one's self. With time, the fear of being alone starts to fade. As we become accustomed to being by ourselves, and taking care of our own emotional needs, the fear no longer terrifies and stifles us. We eventually feel contented and connected in our own company.

Strangely enough, I have felt lonely in the past few years—totally disconnected—even in the company of people whom I've known for several years. Shelby was married and still feeling lonely. It seems that when people say they are lonely, they do not like being in their own company. Being in the company of hundreds of screaming spectators at a football game would not significantly affect how alone one feels. Loneliness seems to happen when we are least tolerant of our own human flaws and frailties. During these periods when we are most sensitive, we simply feel disconnected.

Aloneness is an inescapable part of the human condition. We enter the world alone, we order our lives alone, and we leave the world alone. Surely our lives are joined with others for a time, but we remain separate people. Simply being alone is not something we should panic about; in fact, some actually delight in the thought. Solitude nurtures our emotional maturity, spiritual growth, and inner being. When we are alone, we discover who we are and what we really want. In the stillness, we discover life. I can see now that being alone is not a problem for those who believe that they can take care of their own needs and be happy. It is a problem for those who cannot fathom the possibility.

Buying Worth

SEPTEMBER 2004

Viewing frequent portrayals of fanciful well-heeled lifestyles—ones to which ordinary people could now aspire—stimulated an image of how Trent Mabry should live. For years he was hooked. The cumulative effect of these images would alter Trent's thinking and create a kind of restlessness that would govern his behavior—only the biggest and the best for Trent.

While ordinary people are better off than ever, nevertheless, the super rich have become a permanent fixture in our brains, continuously prodding our sense of what is essential to live happily. Trent, like most children, grew up looking at the images of the flashy American Dream and was fascinated by the magazines and television shows like *Lifestyles of the Rich and Famous* that celebrated the rich. Flashes of $3 million dollar mansions, $120,000 convertibles, Dolce and Gabbana suits, yachting on the French Riviera, dining at five-star restaurants, and bulging stock portfolios were reflected on prime time television and in the movies. As Trent matured, those clever advertisements, infomercials, and billboards continued to appeal to his yearnings, convincing Trent that he needed to buy more to be happy.

Trent, burly and husky-voiced, was a survivor from the ruins of the American Dream. With good fortune and entrepreneurial flair, he'd joined the elite ranks by starting a construction company and making it thrive. At forty-eight, Trent, a pillar in the city, was by all appearances living the dream. In our town, Trent was somewhat of a deity and was considered by most to be the epitome of success: he owned a business, hosted lavish parties, drove expensive cars, and lived the kind of life for which most people only wish. He was a true rags-to-riches story that we could see and feel. Life had not always been rosy for Trent. Trent was all too familiar with the misery of belonging to the wrong class and the ensuing prejudices that accompanied it.

A group of us, including Trent and his wife, had gotten together for the Catauga Fall Festival. After purchasing hot dogs and chips, we all strolled through Cooley Park, admiring the brightly colored leaves on trees near the Tennessee River. As we walked, Trent told me more about his background, and the first thing he said was:

"As a kid, I felt underprivileged, inferior, and envious of others."

The children who attended his school looked down on him and mentally tortured him for being poor, cementing his beliefs. With each passing day, Trent grew increasingly more insecure, watching the gap between his needs and circumstances widen.

"You have no idea what it feels like to grow up with nothing," Trent told me.

Trent's own family slipped in and out of poverty as his dad's employment fluctuated with bouts of heavy drinking. His mother, weighted down with her own vices, could not give her children the love they needed. Trent often dreamed of having nice clothes, toys, and a happy family, like other kids. After growing up with so little, he had every reason to dream of material success above all else.

Like the average American, Trent believed that in order to be on the fringes of what he considered "doing well," a person needed to be very wealthy, have a successful career, a happy marriage, and a measure of panache. More than anything, Trent wanted to be accepted in the right circles of people. In the absence of a better plan, Trent made the pursuit of wealth a primary goal in his life. There was one big problem: Trent believed he lacked the attributes needed to be successful. Growing up, he was not hunk-handsome or popular, and he did not shine on the basketball courts. Plus, Trent was an apathetic student who considered himself a nobody, and this belief kept him in the trenches, at least for a time.

Memories of poverty and rejection fueled Trent's ambition, driving him to prove to the world that it had not defeated him. His path to fame and fortune was like a frenzied cross-country road trip with a few blowouts along the way. After working several dead-end jobs, he landed a gig as a day laborer, where he discovered that he had a knack for construction. Prompted by his supervisor, Trent enrolled in technical school and received his certification in several areas, including carpentry and dry walling. Two years later, with a small business loan and a bond guaranty in hand, he started bidding on construction projects.

Business took off without a hitch and Trent, working with his new partners, transformed untapped residential markets into valuable assets. At its peak the company earned millions. As Trent's income rose, so did his confidence and status in the community. He had only been in business a short time by industry standards and had already received several awards, including two from the Chamber of Commerce.

"Finally, I'm getting the respect from the community," he said.

Most of all, he could afford the kind of life that he always wanted. But this was only part of Trent's goal. The following year he married Raquel, a gorgeous woman who had been the senior prom queen from his high school, and immediately started his family. Raquel was really impressed with his ambition and lifestyle. Trent purchased a pleasing home in a gated community—the best that he could afford—and showered his wife with roses, trips abroad, and expensive gifts. Few knew that his self-worth was invested in what he owned. Finally Trent had arrived; he had achieved the American Dream and now considered himself a success.

Trent told me, absolutely exhilarated, "I have it all! Anyone who's rich and miserable isn't spending his money right!"

With images of the cherished *good life* fastened around Trent's neck tightly, he embarked on frantic shopping sprees rooted in competition—keeping up with the Joneses on a grandiose scale. Making money and buying became as natural for him as breathing. It appeared that Trent hoped to keep up with his neighbors, advance his status, and if possible arrive at some materialistic winning post.

Longing for more of the *good life*, Trent shaped himself into the image of upward mobility, all while conveniently disposing of details of his disadvantaged past. It was his best attempt to ward off ego threats from others. Trent was making his rounds, attending celebrity-type parties, and rubbing shoulders with the big boys.

"I'm hobnobbing with the best people now," Trent said. "I can finally look down on all of the people who have looked down on me."

He loved to compare himself to those who had written him off, like his former classmates with leaner pockets. In Trent's circle people were judged by what they owned and how they looked.

An elated Trent offered, "Powerful men talk about their salaries, beautiful wives, country club memberships, million dollars homes, car collections, and 150-foot luxury yachts." Trent, bursting at the seams, continued, "When you're making a few million a year, that kind of dough just makes you feel powerful and invulnerable. Hell, it seems that I can buy anything I want."

Nothing thrilled him more than flaunting his success. Trent liked the things that his money could buy and he liked to brag about them. In his insecure moments he tried to reassure himself that he was top dog. Using his possessions to define his place in society, Trent began to think that his financial success confirmed that he was as good or better than other people. But beneath his public persona, Trent felt like an imposter in a line-up and lived in fear of being exposed. He was living, what author Henry David Thoreau coined "a life of quiet desperation."

Does Net Worth Equal Self-Worth?

With all of his success, Trent was finally happy; well, almost. Trent was hosting one of his celebrated end-of-summer cookouts, and we talked while he added more shrimp shish kebabs to the grill.

"You're living the life!" I told Trent.

"I have it all!" He responded raising his arms in the air. "I have a successful career, a beautiful wife and two children, a lovely home, and all of the status a man could want. If I'm not happy, then who is?"

"Who is, is right," I said, smiling.

"Honestly, sometimes I'm not sure if I'm happy or not," he said, wiping the perspiration from his face with a white cloth.

"What do you mean, you're not sure?"

"Well, when I earned my first million I was ecstatic, but that feeling didn't last for long."

"Say what?"

"Sure, I love my new lifestyle, but I can't say that I'm much happier than I was before," Trent said, his words very precise. "Sometimes I think that happiness is just an illusion."

"Wealth is good, but maybe happiness is elusive."

"Yeah, something like that," Trent continued. "Life in my circles can get too demanding, too pretentious, and quite exhausting—it's a high price to pay."

I sensed that maintaining his lifestyle and image was rather stressful at times. Still, half the world is killing themselves to get where he had gotten.

"Are you kidding?" I said.

"It's not just the money. I'm not poor by any stretch, but I'm not the richest, either."

"Wanna trade bank accounts?" We both laughed at my reply.

Perhaps even more disturbing for Trent was that he had not tamed his raging insecurities about his looks, growing up in poverty, and not being a part of the inner circle. Whenever he reflected on his childhood, he experienced a profound sense of shame and deprivation. Trent told me, "I would go into debt to escape that feeling."

Wealth, it seemed, had not spared Trent from pain and suffering. Plus, he just couldn't seem to get enough money to feel secure. It is odd; in the absence of economic challenges, we tend to create stress in other areas of our lives.

In truth, Trent was only moderately happier as a success than he had been as a failure. Rich or poor, he lived with a fear of failure and being snubbed by others. Having wealth had failed to make him feel safe and secure; he never experienced a sense of freedom, of letting go. Instead, Trent's new-found status elevated his insecurities and expectations of personal fulfillment. Plus, Trent was still not comfortable in his own skin, so he was still jockeying for acceptance in the top social tier, yearning to be sprayed with their status juice all while feeling like an outsider.

Regardless of what Trent did have, he never stopped thinking of what he did not have. Surely there is nothing wrong with wanting the best, but pursuing excessive wealth and hoping to gain a sense of satisfaction and happiness had yielded the opposite result for Trent.

The party ended and Trent walked his first wave of guests to their cars.

Standing near the end of his driveway, he said, "Hope you had a good time."

"Enjoyed every minute," I said, opening my car door.

He waved good-bye, as I drove away.

The ironic result of Trent's efforts was that he had outstanding business success, two adorable children, and a beautiful, loving wife; and yet none of these things were enough to sustain his happiness.

Great Expectations

Trent's expectations were unrealistic. Whenever he reached one milestone, rather than being content, he would boost his expectations to higher and higher levels. Being better than his former classmates and peers no longer made him feel worthy. Holding the quixotic hope that his next million would spawn everlasting happiness, Trent now needed to be more successful than the multi-millionaires in his country club, who lived in even larger homes and who drove more expensive cars than his; guys who were a few steps higher on the income ladder. A few owned penthouses in New York, classic sports cars, Cessnas, and summer homes in the Hamptons. Seeing life through economic lenses, Trent felt inadequate compared to his peers; their success was his failure. He was now driven to prove that he was as good and successful as they were. So he invested more cash and expanded his business, hired a bigger staff, and worked longer hours.

With longer hours and more risks, his stress level increased. Soon Trent's marriage started to feel the squeeze and his dreams began to fade right before his eyes. Ultimately, the couple separated. Moreover, he had no appreciation for his path to success, what he had already accomplished. Despite all of Trent's tremendous success, his happiness was always short-lived because he never learned to be happy just being himself.

Trent loved himself based on conditions—if he were rich, if he were successful, if he were powerful, if he were happily married, if he were superior to others, etc. So he always had to achieve something bigger and better before he could be happy. Regardless of what he achieved, he never had enough success to prove that he was a minimally acceptable person. Because most of Trent's identity was tied to things—things that made him feel important and superior—the threat of loss was always hovering.

It didn't stop there. Trent also did not believe that anyone else could truly love him—including his wife and children—just for being himself. Looking away from me, he'd said, "How did a loser like me get a beauty like her? I married up for sure. I'm just a poor country boy. I should be living the life of my older brother." His brother was happier than Trent and earned less than $18,000 a year as a short order cook. "Sometimes I feel like a fraud," he'd added.

In a twisted sense of irony, Trent's desperate need to please his wife caused him to be controlling and to shut her out emotionally, which put a wedge in their relationship. Soon after the separation, I ran into Raquel Mabry, and she confided, "The money is nice, but I'd happily live with less to have my husband back. I miss the attention … I miss him."

Feeling that he was not worthy of love, Trent opted to buy love or show people that he was valuable by being more successful than others. (Logically, when others were more successful, Trent's life no longer had meaning.) He used props like his business, cars, and house. Trent's success, spouse, and kids were all possessions that he needed to feel special and worthy. If his wife ever left him permanently or his business crashed, it would be proof that he was a failure as a human being.

A Clearer View

Closely examining Trent's life, it was apparent that his excessive shopping; his need for social mobility; and his hunger for the latest plasma TV, nicest car, and biggest house were merely ways of seeking attention and love, which he was obviously lacking. Maybe Thorstein Veblen, author of *The Theory of the Leisure Class*, was right. Trent's life vividly illustrated that achieving success without a measure of self-worth leaves one feeling like a guppy in an ocean of sharks.

When we do not feel good about ourselves it is like a plague that colors everything. It convinces us that we are inferior, inadequate, and unlovable. We tend to place unreasonable demands on ourselves to prove otherwise. When our self-worth is totally reliant on things that are beyond our immediate control, we will live our lives in bondage to an invisible beast that holds our happiness in its grip. Trent had not realized yet that being honest with ourselves about what we can do and who we are can defeat the demons of self-doubt and low self-confidence. Real self-esteem comes from within, and wholeness comes from accepting all parts of who we are—even those parts that we would like to discard.

Looking Upward and Onward

Over time Trent was slowly grasping that financial security does not contribute more to happiness, although it can buy temporary pleasures. Moreover, it does not offer much of a feeling of individual security—feeling good about one's self. Being totally secure is a myth in an unpredictable world that is rapidly changing, fragmentary, and loose. Our primary sources of security are unstable: jobs are not guaranteed, marriages may end in divorce, and people's opinions are biased. Even wealth can be ephemeral. Companies fold, stock markets crash, banks fail, currencies deflate, and international markets plummet. More, natural laws are at work: there are natural catastrophes, sickness, the loss of loved ones, aging, and eventually death. No amount of money can shield us in this chaotic environment. In this game of life, we are all vulnerable.

I do not claim to be the arbiter of what is deemed successful. Wealth is a good thing and those with less may be momentarily jealous of the lifestyles of the rich and in awe of their social cachet. There is nothing wrong with aspiring to be wealthy or owning nice things. Certainly, material goods can be enjoyable. However, when they are rated too highly, they can incite the opposite emotion, causing us to be miserable (particularly when we can't have them). We often fail to consider that although wealthier people can afford to be self-indulgent, they may not necessarily be happier. Happiness, it seems, is not something we pursue; rather it is a byproduct of many things, including love, optimism, success, and self-worth.

Possibly those who are dissatisfied with their lives before they acquire wealth are not rescued by money. Yet, like Trent, many of us stubbornly cling to the false promise that money will make us safe, happy, valuable, or even immortal.

In looking at Trent and Madison's lives, in some instances their possessions were no less than a crutch or an attempt to compensate for deficiencies in other areas of their lives. Once we are the source of our own worth, we still achieve, buy homes, get married, have children, and do a host of other things, but the intent is different: these things are not done to impress others. At some point in our lives, we have to stop measuring our success against our peers and trying to prove ourselves by some fabricated yardstick.

The American Dream, with its promise of happiness and fulfillment, speaks with certainty of the parameters of happiness, namely success and upward mobility. At this stage, I had seen that the dream, in large measure, was no less than the homogenization of the American experience—a prepackaged idea for all people, which ignores personal happiness. I had also seen that achieving the American Dream does not guarantee happiness for everyone. There were other elements needed to rise to the top of our emotional mountains, namely, a clear view of one's self.

Gauging Our Worth

American life has evolved into a series of never-ending contests, and the realms of our competition have no restrictions. Winning is a prominent aspect of our culture. Being better than others gives us a sense of satisfaction and well-being. Competitive urges are so deeply entrenched in our psyches that our lives are based on one-upmanship. Minute by minute we compete. Trent and Madison's competitive spirit reminded me of Aimee, a programmer analyst whose quest to be on top was in overdrive.

Aimee Chandler was a cornucopia of contradictions with a proclivity for social comparisons. Though she was swathed in syrupy sweetness, her insides were green with envy. Wherever she looked, she was reminded of what she did not have. We often envy our neighbor's possessions more than we would like to admit. Like most, Aimee seemed to be hardwired to judge how well she was doing relative to others in her job and similar settings. Every meeting, conversation, friendship, or interaction became a contest.

With a petite frame, shoulder-length burgundy hair, and a rather bland face, Aimee played a game of one-upmanship with a fervor unmatched by modern women. Yet after years of outwardly living the American Dream, having all of the things that she believed guaranteed her happiness—a professional career, a husband, several children, and a big house in the suburbs—Aimee was drowning in feelings of low worth and she was miserable.

Blame it on human self-delusion or the culture, but Aimee's choices had not been as life-changing as she had hoped they would be. She had failed to predict what would make her happy in the long run, a trap that snares many. As Aimee raised her standards, she needed a bigger house, a pricier car, and a higher salary in order to capture the feel-good high she had initially.

Whenever Aimee perceived the slightest imbalance, e.g., if others were promoted or given pivotal assignments, she would give a performance worthy of an Academy Award. A few months ago, a co-worker was promoted to senior management and Aimee nearly exploded with jealousy. She literally broke down in tears after learning that she was not the chosen one and Mark was. Resentment simmered in her soul. Aimee later publicly expressed regret to Mark after making a total spectacle of herself. "I'm sorry, Mark. Hearing about your good fortune and learning that I wasn't going up the ranks was more than I could take." There's nothing like a little competitive individualism.

Later that day, Aimee and I talked about this incident at the water cooler. After taking a sip of water, she gave her spiel. While she was an expert at maneuvering her anger smoothly beneath her "nice girl" image, this time Aimee's anger managed to seep through her pores.

"I wanted to be happy for Mark, but I just wasn't," she said, fuming. "I deserved that job!"

"Maybe," I said. "But Mark got it."

"I know, I know ... but I was more qualified for the position," she said. "Mark is a run-of-the-mill employee."

This habit of comparing herself to others had begun when Aimee was ten years old. Since that time, her perceived intelligence, talent, beauty, and level of success were defined in relation to others. And their looks and possessions were blaring reminders of what she felt she lacked. Regardless of who Aimee compared herself with, she was generally holding the short end of the stick. And the more unhappy Aimee was with her own life, the more consuming was her envy of other people's looks, possessions, and success.

"The way I see it, competition is only good if it inspires us to improve," I explained. "Otherwise, it's a pain."

"That's your opinion, Kay," she threw in, riled to the hilt. "I don't just want to be the best; I have to be."

Aimee operated in this fashion: If a friend told her about his or her accomplishments, she would quickly brag about how well she was doing at her job. If a female peer got a new haircut, she would go in for a makeover at an expensive trendy salon. And when one got married, she would hate her for snaring a husband that was either richer or better looking than hers.

"Don't you get a bit worn out?" I asked. It seemed that nothing was off-limits for Aimee's competitive zeal.

"No!" she said.

No was right. Whenever Aimee felt "less than," compared to other women, she immediately zoomed in on their imperfections—capped teeth, acne, cellulite, or crow's feet—to even the score.

"That's just the way it is," she said. "I'm not the only one."

No doubt this practice was as common among women as lipstick. Possibly the competitive gene is bred into our cells.

"Well, we can't always be the top shelf," I replied with words more sobering than soothing.

"Whatever!" Aimee remarked, flustered, and walked away.

If Aimee were self-accepting and satisfied with herself and her accomplishments, she would not feel compelled to compete with everyone or to use them as benchmarks for measuring her worth. Apparently, she hadn't learned to value her own accomplishments or her being. Because Aimee lacked self-confidence, she was a bottomless pit, and nothing would ever be enough for her. Trent also had this condition.

Healthy competition is good. But in many ways we compromise our own happiness, inner peace, and feelings of worth by competing and striving to out-do the competition. Ironically, the unrelenting quest to be the victor invariably results in loss: loss of self-esteem and self-love. Most people are running an exhausting race that they are destined to lose. It's often difficult to see the connection between our endless striving and reality, with the media blocking out most anything that has to do with the real lives of ordinary people, particularly their unhappiness. This segment of the population is kept off camera, their voices muted.

Coming Into Focus

Few things can cause us to ache like the unhappiness and envy that occur when we compare ourselves to someone we believe is superior to us in some way. We feel like we've been hit by a boulder. So we quickly look for ways to relieve the pain, like comparing ourselves to someone we deem lesser. These comparisons can go on continuously; they are catalysts for a mental meltdown. Because we learn to traverse social terrain by gauging similarities and differences—comparing and competing—it is often impossible to undo this programming.

Regardless of what we value about ourselves, unfavorable comparisons have a way of making us feel "less than." Entertainers, corporate executives, and professional athletes carp about multi-million dollar salaries because their colleagues or teammates are earning higher salaries or have landed bigger signing bonuses.

Growing up, I was extremely competitive and a sore loser. I believed that I had to win at everything. And although I compete far less at this point, my quest to win did not slow down until I dismissed myself from the race. In my estimation, I was losing at every angle—I wasn't successful, rich, or hitched—so I simply quit. But I was not able to get a big picture of the true nature of unhealthy competition until I observed it in others like Trent, Madison, and Aimee. Then I knew for sure that when we become so engrossed in other people's lives that we lose sight of our own, and deem their lives preferable to our own, we give pieces of our lives away.

Our Competitive Spirit

Trent, Madison, and Aimee were like many Americans. Blame it on the culture or a new influx of reality programming; Americans are competitive status-seekers with a penchant for social comparisons. Although we deliver soapbox speeches about unity and equality, we continue to create hierarchies and jockey for the top position. Our self-esteem and identity are based largely on how well we compare. We are happiest when we are more attractive, smarter, and richer than others. We tend to justify our feelings with thoughts like: "I may not be the best looking, but I am better looking than some," or "Surely there are richer people in the world, but I am in the top tier so I am okay." On the contrary, comparing ourselves to those who are richer, more attractive, or more intelligent than us tends to trigger envy, dissatisfaction, and misery.

Further feeding this frenzy is our tendency to compare upward. In the past we made proximate comparisons, comparing ourselves to people with similar incomes and status. Today we are much more likely to aspire to be like multi-millionaires in the top five percent of U.S. income levels. The super rich have set outrageous precedents for ordinary people and well-heeled lifestyles are considered the norm. Now, BMWs and 10,000-square-foot homes have been elevated to a necessity. We can never quite get enough. As Aimee and Trent showed me, it is a contagion of envy and rank-obsessed thinking that prevents us from feeling any happier or more content. Obviously, comparing is useful in prioritizing and making choices; beyond that it can be problematic.

It seems that we all strive for a sense of superiority, to some degree, whether we care to admit it or not. Maybe it is because most of us feel inferior in some ways, and winning (feeling superior) just for a moment thrills our hearts and brings us joy. Winning, after all, authenticates our superior intellect, beauty, or abilities, which boosts our sense of worth. As expected, our competitive spirits continually spiral out of control. Cleary, comparing condemns us to a lifetime of shaky emotions.

At this point, I was also beginning to see that all human beings have the same needs for love, respect, and acceptance. We also have fears of pain and loss. We feel the same range of human emotions and struggle with the same doubts and insecurities. We differ only by degrees. Now that these similarities were clearer, external differences in people (status, race, gender, age) no longer had much bearing. We are all striving to fashion a life of our own.

Seeing Wealth and Happiness

Does money make us happy? Well, we're not quite sure. "People who say you can't buy happiness never chucked enough dough at their problems," my friend Darryl once said. Though we give unlimited lip service to the popular maxim that "money can't buy happiness," most of us don't believe it. If we did, we wouldn't be working like machines to make more money so that we could buy more things. Money is inextricably linked to our accomplishments, security, status, identity, and sense of worth.

Indeed, wealth can produce some happiness. Earning a million dollars causes the pleasure center of the brain to light up. But that initial surge does not convert to lasting happiness for most people. Still, given the choice of being rich or poor, few of us would opt for poverty. I am certainly not an advocate of poverty. Poverty is quite scary and not on any sane person's wish list. We all want to avoid being grouped with the non-celebrity poor. Dwindled savings, poor health care, substandard housing, mounting debt, and the danger of foreclosure or eviction just are not appealing. Still, there are people who will say, off-handedly, that money isn't everything; and they are likely called "middle-class."

Without question, when money relieves poverty and provides for the basic necessities in life—food, clothing, shelter, and other essentials—it certainly creates happiness. But at the other end of the spectrum, when money is used to buy luxury cars, mansions, and jewels, that level of satisfaction seems to wane a bit.

Americans assume that wealth can soothe all of their problems. Most of us dream of embarking on a satisfying course of our choosing, unfettered by financial constraints stipulated by the next car payment, mortgage, or meal. So we spend our days working ourselves to the bone and sacrificing both leisure and freedom, only to feel drained and frazzled at the end of the day. Experts agree that a lifetime of chasing the dollar seldom raises our level of happiness. Rather, it tends to lead to a life of perpetual struggle.

When we follow the conventional wisdom that a higher income guarantees our happiness, we predictably react to our disillusionment (after getting more money) by concluding that we simply do not have enough. "I need more money." Why? "Other people with money are happy." So the cycle continues without end—hope followed by disillusionment—until a revelation stops it. We are so concerned with making money that we often lose sight of what can really make us happy.

We may be wise to consider that although wealth can offer us great pleasures, it also brings with it heartaches: steep mortgages, higher property taxes, costly property upkeep, lengthy rush hour commutes, longer workdays, and little time for leisure. Even so, we continue to fantasize about levels of comfort that do not really exist, refusing to shed the delusion that we can buy our way to happiness. Maybe we should ask ourselves what we really want. Do we really want more wealth or do we want to be happier and are assuming that more money will do the trick? If what we are in search of is a happier and more meaningful existence, how much money will we need to achieve this? More important, how are we to feel in the meantime?

Caving in to the temptation of money is easy. Money is good. It makes a lot of things possible; but it may not make life any easier. Happiness and satisfaction seem to be, in large measure, a function of how we look at things rather than what we do or what we own.

If you had asked me a few years ago how I defined success, I would have given you a predictable response: a high income, a prestigious job, status, and achievement. But after seeing Madison, Gavin, and Trent, all of whom had the trappings of success and yet were not fulfilled, I knew that I needed to extend my definition or create a new yardstick for measuring success. It was then clear to me that aiming for the American Dream can create a frantic agenda rather than a satisfying one. More, our sense of worth and completeness may not be found by chasing after things.

2 Achievement

A Generation
of High Achievers

FEBRUARY 1997

In our quest to be the best, we have created a generation of high-achieving, highly pressured young adults who often collapse under the stress and sink into despair—not from failing but from getting a B. These same young adults pursue subjects not out of genuine interest but to create an impressive college application. Such students often feel that they will have nothing to live for if they are not admitted to one of the top schools in the country. Some of them may retake national college entrance exams in hopes of getting a perfect score. When these would-be champions do not unequivocally succeed, their self-esteems take a nose dive.

Bailey Fenwick, a classic overachiever who always put her self-esteem to the test, was part of this generation. Since preschool, Bailey had been enrolled in insanely competitive schools, largely due to her mother's brimming maternal ambition—her own ambition that she had turned on Bailey. "It was the only way I knew how to ensure her success," her mom once said succinctly. This kind of high-intensity mothering was like the Olympics, with each contender in danger of being flattened by the competition.

Bailey's parents, with their own unfulfilled aspirations, burdened her with incredibly high goals. They inwardly hoped that Bailey's astonishing achievements would enhance their status and prestige. I had seen scores of parents who were living through their children. Bailey's parents had the surreal expectation that once she gained entry into a premier university, it would open doors to adulthood—doors to the best jobs, the right spouse, and the right social circles. Needless to say, this way of gaining life satisfaction was unfair to Bailey and quite unreliable.

Since elementary school, Bailey had ranked at the top of her class, particularly in math and science. As a child, she was praised for her accomplishments, so she knew how to earn the status that would ensure her acceptance. Her dad gave her $20 for every A on her report card, which may have prompted her to equate academic achievement with financial rewards.

Because Bailey's self-evaluation was based solely on what others thought of her, it was important for her to be perfect all the time. Her parents taught her that stellar performances meant that she was okay, but making mistakes rendered her a failure. She had learned that lesson well. Love was guaranteed as long as Bailey behaved according to her parent's expectations. And their high expectations for Bailey soon became her own. As a child, I was always allowed to speak my mind and to be myself, so this facet of Bailey's life was rather foreign to me.

Bailey had nearly worked herself to death to be successful in other people's eyes. She had an unremitting need for the world to proclaim her as extraordinary and great. As she matured, she continued to raise the bar, expecting more and more of herself, increasing her chances of failing. And to Bailey, there was nothing more dreadful than being merely average, or worse, being branded a loser for life.

An unconventional beauty with layered ash brown hair, almond-shaped eyes, and freckles, Bailey compensated by being a classic apple-polisher who showered the managers with the kind of adulation that made them feel like they were walking on air. Beneath her self-assured veneer, she was a ball of knots who constantly stressed over how she appeared to others. Lacking the psychological resilience to handle failure and rejection, Bailey crumbled whenever she failed to get approval.

Undeterred by notions of an ultra-macho corporate culture and exhausting working hours, Bailey entered the workforce right out of college at full steam, immaculately dressed and ready for the challenge. She had something to prove to herself. "I am going to be more than a no-name, no-experience desk warmer," she said. Relatively new to the company, at twenty-two she landed a position as a systems engineer and was living a comfortable lifestyle.

Bailey was successful in her initial position and was promoted to project leader in systems engineering after three years. Now she was floating on air, proud of her accomplishments. As planned, Bailey was inching up the corporate ladder. She hoped to completely shatter the glass ceiling and exceed the limits of traditional female expectation.

With phenomenal abilities, Bailey was used to approbation and performance highs. And she fully expected to find that kind of stimuli from her engineering position. High achievers all tend to have this flow: phenomenal grades, top honors, and impressive corporate gigs. For Bailey, succeeding had always been a given. "I've never failed at anything," she'd jokingly boast.

Bailey spent an inordinate amount of time checking, revising, and focusing on minute details of her work. She knew the unspoken rule: When women were not on top of their game, it confirms what men think about most women—that they can't cut it. Desperate to avoid appearing brainless or unqualified, which is not unusual for women who are thrust into heaps of responsibility in a testosterone-driven industry, she hardly ever asked questions. Bailey wanted to feel that she belonged.

Although Bailey was a first-rate employee, she had a lot of trouble accepting criticism. When her boss openly criticized some of her electrical schematics and wiring diagrams at one of our group meetings, she quickly countered, "I've done a superb job." So her boss continued to tell her, this time in a much harsher tone, what corrections needed to be made to the project—and Bailey's behavior became even more defensive.

"I'm an excellent employee and you're making me look stupid in front of my staff. Now they won't respect my ability," she'd said.

Bailey had failed to meet her own standards, and, after work, she went home angry and stressed. Her imperfections had been exposed. She cried for hours. She couldn't eat or sleep. Anger soon turned to guilt, insecurity, and depression.

I recognized some of Bailey's traits. It was clear to me that Bailey had fallen into the same trap I had once fallen into, and things were not going to improve for her until she made some internal changes. I was now seeing the error of my former ways quite vividly.

At her boss's recommendation, Bailey entered therapy. According to Bailey, the goal of her sessions was to help her identify, understand, and modify her central beliefs so that her feelings of worth would become more stable. Thankfully, she was making some progress—the boss had been one step from declaring her "disturbed." We talked over lunch several weeks after the incident with her boss, and Bailey told me about her counseling sessions and a few other tidbits.

"How are your sessions?" I inquired.

"Going well, thanks," Bailey replied.

"Did you clear things up?" I went on, taking a bite of my tuna sandwich.

As furrows formed between her eyes, she said, "Sort of. I learned that I have a nagging fear of failure."

Okay, that explained why she hated coming across as an idiot to her boss and her staff, and with good reason: The stakes were high at the job and Bailey's company had zero tolerance for errors.

"That's progress," I said.

"When it happens, I am literally crushed. Obliterated. I can't take it!" Bailey wailed.

"Isn't that a bit severe?"

"Well, maybe," she replied quickly. "When I make mistakes I feel completely worthless; it's like I don't exist."

"We all make our share of mistakes. It's normal."

"I don't," she snapped. "I expect the best from myself and I generally get it."

"But we don't always perform perfectly."

Ignoring my comment, Bailey sputtered, "When you foul up, everyone gets a laugh at your expense. It's so humiliating."

"It can be, but the feeling doesn't last long."

She did have a point; in this country failure is a cardinal sin punishable by an invisible guillotine.

"You're accepted when you're perfect," she said.

One did not have to be a psychologist to see the problem here. To Bailey, not being the best in the group meant that she was not a valuable person. Doing outstanding work made her feel accepted. But it didn't matter how hard she worked; the results were rarely good enough for Bailey.

She continued with added enthusiasm, "When I do excellent work, I get praise from my boss and the group applauds my success. Everybody wins!"

Since none of us performs perfectly all of the time, Bailey was setting herself up to feel bad. With Bailey, there was no mid-ground, no continuum. Mistakes weren't simply mistakes; they were proof that she was flawed. If Bailey could get everything just right then she could feel good about herself. But most of all, she could avoid criticism. Bailey was unwilling to let go of her quest for perfection.

"I've always wanted people to like me," Bailey explained.

"Approval feels good; we all like it," I said. "But we have to learn to like ourselves without it."

I could see clearer now: If other people approved of Bailey she was okay; otherwise she was a failure. Worse, she stopped loving herself whenever her performance was less than perfect.

With her countenance brightening a tad, Bailey said, "Easy for you to say. Listen, I dress perfectly and try to be the best at everything. My cheeks ache from smiling so much."

"You're pulling my leg."

"Thank God for therapy, huh?"

I am a recovering perfectionist so I know, to some degree, how Bailey views life. I did not start to recover until I could see myself more clearly. As I learned to appreciate my capabilities and to recognize my limitations, the sting from the criticism decreased. Believe it or not, seeing ourselves realistically and accurately builds confidence and self-esteem. With this self-knowledge, we tend to like ourselves better.

To some extent, we are all fearful of being judged and found wanting because to us that signifies that we are not worth loving. Coming to the realization that human beings are not perfect offered me a sense of relief. It does not mean that we are incompetent, lazy, or mediocre; it simply means we are human.

A Wider View

Life is about learning, not perfection. In the long run, the morsel of approval that one receives from bartering oneself away seems hardly worth the effort. Besides, approval ratings from family, friends, peers, and colleagues change like the wind. Bailey was coming around, and so was I. She was working hard to make the connection but was still reluctant to abandon the idea that perfection leads to subjective feelings of acceptance.

Bailey was so accustomed to dancing for approval that she was not in tune to her own feelings. She had become alienated from herself and was nearly incapable of having a genuine relationship.

"When you've lived your entire life fitting into other people's expectations and then you finally feel your own experience, it can be startling," Bailey explained. "It's frightening to focus on yourself and what you're feeling. You don't know what you may find out about yourself. Maybe there is no one to find."

What I know for sure is that when we believe that we are valuable people, we can more easily accept our imperfections, and being wrong does not make us any less worthy. But this transformation does not happen right away; it takes time and effort. We help ourselves feel valuable by cutting back on the self-inflicted attacks and reminding ourselves of projects (or any tasks) that we have done well, or other times when we have been successful, so that we maintain balance. This has always helped me.

Now that Bailey was gaining an awareness of how her beliefs governed her feelings of worth, she was slowly revising her map and things were looking up for her. Bailey was learning to rate her performance and to stop rating her total worth as a human being. She was also learning to transcend her need for approval, to take criticism gracefully, and to lead others without the need to feel superior to them. This was particularly hard for Bailey, who was addicted to the self-esteem high that she got when she performed perfectly.

"I don't have all of the answers and that's okay," she told me. She was finally open to the idea of recognizing the benefit of getting perspectives from a diverse group of people.

Bailey had ceded her life to a mélange of expectations, norms, and artifices, all blended for universal acceptability. But she was changing. "I am learning to be my own person," she told me. Though it was difficult to jeopardize her primary source of love and security, Bailey was slowly severing the phantom umbilical cord that attached her to her parents. According to Bailey, her therapist asked that her parents not express any judgment, good or bad. "They were to get to know me, not to fix me," Bailey reported happily. "Maybe people should accept and love me for who I am, not how perfectly I perform."

We finished our sandwiches and Bailey quickly jumped to her feet. "I have a one o'clock meeting," she said, gathering her files. As she walked away, she turned around and waved. I waved back, and then she walked into the elevator.

The stereotype of domineering parents who load their children with high expectations is all too common. But little is reported about permissive, cool parents who offer their children no guidance, parents who are afraid of being rejected, not cool, or overbearing. Often these parents fail to set boundaries and fail to provide their children with the skills critical to helping them find their own interests and navigate successfully through life. Perhaps more troubling is that these children grow up to see privileges and material possessions as inherent rights and are unable to cope whenever life ceases to go their way.

As a result of interacting with Bailey, it was clear to me that conditional self-esteem rises and falls. In order to feel good, we must continually live up to some criteria of excellence. Of course, performing perfectly one hundred percent of the time is impossible, so feelings of worthlessness are unavoidable. Maybe it is because at an early age we are indoctrinated with the message that it is shameful to be wrong and that our self-worth depends on being perfect. This is likely amplified in the office by intense pressures to be smart, assertive, and successful. Clearly, we can contribute so much more to life when we stop trying to impress others and prove to ourselves that we are the greatest. Perhaps that means that we must learn how to live without applause for a time.

After conversing with Bailey and Madison, and seeing them on objective and empathetic levels, I concluded that the high that we get from performing perfectly and making a nice salary does not seem to impact our happiness levels long-term. Surely these momentous events alter our level of happiness for a short time, but we quickly adapt and return to normalcy. Not realizing this truth, we keep chasing success.

Having it All

AUGUST 1997

The culture is in constant flux. While it once glorified full-time mothers and bashed working mothers, it seems to be trying to balance the two, which is commonly known as "having it all." Allie Sharpe, two other friends, and I met at Panera Bread just after summer vacation to discuss this cultural phenomenon. Allie was a part of the Me Generation, which also wanted dynamic careers, rich husbands, fabulous sex, several babies, and designer fashions. She was the type about whom women asked admiringly, "How does she do it?" Now Allie was trying to strike that impossible balance between work and home, pretending that she had gotten it all together.

Allie's life left an indelible impression on me. She had what I considered an ideal life, the fulfilling life that I had envisioned for myself before reality set in. From the outside, Allie had achieved the American Dream: a wonderful marriage, a successful career, three beautiful children, an amazing home, and an active social life. But on the inside, life was quite different for her. It seemed that even Allie, the imagined pinnacle of success, had not achieved the state of longed-for euphoria for which I was searching.

Perhaps I had been fed a sugarcoated version of what motherhood was like, one that omitted the strain, fatigue, compromise, fear, sleepless nights, and over scheduling inherent in the job. Who knows? With the world constantly telling women that being a mommy is the happiest time of their lives, few are willing to admit what they are really feeling.

This generation's obsession with competition, wealth, and perfection has spilled over into motherhood, creating a deleterious blend of anxiety, resentment, and regret. A few of the mothers in Catauga County had gotten soaked.

"I get so tired of hearing about the sexy celebrity mom who 'has it all,'" Allie said, sparking a long discussion.

"Tell me about it," Reese yelped. "They're the ones who brag about how fulfilled they are in their careers and motherhood."

"Everyone knows that they have an army of servants and nannies doing the work for them," I added, taking a sip of tea.

"How are ordinary women supposed to compete with that?" Allie asked, throwing her hands in the air.

"It's all an illusion," I said. "Besides, women do not have equal means, so competing is fruitless."

"How can we not compete?" Allie asked, sipping her cappuccino.

"Ignore them," Britta yawned.

"And how easy is that?" Reese asked.

"It's impossible," Allie continued, visibly frustrated by her inability to model the life of a celebrity mom. "I've been running myself ragged and I still can't seem to get it right."

"Allie, please," I countered. "You're the envy of the pack." Allie's life was the one that everyone wanted, and she was complaining.

All of the friends agreed that the planet is overrun with women who are dazzled about the unending demands of motherhood. Most were flummoxed at how having children can all at once be so wonderful and taxing and so complex and blatantly mind-numbing. Apparently, the chasm between sunglow ideals of perfect motherhood and the reality of motherhood is wide, yet scores of women continue to buy into and perpetuate these romantic fantasies hawked conspicuously by reputable magazines like *Good Housekeeping, Life & Style*, and *People*.

"Being a mother is supposed to be so natural," Reese said, taking a bite of her chicken sandwich.

"Anyone who thinks that motherhood is a snap lives in NeverNeverLand," said Allie.

"Ahh, the pleasures of colic, whining, and temper tantrums," Britta threw in.

"And sleep deprivation, weight gain, and a never-ending demand for your time," Allie continued.

Anxious to add another three cents to the discussion, Reese threw in, "My girlish figure has been replaced with varicose veins, stretch marks, droopy breasts, and a flabby stomach." Allie and Britta both laughed and nodded their heads in agreement.

These women were slowly splattering ink all over my ideal watercolor painting of motherhood. Though each of them abhorred the pace of their lives, they could not get out of the harried roller derby and risk being a failure as a mother. "What would the other parents think?" There was no way that we could cover this topic in one sitting, so we ended the discussion and said our good-byes. I rode the shuttle back to Catauga Power.

Much like Bailey's life, Allie's life proceeded through a series of picture-perfect images, down to her overly coiffed hair, trim body, and mannequin-like appearance. She played soccer with her children, baked cookies for the PTA, kept a spotless house, and never quarreled with her husband. Allie's life seemed to operate like clockwork, without ever veering from her schedule. "I pride myself on being efficient!" she told us almost daily. Quite naturally we were puzzled by her remarks. If Allie was not living the dream, then who was? A clearer picture was coming into focus. Allie did not want things to be good, she wanted them to be perfect. So Allie employed a rigorous program of pol-ishing, rearranging, and fervently perfecting her life.

The quest to be the perfect wife reached its pinnacle in the 1960s with the help of Helen B. Andelin's book *Fascinating Womanhood*, written with the sole purpose of teaching women how to be happy in marriage. Women were instructed how to be totally submissive, compliant, and overly happy in their robot-like Stepford state. According to the book, only women who achieved the goal of being perfect housekeepers, wives, and mothers were considered ideal. Fulfilling their role as the perfect wife and mother offered women satis-faction, self-worth, and social approval. Remnants of this pursuit linger in this new era; but now women have added to the magical imagery.

Forty years later, women are still aiming for the pinnacle of perfection—only the equation has changed. Women have now entered the workforce big time and are trying to balance it all. But layering care-giving roles on top of moneymaking roles often leaves them frazzled. It is a strain to always perform at peak level when you are worried about sick children, childcare, and dust balls under the sofa.

The Balancing Act

Allie—stockbroker, wife, and mother of three—could finagle multimillion dollar accounts and get herself and her children dressed and into her SUV in an hour. "I juggle tasks like a performer on a tightrope," she once exclaimed.

Allie's life operated via a Palm Pilot; there were noonday Pilates classes, soccer games, ballet lessons, quarterly doctor visits, and evening gymnastics classes for the children. Even the Sabbath, a day of rest, was filled with endless labor. "Every day I work like a programmed robot from nine to five; then I go home exhausted and start anew," she told me. "I'm always pushing myself to achieve more and to have more."

Changing gears between home and work was so abrupt that Allie got whiplash. But Allie was adept at discarding her work-self and assuming a June Cleaver-like persona. The moment Allie walked in the door, the kids were demanding her attention and she was faced with a pile of daily laundry, a stack of junk mail, a few dirty dishes, fingerprints on her glass surfaces, and a bathroom destroyed by her five-year-old. "My children are at risk for bubonic plague!" Nonetheless, an enthusiastic Allie inquired about her children's day and asked what they would like for dinner before she started her nightly cleaning. Allie's life was a far cry from the paradise that she envisioned before getting married. Her joy, it seemed, had been displaced by stress, never-ending activities, and taking care of other people's lives. Hiring a housekeeper was out of the question.

Then there was the matter of Allie's overly doting mother-in-law, who Allie considered judge and jury, who had charged Allie with abdicating her role as mother to pursue her own ends and compensating by giving her children material things. Allie believed that her mother-in-law was just a typical grandparent with an unfulfilled life, trying to recapture the gift of being alive, wanted, and adored through her grandchildren. "No doubt she's angry that I'm succeeding where she failed," she'd snapped, clearly peeved by the verdict.

Under the strain of trying to have it all, Allie was on the verge of a mental collapse. Already snowed under with a stalled marriage and energetic children, she accepted a new position with more responsibility and longer hours. Then Allie felt really guilty about how little time she spent with her husband and children. She had no love life. The sitter cuddled with her children, knew their moods, and cooked their favorite foods. To Allie, all of this was embarrassing. "My children are supposed to love me best," she'd cried. Although Allie often considered leaving her job, she enjoyed the boost she got from earning millions in the market.

But there was another side of work that Allie abhorred: the gender politics. Working women with children were deemed lesser in the office, and Allie was ticked by the double standard. In Allie's office, women were considered negligent because, after all, they should be home with their children. And heaven forbid that Allie's children should get sick. Women who had to leave the office to care for a sick child were judged to be scatterbrained and irresponsible. But men had it easy. "Men with children are considered good providers and rewarded with huge bonuses for less than stellar results, thanks to the current bastard (boss) in residence," Allie had protested. She hated the disparity.

Every day there was something new for Allie to grumble about. Her children were lazy, her husband was a procrastinator, her co-workers were incompetent, etc. Even when people did their part, it was seldom to Allie's satisfaction. It was never good work. Allie's need for absolute perfection kept her in a frequent state of angst and frustration as people often failed to meet her expectations. Although she tried to lower her expectations and tolerate other people's mediocrity, it never seemed to work.

Allie's romantic life was also waning. It appeared that Allie was the typical high-achieving female who seemed to have time for everything but pleasure. Near the end of August, we attended the Annual Women of Distinction Awards Banquet. Allie walked over to my table not long after the banquet ended; we exchanged pleasantries and Allie gave me the rundown.

"I read in *Cosmo* last month that marriages are crumbling because of attention famine," Allie said with a disconcerted look. "According to the article, husbands are threatening to leave their wives because they want more sex."

"I'll bet that's a lot of hype," I said.

"Well, it's hard to be a steamy love goddess with so many things to do in a day," she laughed nervously.

Allie told me that she would sometimes prolong her stay in the bathroom, methodically flossing each tooth twice, hoping that her husband would fall asleep so that she could forego having sex for the night. Though Allie had planned several romantic weekends, finding a sitter was taxing, and free time felt like stealing. So she settled for a relaxing long bath and a cup of cappuccino.

Allie often envied single women with freedom to shop, travel, date, get body massages, and have cocktails after work. "I miss the freedom to go wherever I want without having to consider child care or time."

"Indeed, freedom is the zenith of the single life," I freely acknowledged.

"Single women can go to the bathroom alone, without their children in tow, and sleep for eight hours," an exhausted Allie offered.

"All true," I agreed.

"Perhaps more fantastic, they get to lead a life of their own choosing without interference."

"Well, there are benefits to being single and benefits to being married," I told her. "But we have a tendency to focus on what we are missing, which keeps us from enjoying what we have."

"How reflective," Allie replied halfheartedly.

One day the weight of trying to be perfect got too heavy and Allie, the superwoman, snapped. "My schedule is insane!" Allie bellowed. "I can't take anymore. I'm worn out and overworked. My marriage is falling apart. Nothing in my life is working!"

Allie had bottomed out. And the newest baby failed to revitalize Allie's tattered marriage. The combined stress of working full time, caring for three children, cooking dinner, cleaning, shopping, and trying to meet her husband's needs and her own had thrown her perfect life out of balance.

Several months later, like a miracle from God, life changed for Allie. I ran into Allie at the Food Mart, and we talked while we were cruising the aisles.

"I was enormously stressed out by trying to live a Hollywood image of perfection," Allie said, somewhat relieved.

Allie believed that she had to be the best at everything. She had equated maintaining a spotless house, perfect body, and ideal marriage with being a perfect mother/wife/person. So if the house was in shambles and her children were not behaving, or her marriage had lost its spark, then she was to blame— and also imperfect. More than that, people would surely think less of her for not keeping a spotless house and having model children. All of this caused Allie to feel weighed down and miserable.

Thankfully, Allie's life was improving; she had adjusted her expectations for her career and her family.

"I'm more reasonable now. I know what's doable with my abilities, means, and circumstances," Allie said with delight.

She had also hired a housekeeper, given the kids a few chores, and joined the neighborhood carpool. And she'd stopped declaring that her husband was clinging to male privilege and now let him pitch in a bit more. Releasing her time-honored housekeeping duties had been difficult. But Allie was slowly realizing that it was okay to be imperfect.

It is rather ironic; the self-acceptance and contentment that Allie was pursuing by being perfect could not be achieved long-term because she was too stressed out and exhausted. Clearly, society's perpetuation of the perfect mom icon is a pernicious ideal that renders all others mediocre. It not only pits stay-at-home moms against working moms, but it leaves both wondering why they cannot measure up to the standards. By setting standards that are beyond our reach, the perfect mom myth primes all women for failure.

Allie's life revealed to me that while it was possible to have it all, it was not possible to have it all at once. Still, this vision of *having it all* will not go away; it remains a dream that many women are in search of today. And this partly explains the rising number of Prozac-and Ritalin-addicted moms.

Interestingly enough, I had another friend, Sophia, who was a stay-at-home mom. Sophia's husband, Paul, worked for Catauga Power Company; I had met her at a company picnic. To Sophia Denson, this concept of *having it all* seemed ludicrous, even insulting, because she was home all day caring for five high-spirited children with no respite. One Saturday afternoon I joined Sophia and her children at Cooley Park for a day of fun. We talked as the children splashed in the water and rode on the carousel. Sophia was practical and plain. Nearly six feet tall, she wore a pair of khaki shorts and a sleeveless floral-printed shirt. Sophia was not at all pleased by the way she'd been treated at her husband's company functions.

"Sometimes I wonder if not working is the right choice," Sophia said.

"I thought you liked being a stay-at-home mom?" I said.

"I do," she replied. "But it gets a bit tiring and lonely."

"Working women experience those same feelings."

"Yeah, but at least you all get public approval for what you do."

"I guess."

"This society does not applaud women like me who stay at home and home school their children," Sophia said, chagrined. "Instead, it leans towards a hierarchy that confers status on women with incomes."

"Really?"

"We are totally ignored at office parties and picnics."

"That's pretty tacky."

"Because we don't have a salary or a job title, people assume that we're insipid airheads."

"Talk about clinging to jaded stereotypes."

"You said a mouthful," she said. "Sleek working women, well-dressed with fulfilling careers, get all of the glory."

In the brutal competition over who's the better mother, each seems to view the other with a mixture of envy and angst. Now I was wondering, *Is anybody happy?* After Sophia fed the kids a quick snack, I said good-bye. Listening to Sophia's experiences helped to widen my perspective.

If magazine covers and movies are social meters, the cultural pendulum is swinging again. The media is beginning to glorify motherhood once more, making children and homemaking more appealing than having a career. Possibly "the grass is greener" adage is still very much alive and kicking. Still, whether a working mom or stay-at-home mom, it is best to be successful on one's own terms. Otherwise, you may shine for the masses, but you feel hollow inside, which is not successful by any terms. Something else was clear: If a woman is unable to get satisfaction from her own life, children and a husband may not help much.

Our Obsession with Time

Complaints about not having any time or enough time are fairly common. Nonetheless, not having any free time is often an indisputable badge of honor. We frequently seek fulfillment via an overbooked schedule. Scrambling with our cell phones and pagers, we constantly stress about losing our competitive edge or missing an opportunity. Even leisurely activities are judged and children's activities are scheduled.

Our lives, it seems, have been systematically stunted by over-scheduling. No more hanging out, day trips to the beach, or lying on the grass, staring at a summer sky. We are racing through life, driven to get the maximum results in the shortest time. Idle time boosts our insecurities. Inching our way ahead, we do not want to be left behind. It is no wonder that we seldom experience contentment. We seem to have forgotten that life is to be lived and not experienced like an Indy 500 race where the winner arrives at the finish line first. We have muddled up the value of time with our own self-worth.

When Our Best Isn't Good Enough

Where did we ever get the idea that we have to be perfect to be worthy of admiration and love? Perhaps it is because we think that any form of weakness or failure gives people reason to reject us. Or maybe we hope to compensate for our weaknesses by being perfect. Still, trying to achieve this *having it all* ideal makes one anxious, striving to be the perfect mom, the successful career woman, and the sexy wife. It is no wonder that self-help books focus on carving out a time slot to find out who one is. Thankfully, *having it all* seems to be evolving towards a notion of balance. The new version involves compromise, setting limitations, self-understanding, and self-acceptance.

Though perfectionism is flaunted as an asset, like workaholism, it is fear masquerading as strength. Wanting people and things to be perfect is a frantic attempt to mask insecurities. Allie hid in a cocoon of perfection to gratifyingly numb the uncomfortable knowledge that she felt inadequate. But life did not improve until she was willing to acknowledge her fears. I had once hidden in that same cocoon.

For years I was overly competitive and a master at stressing over obligations and inventing catastrophic fantasies about what could go wrong. I would spend hours cleaning (tampering with what my mother and father sought to make a comfortable and welcoming home) and rewriting my assignments until they were perfect. Getting anything less than an A sent me spiraling.

Though I managed to maintain a spotless house and to make good grades, somehow I generally fell short of my own expectations. Pop psychology attributes perfectionism to demanding parents, and that may be true for some; but for me it largely stemmed from the widely held belief that only the best will succeed. Allie had this belief, and so did Bailey.

Every day I still hear people boasting about being perfectionists—"I have to be the best!"—when this quest is actually destroying their health and making them miserable. Daily reports about successful people highlight the myth that their perfectionism put them on top, rather than their intellect and fervor.

Living life as a perfectionist can be a vicious cycle that sets people up for continuous rejection and utter letdown. No matter how hard people work to attain their goals, they can never quite reach them. It is as if someone is always moving the mark and the standards are out of bounds. Overcoming perfectionism requires courage. It means accepting our imperfections and humanness, which is difficult at best in a culture that promotes and applauds perfection. We often wish for our lives to be perfect. But if they were perfect, life would probably be meaningless as it would no longer teach us anything. Much like mermaids, the perfect human is both an attractive and mythical concept.

Great Expectations

Jolie Larrieux had a secret dream of becoming a corporate success. She had grown up in a middle-class suburb in Pennsylvania and used her college network to land a position with Dun and Brunstreet. Jolie and I attended the same graduate school, and in many ways her experiences in corporate America were similar to my own. This revelation was apparent to me only in hindsight.

After graduating from college, I entered the workplace brimming with excitement and eager to make major contributions to the company. Inspired by Gavin and others, I had worked overtime, skipped lunches and vacations, and did all of the things that I had been taught would assure my success. But the big success never came; in fact, it was replaced by a series of disappointments.

I had high hopes that with hard work I would one day be offered a big salary and a position in corporate management. I was eager to contribute and to make my mark early on. I wanted to move up the ranks. Didn't everyone? Having a position that was fun and interesting was not important. At the time I wanted money. Money was the magical box that contained happiness and freedom. This was the ethos of the business world, and I believed it—we all did.

Jolie was of French-Creole lineage with a sun glitz complexion and curly brown hair. Mid-thirties with a chiseled face and a big smile, she looked ten years younger. When Jolie entered the workplace, she expected it to be a very wonderful place—warm and supportive; but instead she found it cold and often brutal. Undoubtedly, she grossly underestimated the impact of working in a toxic environment. One afternoon, I got an unexpected call from Jolie, who was clearly distressed.

"Hey, Kay," she said. "Are you busy?"

"No, not at the moment," I replied.

"How's everything going?" she asked.

"Not bad," I said.

"Wish that I could say the same," Jolie said, irritated. "My office is a battle zone filled with insecure people masquerading as overachievers."

"Greed and ambition go with the corporate turf," I teased.

"No matter how hard I try, I can rarely get buy-in from this group," she snapped.

"Try bribing them with perks like $20 gift cards or movie tickets?"

"Cute," Jolie remarked. "I just don't get it. It's terribly frustrating to work with people who don't know the meaning of team."

"The team concept gets lost in the shuffle," I said.

"I'll say," Jolie said. "Every day I watch men and women maneuver for position using the basest forms of office politics on Earth, while the rest of us—a tiny handful—think that we can do our best and merit will have its own reward."

"Merit does have its own reward. Think about the progress you've made," I said.

"I guess," she said warily. "But cattiness seems to propel one further up the ranks."

"Oh, and don't leave out backbiting, lying, and sex," I added.

"Yeah, and that too," echoed Jolie.

"Ah, what would we do with ourselves, deprived of office hierarchies?" I asked with a Grinch-like voice.

As the economy slumped and competition tightened, Jolie was in a world with fierce co-workers and no close relatives or friends nearby; she had no safety net. There is no such thing as friendly competition and Jolie learned that lesson the hard way. She lived in a world of brute competition where her boss gained sadistic pleasure from watching his employees scramble for limited promotions and minimal rewards. But soon friction mounted and tempers flared, causing a meltdown.

During Jolie's tenure on the job, working for a Fortune 500 company, she had risen from staff level to a manager. Life was good and the salary and bonuses made the daily sacrifices all worthwhile. At the height of her career, Jolie had the task of leading a huge project. By all accounts she had the formula for success—she was management material. However, when she most needed to succeed, Jolie was unable to garner backing for her new business initiatives.

Her colleagues did everything in their power to discredit and sabotage her efforts. They deliberately tried to take credit for Jolie's work, held meetings that were related to her project but didn't include her, withheld important information, and a host of other things. Regrettably for Jolie, the result was operational chaos, angry customers, plummeting sales, and poor morale.

"I did everything by the book, just right. I don't understand," Jolie lamented.

Viewing colleagues and teammates as competitors, fierce opponents, or enemies makes us feel like we have got to beat them in order to protect our status or keep our position in the company or in the field. We often feel too threatened by other people's talents to share power, to share inside information, or to give recognition. After all, there is only so much to go around and we've got to get ours first. Right?

Jolie was hired to develop her employees and to streamline the operations in her organization, but she had failed to accomplish both. She had fallen into the sabotage trap that snares hundreds and keeps them from succeeding in the workplace. Regardless of the circumstances, she had failed to perform according to her boss's (and her own) expectations.

Clutching radical individualist thinking, which tells us "If we work hard, we will succeed," Jolie was crushed. Because this kind of thinking neglects to offer an adequate explanation for when we fail, she concluded that something was wrong with her and blamed herself unmercifully.

"I'm a failure. I'm so stupid!" she'd said before ending the call.

In truth she wasn't a failure; rather, she had not succeeded due to a broader range of snags, glitches, and deficiencies. Jolie defined herself by what she accomplished and that restricted equation quickly equaled failure. She needed to integrate other aspects of her being into that definition to feel okay.

Aha! After comparing my experience with Jolie's, it was clear to me that my own inflated expectations were to blame for my bad feelings. Expectations play a dramatic role in our lives and partly determine how we see the world and relate to others. Our hopes, dreams, and fears often become self-fulfilling prophecies and affect our future to some extent. But something else was apparent: We learn as much from our failures as we do from our success. Experiences, both good and bad, teach us lessons.

Shortsighted View of Failure

I was working in what I considered an intolerable environment, and to save my sanity I drew an imaginary line in the sand around my cubicle. Though I was not in a management position, I'd had my share of rude, backstabbing co-workers. Surely not the rule, but a few seem to pop up in every office, particularly where the competition to move up the ranks is fierce. Initially, I had assumed their sole aim was to knock me out of the insidious race up the corporate ranks. Now I was widening my view.

Like me, Jolie never considered that there were several ways to interpret her colleagues' behavior. She simply believed they were out to destroy her. By personalizing the situation, as if it were being purposely committed against her, she added to her pain. There were other possible explanations, like they were jealous of her position, they were insecure and petty, or they were simply afraid that a success for her would impede their own professional goals. Perhaps they viewed her as a threat or they were just acting in their own best interest.

The high side of this experience was that failure provided Jolie with an opportunity to see herself from a wider perspective. Had she been willing to see how she may have contributed to the problem, she could have learned something worthwhile and tried another approach. Instead, Jolie felt sorry for herself and was devastated. She was somehow unable to bolster herself with the fact that she had done her best.

On many occasions, I had done the same: berated myself for my failures and dwelled disproportionately on what had gone wrong—we probably all have. Seeing Jolie's experience through new lenses was truly a gift for me. Suddenly, all of the guilt that I had been carrying around about not being the best at everything started to fall away. I had done my best at that time, and this knowledge made me feel lighter. It is often incredibly tempting to dismiss those things that we can do well, those very likable qualities about ourselves that we take for granted.

We can perform better than ever and still suffer defeat. Living in a society that thrives on competition and breeds divisiveness, one that extols winners and reviles losers, it is easy for the outcome (winning, achieving one's goal) to become the sole arbiter of success. In this setting, our sense of worth can be wrongly devalued. Challenges and defeats are a universal part of human existence. Still, we all want to be successful to avoid the feelings of insecurity that accompany failure. Perhaps Jolie and I needed to redefine the meanings of success and failure as they relate to individual effort, so that when failure occurs, it is seen as simply falling short of one's goals and not failing as a person.

When we make winning our life—and our entire sense of value is based on winning—we have to keep on winning. In the same vein, if we are nothing without winning, we can never win enough.

Failure can mean a loss of status in the eyes of others or a loss of self-respect, but it can also be a time of transformation and survival. It can teach us more about courage, determination, and limits. The reality is that colleagues will not always be supportive, ideas may not be accepted, and projects may not go according to plan; but one must retain the willingness to do the things that one believes.

A New Angle

Expectations tend to hold us hostage to predetermined scripts. They can trip us at every turn, ruin our days, and set us up for continuous disappointment. They were a factor in Jolie's unhappiness. The discrepancies between our expectations and reality determine how happy we are with our lives and ourselves. Generally, if we get what we expected, we are happy. All human beings have the capacity to dream of happiness; in fact, positive expectation is a part of our nature. But our dreams will not always be fulfilled according to our plans and desires. Disappointment is inevitable. I bet that all of us could make a list of our unfulfilled wishes and seeds planted which never grew.

That old familiar adage "If you work hard enough, you can do anything" is misleading and false, though it encourages us to make the most of our abilities. For instance, people with zero athletic ability will never be professional athletes no matter how much they try. So it is both harsh and unfair for those people to cast self-blame when they fail. They simply do not have the capacity. The same is true for all of us. We each have a unique set of abilities.

Life is filled with criticism and obstacles, and hard work does not always produce the desired results. Sure, working hard will increase one's chances of succeeding, but success is not guaranteed. We can do everything right and still not get what we want. There are a multitude of events in our lives over which we have very minimal control. Believing that we must succeed at everything to be happy is like an emotional death sentence because failure is bound to happen. It also leads us to conclude that when we do not succeed, we are somehow inadequate or flawed, which can damage self-esteem. Every setback in life contains kernels of information about how we can change or mature. Identifying these kernels, learning from them, and using this information will help us avoid similar stumbles in the future.

How we see a situation often determines the outcome. We may label ourselves as failures, but chances are that if we made a list of all of our failures and successes, we could just as easily label ourselves as successes. It is merely a matter of perception. Quite possibly, we are not actually failing; rather, our thoughts are failing us. When we give our best in every circumstance, we have no reason to judge ourselves harshly.

There is a kind of undetectable catch-22 in the realm of expectations. We don't want to set our sights so low that we sacrifice the opportunity to challenge our limits and to achieve our highest potential. Then again, we also don't want to set our expectations so high that we are continually disappointed. Hope is essential for life and growth. Finding a balance between expectations and reality is essential. Expectations are no more than wishes or anticipation; they are not written in stone. Therefore, we would be wise not to empower our expectations with preferential treatment or see them as permanent fixtures that cannot be removed or changed.

Looking carefully at Gavin, Madison, and Jolie, it was clear to me that we often believe that we must constantly prove our worth, to somehow show others that we deserve their high regard. We want to achieve and admire the accomplishments of others, which is natural, but using our productivity and performance as grounds for our self-esteem is where the trouble starts. More goals always surface, which results in a continuous flurry of activities in order to maintain self-worth. If these activities end, the need to accomplish more goes unsatisfied, and feelings of worth plummet and the cycle continues. Eventually, what we consider living our lives will be no more than a search for external validation.

Dancing with Fear

FEBRUARY 2001

We are plagued by the many faces of fear; not the subtle kind of fear that surfaces as nervous tremors, night sweats, and nail biting, but the kind that manifests as negativity, anxiety, and depression. Our old fears of spiders, flying, and public speaking have been usurped by fears of getting old, being rejected, being inadequate, being alone, and a host of other fears. Somehow we hope that by fretting about bad things, we can think them into submission. Driving this fear is deep-seated fear that if something bad occurred, we could not survive and would be miserable for the rest of our lives.

Have you ever wanted to pursue a goal or achieve something but your own inner voice offered up hundreds of excuses of why you would fail? We often let our fear of failure keep us from attempting new things. Procrastination springs from fear, so we delay doing those things that make us afraid, like starting a project, finding a new job, or confronting quandaries with a family member. Ultimately, fear spoils our happiness and interferes with our ability to create the kind of lives that we want.

Myles Colburn was living in fear and fighting the imp of self-doubt, but he didn't know it. After hearing his story, I knew that we were kindred spirits. Myles was at a crossroad where he had to decide between a salary and his mental well-being. He and I attended the same work-related conferences every year. We'd met in New York for a three-day training session. After we had each picked up a muffin and a glass of orange juice from the complimentary breakfast bar, we found two seats in the center row of the conference room and sat down a comfortable distance away from the speakers. The large room was elegant, complemented by light beech-paneled walls and hand-tufted tan-colored carpet. I had already given him a quick spiel on how things were with me; now it was his turn to fill me in.

"Feels like I'm on Mars with no return rocket," Myles said, as if he were heading to an execution.

"Oh, yeah?" I asked.

"My former good life is gone forever. Today, I'm just a brain on a stick," he said, running his hand through his close-cropped black curls.

"What's going on?" I asked, fishing for details.

With his face draining, Myles answered, "Work is a nightmare."

Since Myles' first year at Northern Company, the job had been horrid. The bond between him and his boss had never jelled properly. Myles was just like scores of others who were uninspired by their bosses and their jobs.

Going to work had become a real chore for Myles. The alarm clock rang at five thirty a.m. and immediately that old familiar feeling of dread crept into Myles' psyche.

"I'm drained before I climb out of bed," he said.

More, his head ached, his teeth were on edge, and his stomach felt queasy. At the end of each day, he was empty. Years of stagnation in a job that Myles did not consider worthwhile or interesting had finally left their mark.

"I know that I ought to be glad to have a job, but sometimes I think, screw it; I'll quit this job and become a street sweeper. At least then I won't have to deal with people who are candidates for drug testing," Myles said, managing a smile.

"My boss made lots of promises when I was hired," Myles continued, frustration flitting in his eyes. "Now that I have the position, she gives me assignments for dummies, which offer me zero opportunities for growth."

Myles was being subjected to brainless tasks and other forms of emotional torture, with no forthcoming payoff. According to Myles, he had never gotten credit for his good work even when credit was due.

"Have you discussed your situation with your boss?" I prodded.

"Yeah, and she dismissed my legitimate complaints as whining," he said.

Noticing a familiar ring, I responded, "Of course. And managers are always right."

Hesitating for a moment, Myles said, "You bet."

"Failures and screw-ups are naturally someone else's fault."

"Now you're talking," he said. "And I work for a class-A bitch who suffers with penis envy and has the IQ of an eraser."

"Bad, bad combination."

"She'd take credit for the sunshine."

In a burst of laughter, I said, "I've seen that kind of mythic self-confidence."

"This job has 'dead-end' written all over it," Myles said.

It was hard for Myles to believe that he had graduated at the top of the class.

"Hell, maybe I didn't work hard enough," he said, downhearted. "I hate myself for being a nobody."

Myles had been robbed at pen point. Musing over the endlessness of each day, he wondered, *How can I stand it for the next eight hours?* The passion was gone.

We talked for a while longer about the possibility of his soliciting more challenging assignments or seeking opportunities with another group or company. His brain needed to be stimulated. Drenched in fear, Myles elected to play it safe and remain in a rut rather than to risk feeling more incompetent and leaving the job that he loathed in pursuit of one that interested him.

"Try finding another job?" I suggested.

"What's the use?" he asked. "Anyway, I've done a poor job of networking."

"The market isn't booming, but there are prospects outside of Northern Company," I said with confidence. "It's easy for our sense of security to come from predictable routines."

"It won't be any better at another company."

"What's the worst that can happen?" I asked, but didn't get a reply.

All employees run the risk of being tossed around like hot potatoes. No one is indispensable. Myles was giving up and it was taking a toll on his health. He had trouble concentrating and nothing made him happy. Myles was disgusted by his inability to adjust.

Myles said, visibly upset, "Everything is my fault. I feel like a total moron. And to think I was mad at my dad for calling me a loser. He was right. I have wasted my life."

Work had been a huge disappointment for Myles, and everyone was curious why he hadn't quit.

Myles' response was typical, "Obviously I'm a fool or a glutton for punishment. Or maybe I just want the paycheck and health insurance," he explained.

It ticked Myles off to always have to settle for second best. After a few years of having his options stripped away, along with his confidence, Myles felt like he was in prison. At thirty-two, he wasn't even close to retirement age. Worse, he didn't have any goals; and without them he was going nowhere. Myles really wanted to pursue other avenues, but the idea of putting himself out there in the market was terrifying for him.

"I need a safety net," Myles said with resignation and sad puppy-dog eyes.

"In today's market everyone is a replaceable commodity and few people have any real job security," I said.

This conversation was on a fast track to nowhere. I tried to assure Myles that most of our skills in this business were transferable, but that didn't seem to matter.

"I haven't been challenged on the job in years so I'm unsure of my capabilities, which only compounds my predicament," he said.

Aha! The core problem with Myles isn't the job or his boss, but the fact that he feels ill-equipped to change his circumstances, I thought, slapping my hand against my forehead. Myles' lamentations continued for another fifteen minutes. At that point, any interest I had in becoming a licensed therapist was starting to dissipate.

All human beings want to feel like what they've done, either at home or at work, served an important purpose or had meaning. When either of those feelings is missing, life seems pointless. But work wasn't all that was troubling Myles. His girlfriend of two years was pressing him to get married. Myles wanted a family, but the timing was off.

"I can't marry her now; I'm just not ready. She's just settling, anyway," said Myles.

In truth, he was reluctant to accept the burden of heading a family in his state. But Myles also had a fear of growing old alone.

Grabbing his head, he protested, "Look at me! What the hell have I got? Nothing, that's what—no money, no family, and no future … nothing to look forward to. I'll never have a normal life."

"Life doesn't always flow the way we want it to," I said.

"You're shittin' me," he said with mock incredulity.

"My life is a tad off track too," I confessed.

Myles looked surprised. "No way!"

"Yes. So let's try to make the best of it," I said.

"Sure," he said, his eyes darting. "That's not so easy anymore. Sometimes I feel like a hunted animal."

"Night terrors, huh?" I said. "Man, have you been drinking?"

"No," he smiled, "but that sounds like a great idea. I could certainly use a beer."

The session ended at five o'clock and I retired to my room for the evening. After listening to more than six hours of speeches, I ordered room service and called it a night.

Myles' notions of failure had been molded by popular images of failure, which focused on matters that were observably his own: no ambition, tedium, a loss of independence, a dead-end job, no wealth, no family, stagnation, and the stigma of being second-rate. Like most Americans, Myles had once believed that he shaped his own destiny; now he'd lost all hope of winning.

Myles was unable to see that his preoccupation with worry, failing, and being perfect was actually diminishing his ability to cope. "Blind in one eye and can't see out of the other," as the adage goes. Compounding his dilemma was the fact that Myles had traded a challenging job with a measure of responsibility for a higher salary and sheer boredom. Now his dream of getting outstanding evaluations and frequent promotions was trapped in layers of "bureaucracy and bullshit."

Lacking the courage to pursue his dreams, he settled for a cheerless life. He had failed to upgrade his skills and fully develop his talents, and now he was stuck doing mundane work for a job that didn't matter. Myles needed a mission, a calling, some meaningful engagement in the world. He would probably have been happier if he had a challenging position that utilized his talents and offered him a degree of autonomy and flexibility. He could easily have easily improved his technical competence via continuing education courses and work-related seminars. Life flows better when we engage our skills and talents optimally in a carefully balanced position between boredom and stress. In this spot, we tend to feel satisfied and in control.

I was totally empathetic with Myles and grateful for our conversation. Suddenly I didn't feel so alone in my struggles anymore. My own experiences were clearer to me and I had a renewed sense of hope and confidence. It's odd really—no matter how unpalatable one's job becomes, feelings of inadequacy and guilt are almost never enough to stir someone to take the bull by the horns and quit. That's the power of fear, and I knew it well. Fear keeps us from taking risks, and by not taking risks we fail to develop our self-esteem and confidence. If we're not careful, fear stifles our lives like an attempted suicide.

Immediately after speaking with Myles I recalled how badly I wanted to leave my job, but my competitive, stick-it-out nature made me hold quitting in such low regard that is was not a viable option. Just when I thought that I was ready to move up the ranks, I got a new chief whose cowardice could only be matched by his lack of management ability. Adept at wriggling out of his share of the blame, Mike would do just about anything to enjoy even a modicum of power. He was only one of many power-seeking piranhas in the corporate basin.

All of Mike's days were spent trying to impress upper management and trying to gain a position of prominence in the company. Working for him, things started to decline. Sure he pattered on about autonomy, thinking outside of the box, and inclusion; yet he demanded obedience and strict conformity. Those who failed to deliver these essential properties were ejected from the group. True to form, the underlings on staff were jumping through hoops like circus poodles trying to win his favor. Living in an insular bubble of adulation, Mike adored sycophants and he expected all of his subordinates to laugh at his jokes, no matter how unsavory. Unfortunately, superficial amity had never been one of my strong points.

It did not take long for me to see where things had veered off course in my own job. I worked for Mike, who was a master at creating friction among staff and damaging morale—the type we'd fire on the spot if we had the chance. Undermining employees was his game, as other people's strengths could not be tolerated on his turf. Whenever I submitted a project to the "king of micro-management," he'd return it filled with tick marks, superfluous comments, and red crosses. Feeling in charge quelled his insecurities. Mike compulsively nit-picked every line, and over time I ended up feeling that what I was doing was pointless. What a dip weed! My thoughts about work were, *Why bother?* Finally the cumulative effect of months of continual and unsolvable frustrations had taken its toll on me.

Just when I thought that things could not get any worse, Mike stopped delegating projects that warranted recognition or promotion. Ultimately working in this environment caused me to lose my focus, along with my plans for a fulfilling career. Once one of the brightest bulbs, I was running on one watt with no resiliency to recharge. I resolved that life wasn't going to get any better than this. Lacking the energy to participate fully on my job, my knowledge remained untapped, my talents remained dormant, and all of my potential was squandered as my malaise weakened my motivation.

Initially, I blamed everyone I knew for my dilemma, particularly those psychotic bosses whose need for control and superiority spilled over and put a damper on my life. Then I blamed myself, which proved to be an injurious choice.

Processing my state, I began to notice that quite a few people in my age group—intelligent, talented, and creative—are operating below capacity and still searching for their niche in the world. They are still miles away from reaching their potential. I believed that I could find my niche intellectually, but there's more to it than that. Consequently I was once frustrated to the hilt and distracted by those with very definite careers goals and phenomenal track records.

Reflecting on Myles' situation, I could see that though we can temporarily solve our problems by flying the coop, that is not usually the best solution.

Perhaps a better solution would be to address our challenges head-on and manage as best we can. We may not solve all of our problems, but we would be fully engaged in life and taking risks. Logical thinking and self-control enable us to endure most situations.

Fear: The Green-Headed Monster

Fear is the body's natural alarm, aroused by an awareness of danger. It sneaks up on us like an unseen warrior and clamps down on our rational thoughts, distorts perceptions, and riddles our thoughts with negativity. Fear urges one to flight or fight. The problem is that we fly, and we are often conquered by our fears. As Myles' experiences showed, fear can stem from self-doubt, feeling that we are not good enough. Therefore, we do not readily emerge from the fear of rejection, loss, suffering, or humiliation; rather, we cling to these feelings. We are afraid of our ability to endure discomfort and feelings of low worth. Because he lacked faith in his own coping abilities, Myles was convinced that he would suffer dire consequences if he took a risk. Like me, he needed courage to face the possibility of failure without being destroyed.

Shining Light on Fear

Fear acts as a diversion, which keeps us from accepting responsibility for solving our own problems and pursuing our fondest dreams. Though there are always going to be fears, we can better cope by facing our fears as if we are capable of enduring them. That kind of tenacity builds our self-confidence and it helps us to transcend our fears. When the next difficulty arises, we are better equipped to handle it. We can *hug the shoreline* for safety, but at the end of our lives we will be more disappointed by the things we did not do than by the ones we did.

Recipe for Resilience

MARCH 2004

Faces of new heroes line my walls. They are no longer simply the rich and the beautiful, but people who have gone through the storms and not only endured them but have become stronger people. People who have led easy lives tend to be dull, weak, and uninteresting. Listening to stories of hardship and courage has had a profound impact on my reality.

Though courage can be admired from afar, it can only be revealed through experience; it is most often preceded by adversity, disappointment, or loss. I was rediscovering my courage, but Naomi had already revealed hers. Naomi had endured her own private hell, yet she still found life worth living. She had the kind of courage that is not found in things or other people, but within each of us. Naomi Burroughs, full-figured with a zest for life, was a claims processor for Red Cross Insurance Company; which was located in downtown Catauga County, near the riverfront. Her wispy hair was always stylishly cut. She and I had worked for the same company a few years ago. With a terrific sense of humor, Naomi was an optimist, which provided her with resistance, strength, and a capacity for regeneration. She was living proof that happiness resulted not from the hand you are dealt but from how you play your hand.

Naomi's life was hardly the stuff of which Disney movies are made. She grew up living on the American margin, seemingly destined for the welfare rolls or a life on the streets. The fifth child of six born to a single parent,

Naomi lived in one of the city's poorest neighborhoods, surrounded by crumbled concrete, overfilled dumpsters, and the stench of raw sewage. Her mom had cycled through three rocky marriages prior to Naomi's birth, before throwing in the hat. Matrimony had lost its appeal.

Naomi and I met at Chili's Grill & Bar for happy hour one Friday evening, and we laughed over margaritas about work, men, and life in general. I was so awed with the way that she had overcome obstacles and bounced back from failure that I had to tell her story. Growing up, Naomi wasn't really sure of her worth, and she wanted to be anything other than poor and fatherless in a place that valued neither state.

"It's hell being poor in a rich country," Naomi said.

"Which is why everyone wants to be rich with an ideal life," I said.

"Money does have its privileges," she concurred, reaching for the salsa.

Determined to secure a chance at a better life for her children—a life poverty had denied her—Naomi worked hard rewriting the script she was handed. She longed for the happy, whole family she never had.

"We were so poor that I washed my hair with bar soap," Naomi remarked quite plainly. "I didn't know that shampoo existed until I was a teenager."

"Get out of here!" I said.

"My mom did the best she could, but she wasn't the most nurturing mother in the world."

"With six children, she was probably exhausted."

Naomi didn't feel wanted at home, so she looked for love in other places.

"I spent my life with the wrong men and the wrong birth control devices," she said, shaking her head.

"Sorry, you're not a trailblazer."

Naomi tried to assure herself that she had merit by sleeping with guys who wanted her.

"I thought men were the answer," she said, fluttering her leaf-shaped eyes. "All that got me was four children before my twentieth birthday."

I smiled, shrugged, and sipped my water.

"It was sheer hell trying to buy food, diapers, and clothing for four children with pennies."

"I bet," I said.

"Only the Christ has that kind of talent," she said, tossing her head back and laughing.

Naomi did marry. It was all very fast. He proposed on Tuesday, and they were married the next day at the courthouse. Naomi wore a new dress and held a fresh bouquet of mixed flowers, and her husband wore a cheesy blue suit.

"Grinning like two Cheshire cats, we stood in front of the judge and said our vows," Naomi recalled.

Most newlyweds were happy about being married, but Naomi was just glad to be able to buy toilet paper when they ran out. She didn't always have that luxury growing up.

When Naomi turned twenty-three she got a lucky break and was hired on at Wellan Foundry as a unit clerk. There she took advantage of the company's college reimbursement plan and earned a degree in business. For nearly thirteen years, her career with Wellan was good, with a few promotions along the way. It seemed that things were really going well for Naomi—at least for a while.

"Just when I'd thought that things were going smoothly, my daughter flipped her lid," Naomi explained.

"Oh, no," I said.

"Oh, yes," Naomi said. "She started hearing voices, running naked in the streets, and talking out of her head."

Less than a year later, Naomi's daughter was diagnosed with schizophrenia.

"I couldn't talk with her because mentally she was on the moon, and I was on Earth," she told me.

"Yeah, I bet."

"When she flips, she's as strong as a prizefighter on Angel Dust," Naomi chortled. "It's like a scene from *One Flew over the Cuckoo's Nest*."

We both laughed heartily.

"You're a hoot," I said.

It took Naomi a while to get over the initial shock of her daughter's diagnosis and to come to terms with the reality of her situation.

"I had to accept that my daughter's life would never be the same," she said. "She would never fulfill the dreams that I had for her."

With counseling, Naomi managed to unload some of the grief and guilt. She wasn't a bad mother, and this illness was not God's way of punishing her. Taking time off to care for her daughter, Naomi missed too many days from work and the company sent her packing.

"I was starting to feel like Job," Naomi told me.

"I can imagine," I said.

"I was sure that God had me on His hit list."

"Not a chance."

"I was frantically asking, 'Why me? What did I do wrong?' Then I realized that I hadn't done anything; this was just life."

"You're right."

"Sometimes I wonder how I've lasted this long, touching the hem of insanity."

"I often ask myself the same thing."

"It's hard trying to stay afloat when life keeps knockin' you on your ass."

Thankfully, Naomi got another job and her daughter has gotten treatment. I guess you can say life is back on track—for now, at least. Naomi was looking forward to lying back, watching old movies, dancing in the snow, making love, and having happy endings.

"I believe in God and prayer. God is able when we are not," Naomi said, her eyes welling with gratitude.

Naomi now looks down the corridor of her past with love and understanding.

"I've learned to reinterpret my life, to take lessons from it and leave most of the pain behind," she said.

"That's excellent," I said.

The waiter brought our checks and we paid for our meals. He thanked us and walked away.

"We'd better go," she said.

"You're right," I said, and we both got up from our seats.

"I'll call you tomorrow."

"Okay, later," I said, waving good-bye.

Remarkably, Naomi had achieved courage, amid adversity, that allowed her to see that even when life seemed to have betrayed her, life was still good. Because Naomi housed a well of courage within, she was never totally diminished by the events in her life. Her attitude taught me to view hardship in an entirely different light. Life is not always easy. But things only hurt when we can't accept them. Once we adopt that view, we realize that we are still lovable and valuable, and life tends to change for the better. There is enormous relief in surrendering to life. Whenever we can detach from life's painful stories and accept the truth of our lives, happiness seems to emerge out of nowhere. Most of all, I learned that though resilient people feel pain and loss, they don't allow those feelings to become permanent.

Happiness comes from loving the moment you are in rather than mourning what you have lost. That kind of acceptance often requires changing your view of life so that you appreciate all of the good in it. Sometimes we look for love and happiness in all of the wrong places before we realize that we have had both within us all along.

Gratitude is rare in our self-entitled society that tells us that we deserve the best in life just for being such wonderful people. We have to learn to be appreciative for even the small gifts in life. It is having a sense of gratitude that releases the richness of life. Gratitude transforms what we have into enough. Our standard education, modest homes, mediocre jobs, unruly children, unpretentious communities, average friends, and ordinary spouses/partners are suddenly all that we need.

Born with a Silver Spoon

Ivy's childhood was the antithesis of Naomi's. A fresh-faced beauty with short brown hair and green eyes, Ivy was stylish and exuded a brand of flavorful affluence. Ivy Leers, a friend from college, grew up cushioned by wealth in a moneyed community in Los Angeles, surrounded by mansions, servants, chauffeurs, nannies, and Bentleys. It was the kind of lifestyle that most only get a glimpse of on television. In the Leer's household, rules were scarce and Prozac was consumed like candy. Ivy's parents were part of the feel-good movement. In three years, Ivy partied her way in and out of college and straight into a detox center.

With memories of homemade cupcakes and summers on the beach wafting through their minds, her parents had hoped to create a similar childhood for Ivy, one that was happy, safe, and complete. They wanted Ivy to have a perfect life, which meant that they had to be perfect parents. Determined that their progeny maintain a leg up on the world, they sent Ivy to ballet lessons, piano recitals, and acting classes. Overflowing with parental pride, they loved to parade Ivy's talents: "Ivy, everyone wants to hear you play a bit of Chopin on piano." "Show Dan and Claire your Diana Ross impression." After years of having parents who oohed and aahed over her every move, every word, and every creation, Ivy overdosed on junk praise.

"My parents thought that everything I did was wonderful, even when I totally bombed out!" she'd once said. "Parents really know how to screw up their kids."

Elevated above the masses at birth, Ivy grew accustomed to having her parents buffer all of her mistakes and pull strings to get her out of a pinch. Heaven forbid that she should fail at something. Being cushioned from bad feelings and hard knocks robbed her of valuable coping skills. Because Ivy was never allowed to find her own answers or to solve her own problems, her self-confidence was trampled.

After a lifetime of receiving special privileges, pricey gifts, and loads of attention, Ivy believed that the world would confer her with a similar kind of admiration and treatment. In those rare instances when life refused to acquiesce to her wishes and she was not the center of the universe, her world fell apart. With a false sense of reality, it was no accident that she suffered with depression when things went sour. Ivy was also sort of a loner, which added to her troubles. She was never quite sure if people were interested in her or her money.

Growing up in affluence with people catering to her every whim, Ivy expected privilege and luxury. Those expectations backfired, making her ungrateful, cynical, and weak. Low self-esteem was also an issue. Even as an adult, Ivy lacked a sense of self and a passion for life. Everything was handed to her on a silver spoon, so she had no incentive to work or develop her own potential.

"I know that I should be doing more with my life, but I can't seem to get off the ground. Nothing turns me on," she'd lamented after we'd known each other for a while.

Like other apparent heirs, Ivy had not earned her money, so she didn't know if she could make a living on her own. She was always asking herself, *What am I doing here?* This often led to the blues, which was quickly lifted by her choice of delights: sex, drugs, partying, alcohol, or shopping. Ivy's life emphasized the fact that no one gets a free ride in this life, not even those who believe they should because they can afford the price of the ticket.

At times, we seem so eager to eliminate all of life's challenges; yet solving problems, developing relationships, and making things work is part of our innate design. Although our hope is that money will create a life of ease, disregarding the details of our lives actually makes us feel more insecure, not less. Humans tend to be easily bored with a life of total satisfaction.

From birth to maturity, our natural instincts often cause us to seek more and more independence. Most of us derive a great sense of fulfillment from our own efforts, not from being handed life on a silver platter. It is the struggles in life that often help us to become more responsible and independent, traits that offer us a different kind of wealth. Overcoming challenges makes us feel competent and courageous. That is something that money can't buy.

3 Appearance

Eclipsed by the Beautiful

APRIL 2002

We see the face as a symbol of the way we are. Our view of self is largely the result of views from our cultural mirror, which is reinforced by our bathroom mirror. Years of negative feedback can readily and easily distort our impression of who we really are. By the time most of us reach young adulthood, we are often largely dissatisfied with our appearance.

Who among us did not experience the horrors of high school taunting? I did for sure. I was teased mercilessly about my glittering braces and my voluptuous body—actually, the lack of a voluptuous body. People would hurl names at me like "wire head" and "metal mouth." Once a guy hollered down the hallway, "Kay is so skinny that her mother must be a sparrow! I could pick my teeth with those legs." Too bad I was thin before it was in style. Though I was never destroyed by the comments, I was bugged by the teasing and countered with scathing snaps, which I will not quote in this work.

Albert Kincaid's story is one to which we can all relate. Like most teens in high school, Albert was chided for his imperfections; but, unlike me, he didn't have enough cushion (self-esteem) to withstand the slights and was nearly destroyed by the experience. Moreover, he never counter-attacked, so he was a perfect target for all types of predators.

I met Albert on a cold winter morning in 2002, while struggling up the stairs on crutches after I had broken my foot. Albert was an intern at Catauga

Power Company, and he volunteered to chauffeur me around the complex in a wheelchair during work hours and to help me get in and out of the building when it rained or snowed. He was really a nice guy.

For six weeks Albert and I talked about everything from stem cell research to his childhood, and it did not take me long to realize why Albert was so withdrawn. Albert had been criticized for not being one of the "beautiful people," and I sensed immediately that his self-esteem was splintered. I knew from personal experiences that body image is often linked to self-esteem. Emotional scars can take a lifetime to heal and often they don't heal at all. I had met scores of adults who were still hurting over something that happened to them as teens. Their self-image was so warped that it distorted all information about who they were and controlled their every move. Albert was included in that number.

Most of us can vividly recall the sting of comments offered by insulting peers, parents, or others in society. Insulting remarks are offered to children— "stupid," "ugly," "fatty"—that few would say to an adult. Children are mocked and made to feel ashamed for being unattractive, poor, cross-eyed, thin, overweight, bad students, unpopular, nerds, and a host of other things. For some, these comments become a hidden ogre that wrecks their social life and blocks their joy. Those who fail to accept themselves give rejection a clear path to their emotions.

Eye Strain

Our daily encounters during this period provided me with plenty of insight relative to Albert's background. Albert Kincaid suffered from a near-crippling body image problem that separated him from himself and inhibited him from forming close relationships with others. He almost never smiled and covered his mouth when he spoke to conceal his protruding teeth. According to Albert, he was so ashamed of his teeth and body that a glance in the mirror conjured up self-hatred.

As a teenager, Albert often skipped class and avoided dating because he could not bear to be looked at, and he scribbled all over his tablets "I'm so ugly" and "No one likes me." He knew all too well the pain of peer rejection and of wanting to be special and loved. For most of his life Albert felt alone. When he tried to seek help from his father, his words of advice were, "Be a man and suck it up." And Albert knew better than to question his dad, who was always the final authority.

When Albert entered high school, his peers cruelly taunted him about his buck teeth and tall, gangly body. Initially, he ignored the cruelty, but later he started to believe what they were saying and to question his own worth. "The kids at school would take digs at me and jokingly call me Beetle Juice and Stick Man," Albert once said, dispirited. To Albert, those remarks were as funny as a train wreck. "I'm very good at hiding my feelings when they call me names. I never show how much it crushes me inside," he confessed. He knew that it was only safe for men to show emotions in a dark theater, protected from society's shaming gaze.

Albert let his tormentors prove to him that they were right about him and he essentially joined in dogging himself. He never considered that they were desperately trying to soothe their own wounded egos and mask their own fears.

College did not provide him with much relief. Once at a campus party, his peers chided him unmercifully. "Look at Albert, his teeth are so bucked his mom must have had an affair with a mule" and "Albert looks like an emaciated skeleton." These remarks burned like acid and ate away at his self-esteem and confidence. Albert soon grew tired of the callous remarks and being pushed around, so he retreated to his dorm room. The endless clobbering that Albert received his first year in college had done more to damage his self-worth than the brutal years of grammar school that preceded it.

Insulting remarks from his peers—the mocking, laughing, pointing, staring, and persistent teasing—nearly destroyed him. Albert started to hate himself because he felt that no one else loved him. Because he did not love himself, he dismissed compliments as ridicule and created a wall between himself and the world. Isolated by a snobbishness formed by pain, Albert's pattern as a loner had begun.

Albert wholly believed all of the bad press that others had ascribed to him. So it was no surprise that Albert considered everyone else more likeable, attractive, and cool than he. After repeatedly telling himself that he was inferior to others, he knew that people would reject him in some way. "Once I attended a party and I ended up alone all night. I'm definitely not a chick magnet," he'd said. Soon he stopped going out at all. Instead, he entertained himself reading science fiction books and playing video games.

The real problem was not that Albert was unlovable; rather, it was that he believed that he was not lovable or worthy of acceptance. It was more his thinking than his circumstances that caused him to feel alienated. There were tons of other people to befriend in life; he had only met a few. Albert's thoughts were cloudy. One bad experience meant that whenever he was in a similar situation, he would repeat the bad experience. If a girl turned him down for a dance once, he concluded "No girl will ever want to dance with me again." His beliefs were in need of tweaking.

Living in a shell of his own design, few people got to see that Albert was a truly delightful and brilliant person. Albert was a vivid reminder of how character is often eclipsed by appearance. Albert had the phenomenal ability to gauge the stock market, and once he was employed, he would surely make millions. He was also a computer whiz with a gift for hacking and programming in a variety of languages including PHP, XML, JAVA, and Dot.net technologies. "Understanding, manipulating, and mastering complex structures occupy most of my time," Albert once told me.

Feeling Insecure

Few things have the power to send one spiraling into a pit like grave insecurities about one's appearance. Think you're too thin, too fat, not attractive enough, not loved enough, or not good enough? Welcome to the insecurity club. There are a trillion issues available to make one feel insecure. Harboring outrageous expectations, narrow standards, and zany comparisons can make life really complicated.

Albert's story reminded me of Riley, another friend whom I met while taking an art course at the community college in Catauga. Riley Chilton suffered with skin eruptions that left her face slightly scarred. Her condition was another one that I could relate to. Although I never had severe acne, I did have oily skin, what I considered large pores, and chicken pox scars from a horrible outbreak in my early twenties, all of which were a source of discontentment for me for years. I spent hundreds of dollars on pore minimizing creams and oil blotters before I realized that I was fighting a losing battle with the oil. The genes always win. Thankfully, my dermatologist offered me a ray of sunshine. He assured me that in time, I would come to appreciate these qualities, because oily skin doesn't wrinkle fast.

Riley was a lot like Albert. She was extremely shy and self-conscious. Riley had skin disorders and called herself "Crater Face." Since her thirteenth birthday, she had endured insults and ostracism from her peers. Inevitably she felt alone in the company of her genetically gifted and popular peers. Riley's confidence received further battering when her attempts at dating proved fruitless. Things never seemed to work out. At thirty-four, the pain lingered on.

We had gone shopping one Saturday afternoon at Hamilton Mill Mall. After hours of browsing the racks and trying on clothes in Ann Taylor and

Banana Republic, Riley and I purchased two milkshakes and plopped down at a small table in the food court.

"I'm not one of the beauties," Riley said with venom.

"Ah, stop whining," I said. "You look fine."

"My looks are repulsive," Riled cried and then continued her self-pity tirade. "I have more craters in my skin than the moon. The last guy that I went out with spent all of his time staring at my skin and commenting on every inch of it. 'Can't you do something about those zits?' What a jerk! I may as well deal with the fact that I'll be living the single life forever. Flawless skin rules—just look at the commercials. I really hate my face."

"This kind of bashing should be illegal," I said.

"Oh, please," Riley said.

"If it were possible to be locked up for ingratitude, you'd be behind bars."

"You're not funny."

Riley whined for another thirty minutes about her skin condition and her regrettable life, until it was time for me to leave.

"Listen up. I have a wedding to attend this evening," I said. "I'd better get going."

"Catch you on the flip side," she said.

"Right," I smiled, tossing my cup in the trash bin.

Riley's vast insecurities produced such sensitivity that almost any critical comment sounded like blanket condemnation. When we do not accept ourselves, we believe that no one else can either. Riley replayed these torturous dialogues in her head day after day and wondered why she was never happy or content. In fact, she listened so closely that she could not hear the good things that people were saying. Riley played this tape over and over in her head until she actually believed it. Hell, she had even convinced a few others that she was horrid. That's the power of language, and of her thoughts and beliefs. Her language was the spoken expression of her beliefs.

That recording was so embedded in Riley's self-image that she resisted any new lyrics that didn't have that familiar ring. Riley didn't bother to put a new tape in; rather, she allowed her inner critic to run unbridled, which zapped her energy and eroded her confidence and self-esteem. Getting her to shift her views was like pulling rat's teeth with tweezers. Regardless of whether Riley's labels were truly applicable, they yielded a tremendous influence on her perception.

The somewhat exaggerated descriptions that others offered Albert and Riley had flown in the face of their self-image and they were flattened. Perhaps if they thought of themselves as more than the sum total of their physical characteristics, their egos would have been salvaged. Though labels shape the way we act and feel—and the way people act and feel towards us—they are often misleading and, for sure, they fail to wholly describe the multi-faceted human beings that we all are.

Although Riley had a few minor scars, she was still attractive, not to mention a gifted musician with a promising career as a classical pianist. She also had an amiable personality. But these qualities she ignored. Rather, she had come to see herself as nothing more than a face. Riley was split between clashing desires in her soul, desires that pervade most of us: wanting to be loved for who she was while yearning to look perfect.

Both Albert and Riley had distorted views of themselves that most likely developed based on some misinterpretations about their faces/bodies or from their interactions with others. They were struggling for a positive identity apart from commercial and social dictates. The tragedy of their situation, however, was not buck teeth or acne, but the pain of feeling ugly. Wrapped in self-loathing, it was hard for them to imagine that anyone could love them or want to be in their company—because they did not love themselves. So their own negative vibes were blocking their connection with others.

One thing was clear: this society has a way of devaluing and marginalizing people who do not fit the cultural standards for attractiveness. But our response to criticism depends largely on how we feel about ourselves. If we lack a solid sense of self, we repeatedly fall prey to the comments and actions of others. Others will tear away at our feelings of worth like vultures on a carcass.

I too was guilty of beating up on myself with the belief that I was challenging myself to improve. I will admit, it was a chore trying to be happy when the relentless bombardment of messages tells us that we should be thin, young, beautiful, fashionably dressed, and tall, with perfect teeth and blemish free skin. After knowing Albert and Riley, I was more aware of that critical voice in my head. I have slacked off of the criticism; the world does a good job of that. I now work harder to replace the bad thoughts with appreciative thoughts, and things are looking up.

Albert and Riley made me aware of what can happen when one's self-concept mirrors other people's negative opinions or largely reflects cultural models. The truth struck me like a bolt of lightning. When we derive our sense of self from reflections in other people's minds, we are precariously dependent on their perceptions. Every glance holds the power to affirm or destroy us. Since people's opinions are not always accurate, it seemed wiser to create a self-concept based on one's own ideals.

We have many desirable qualities, so why rate ourselves on just one? Physical appearance is only a part of attractiveness and a part of who we are. Intelligence, charm, wit, values, and warmth—those non-physical traits that truly make us individuals—are also in the mix. Some aspects of our self-concept are stable, while other aspects change from moment to moment. We may feel attractive after receiving a compliment and unattractive after being ditched by a lover. It's a safe bet to say that few of us consider ourselves perfect.

Our sense of self is whatever we believe it is. We have the capacity to judge ourselves as attractive and popular or ugly and hated. The latter leads to low self-esteem, which detrimentally impacts the most important relationship that we have in our lives: our relationship with ourselves. Accepting who we are physically is the key to a healthy body image. It means that we can love ourselves with crooked teeth, rail-thin bodies, and zits. By accepting ourselves, we can still work on ourselves at the same time. For instance, Albert could get orthodontic work to straighten his teeth, and Riley could see a dermatologist to improve her skin. But if that never happens, by accepting themselves for who they are (and not simply what they look like), they could fundamentally know that they are okay.

Clearly, our worth as human beings goes far deeper than our outward appearance. Life is filled with examples of aesthetically-challenged people who made extraordinary contributions to the world and achieved success and happiness without the assistance of conventional good looks. People like Albert Einstein, Golda Meier, Fannie Lou Hamer, Ludwig Beethoven, James Baldwin, Abraham Lincoln, Eleanor Roosevelt, and others were hardly considered attractive by cultural standards—in fact they were considered by many to be ugly. There are scores of actors, entertainers, artists, and athletes who are quite ordinary looking and yet very successful. Hard work and determination can help one overcome most things.

God does not seem to be a big fan of absolutes. There are those who seemed destined to be successful and happy but whose plans were derailed, and those who didn't seem to have a prayer but were remarkable success stories. Consider this: we don't pick our genetic traits; we inherit them. How we look is largely the result of the spin of the genetic wheel, which we don't control. Realizing this truth, we should approach life very differently, without gauges to determine our worth.

Life does not always deliver us in a perfect form. Sometimes we are not as tall, muscular, shapely, thin, or attractive as we wish to be. But it is our imperfect form that affords us the opportunity to grow in wisdom and love.

The Relentless Pursuit of Thinness

JULY 2002

The heat is on to achieve a rail-like appearance. Cultural messages have catapulted millions of women into the diet zone. Waif-like models, peddling a myriad of products and lifestyles, have glamorized eating disorders. Attention grabbing ads, promoting concepts of worth, success, and sexuality, reveal to us who we are and who we should be. Many women feel pressured to mirror celebrities who appear to be shrinking as their popularity and bank accounts grow. They fantasize about the perfect life that these images suggest: "If you're thin, you'll be adored, popular, successful, and always happy."

Thin is our cry and dieting is the plinth that underlies our self-esteem. Our obsession with sylphlike bodies is so extreme that some women are dying to achieve them. Young girls literally weigh their worth. As they flip through the pages of magazines, they long to look like the striking models with slim bodies, flawless skin, and silky hair, who are cuddled with muscular gods. There was a time when I flipped through the pages and didn't give any thought to the rail-thin bodies because I had one. But all of that changed.

It happened while I wasn't watching. Less than six months after starting steroid treatments for a medical condition, I gained more than forty pounds and my once defined jawline was now obscured under a layer of fat. The medication made me swell in the face and body to the point where people who had not seen me in a while didn't recognize me. It was truly an ego-shattering experience.

I went through periods related to grief and loss for the next few months, feeling sorry for myself one minute and then getting angry the next. When I met Sandy Warren, I understood, to some degree, how she felt. Like scores of others, Sandy had waged an agonizing battle over her weight based on a market-driven concept of perfection. Beauty brokers were making a mint on Sandy and others like her by trading on their fears, insecurities, and fantasies.

Sandy was one of the estimated millions of women who did not like the way she looked. She cringed at a glimpse of her reflection. Hoping to gain more confidence and to improve her love life, Sandy joined the dieter's brigade. Dieting for her was an all-purpose panacea and she'd tried every fad diet in the book: Atkins, Grapefruit 45, Sugar Busters … you name it. Not dieting or exercising was nearly immoral.

Worshipping the perfect-figure gods, Sandy subjected herself to a number of body hating rituals. She weighed herself a dozen times a day, exercised fanatically, and scrutinized the contents of every morsel she ate in search of an extra gram of carbohydrate or fat. To her, life was not worth living unless she was thin. Beneath all of the fanatical exercising, primping, and dieting was a sense of shame and the feeling that in order to be loved she had to be perfect. The price for not measuring up was a deep self-loathing. Just as I was preparing to leave the office for the day, Sandy walked over to my cubicle to talk, and talk she did. Taking a seat, she began.

"Look at you; you've lost weight," Sandy said, grinning.

"Yeah, a few pounds," I said. "But I'm not bikini material."

Sandy laughed. "How'd you do it?"

"I walk a few days a week," I said, "and I've cut back on the fries."

"I've struggled with my weight since high school," said Sandy, squirming in her chair.

"We all struggle with something."

"Not like me," she fretted. "I was self-hating and miserable as a chubby girl. I never got asked out on dates and everyone teased me about my weight. Plus, I could never find clothes that fit properly."

"I'm sorry to hear that."

"My body was destroying my life and my chances of being happy," she groused.

To add insult to injury, Sandy had three sisters, all of whom were thin and gorgeous with guys constantly hanging off of them. Compared to them, Sandy felt invisible … like a ghost.

"No one ever paid attention to me. It was so painful," she continued.

"I can imagine."

"A guy once told me that he wouldn't be seen in public with someone like me. 'What would my friends think?'"

"How thoughtless!"

"I started taking Fen-phen and lost weight," said Sandy.

"How'd that work?"

Biting her lip, a sure sign of insecurity, Sandy replied, "I've lost sixty pounds, which I've managed to keep off for a while."

"Congratulations on achieving your weight loss goal," I said, clapping my hands.

Peering at me earnestly she said, "Staying thin is hard work."

"Sure it is."

"It hasn't really been worth the time or effort," she said ruefully.

"Why not?"

"Sure, I have a thinner body, but I don't like myself any better."

"Oh no?"

"Duh, because I'm still single, lonely, and bored stiff," she insisted, as a cauldron of merciless criticism and despair brewed within her.

Sandy had hoped that her new life would begin after she lost weight, but that hadn't happened. Though Sandy's friends and colleagues raved about her thinner body, the approval high didn't sustain her for long. More, she hadn't had much luck attracting romantic attention of a desirable sort. Sandy was attracting odd types with food stains on their shirts and pocket protectors, and those who wore pants that were five inches above their ankles. I started to see the big picture: Quite often a woman's feeling of worth is based solely on the kind of man that she can attract. Sandy was not catching the eye of the top-shelf men, so her self-esteem was bottoming out. Further, since women are expected to be wives and mothers, Sandy could not fulfill her traditional roles in life without attracting the right man. Lacking the ultimate spoils of femininity—a husband, a child, and the male gaze—she thought that she was nothing. No wonder Sandy was obsessed with her appearance.

Looking away from me in disgust, Sandy said, "When I do get asked out on a date by a handsome guy, which is rare, I always think that he wishes I were thinner and prettier."

"Oh, now let's not call on the Fairy Godmother of excuses," I said with a bright smile. "Guys who are interested in you will not care about your weight, just your health and happiness."

"I'm not making excuses," Sandy said, obviously ticked by my comment.

"I'm sorry to tell you that you can't like yourself when you're thinner unless you also like yourself when you're heavier," I countered and there was an awkward lull following the venomous truth.

This would be no easy task with popular media depicting heavier people as unattractive, lazy, and self-indulgent. Undeniably, there are women who are considered heavy who are happily involved in relationships. With warm smiles, great personalities, and a zest for life, these women attract men as readily as model types. The singles are also enjoying life and not waiting for happiness to magically appear.

"I know, and thank you, Mary Poppins," she said.

"You're welcome."

I could not cut through the negative programming and convince her that she was okay. After all, most of her full-figured idols had undergone gastric bypass surgery.

"Without a doubt, thinner is better," Sandy volunteered.

Sometimes weight is just a convenient excuse for people's unhappiness. I have never read any published reports that thinner women live happier lives. Have you? Thin people get divorced, booze it up, lose jobs, commit suicide, and die, the same as heavier people. A thin body does not guarantee happiness. But no one talks about this sort of thing. Of course not; it shatters the illusion. I think it's a myth that a thin body solves all of our problems. I was razor thin once and my life was certainly not completely happy-go-lucky.

"Happiness depends on more than sticking with a diet regiment and finding a man," I said, leaning back in the chair.

"Oh, yeah," she replied skeptically leaning towards me. "Well, I disagree."

"You're a whole person," I said. "So, why neglect other parts of your being just because you're not dating?"

Flustered, Sandy flopped her arms by her side and hesitated. "Well, since you put it that way."

Sandy had not learned to counter self-criticism or do the things that made her feel good. Shedding pounds is no easy feat, but if we make our meals sensible, not restrictive and punishing, we will likely develop leaner physiques. Adding fruits and vegetables to our diets and cutting back on salts, sugars, and fats also work well. Good health is the goal; food is not the enemy. If we hit the gym a few times a week, we can raise our energy levels and burn off extra pounds.

"Savor the feeling of being alive!" I said.

"Okay," she said, her expression tinged with inspiration.

"If you enjoy painting, theatre, apple martinis, jazz, scented candles, or massages, treat yourself to a few of these delights," I suggested.

Feeling a spark of optimism, Sandy's face brightened. "I can do that."

"You can live happily, single and full-figured," I said. "If not, there's always Matchmaker.com. Fall in love via a questionnaire and one click of the mouse."

"You're hysterical," she said. "Actually, I'd rather have Lily's life; she's always bubbly and happy."

"Lily?" I asked. "Is that so?"

"Yeah," Sandy said. "Lily is perfect. She eats like a bird and is razor thin with perky boobs, which gets her tons of lovers."

"And not much love."

I'd seen her bawling in the ladies' room a few mornings after dates went sour.

"I never thought about that," Sandy said.

"She's as slim as a Palm Beach mannequin," I said. "And excessive dieting is certainly not the mark of a happy camper."

"Umph."

She paused for a minute or two. "Are you spending the night at your desk?" Sandy asked, smiling.

"I'm leaving in a minute."

"Okay, I'll see you tomorrow," she said before she left my cubicle.

"Good night."

Our culture is so obsessed with being thin that we tend to blame most things on weight. If we don't get a promotion, don't have any friends, don't have anyone to date, don't have an interesting life, etc., then weight becomes the natural culprit. The gods adore those who adore themselves. Honestly, I don't think it's wise for women to conceive of their lives as complete once they are wedded, or to consider that they are wholly valued for their beauty. Women are valued for a myriad of things, like their minds, nifty ideas, careers, and personalities. They may do themselves a favor and take a break from the "Build a sleeker, sexier you" and "Wouldn't you like to have a beautiful body?" advertisements. Surely, there's more to life than a starved twig-like body. It is fascinating to watch the beauty pendulum swing back and forth every decade from fuller to thinner.

Starving for Attention

Concerns about body image appear to be surfacing much earlier than in prior generations. Some of my younger cousins, barely ten, are beginning to show a preoccupation with their body shape and size. Young girls are trying to shed pounds that they do not have to spare. Some girls are on a full collision course to an eating disorder like bulimia or anorexia. Alexa, age sixteen, was a junior in high school and part of the Kid Exec mentoring program sponsored by my company. Conscientious and eager to please, she too had been devoured by the body image demons. Alexa often wore black spandex pants to make her legs look thinner, but she seemed unaware that she hardly had the stamina to make it across a room.

At five feet five and scarcely ninety pounds, Alexa considered herself fat and existed on a diet of sugar-free Jello, salads, and chicken broth. She seemed willing to sacrifice her health for her looks. During the Kid Exec's luncheon, Alexa told me, "I've been trying to maintain the perfect weight. I don't want the kids at school to tease me about my size." But weight was just one of the things that she didn't like about herself. Alexa also considered herself a "dork" and an "idiot." She wasn't enough of anything to suit herself. To her, absolute perfection guaranteed acceptance, so she was doomed to failure for being imperfect. "Everyone hates me," Alexa whimpered.

Though women's fashion magazines are frequently lambasted for glorifying slenderness, they are not entirely to blame for women's body dissatisfaction. If a woman is overweight, unpopular, or ending a relationship, being bombarded with images of thinness merely influences her thought process. Most don't consider that these perfect images often do not look like the real model or celebrity. They rarely consider the hours of hair and makeup preparation, photo retouching, and special lighting helped to enhance those photographs.

A Lucid View of Eating Disorders

Eating disorders often result from the way girls see themselves in relation to others and the world. By not eating, some girls hope to magically shrink their bodies into images of perfection, their promised ticket to love and happiness. Though the medical profession has yet to pinpoint the exact causes for eating disorders, one premise is that anorexia stems from a dire fear of being inadequate, unloved, or disregarded. Anorexia involves the self-esteem, and not eating seems to be less about not satisfying hunger and more a function of satisfying the expectations of others. Another premise is that anorexia may result from an inability to cope with life's stressors. Oddly, when women obsess about their weight it makes their world more manageable. Therefore, their weight becomes one of the things they can control.

It seems that growing up in a consumer-driven culture intensifies our self-scrutiny. For most of us it is automatic. We are conscious of our weight, bad breath, large pores, wrinkles, and a host of other things. With the culture initiating girls to feelings of inadequacy very early—girls who lack fully-formed identities—it may be very difficult to undo the negative programming. Perhaps we need to redefine attractiveness with wider parameters that span beyond a thin body. We are so much more than thin or thick, heavy or light. We are also thoughts, feelings, talents, personality, and a host of other qualities.

It is quite ironic: When I talk to guys about women and their troubles, the men don't seem to understand why women are so obsessed with their looks. Most guys are tired of hearing women complain about their butts and breasts and of their continual need for reassurance that they look okay. These guys, overall, prefer women who like themselves and who are comfortable with who they are. Understandably, these women are happier and make for more enjoyable company than those who are constantly starving themselves and trying to hide their insecurities and feelings of inadequacy. People who think that they have to be attractive to feel worthy will be insecure no matter how attractive they are. Looks fade, bodies change, and beautiful people abound. Sadly, most people who equate their appearance with their sense of worth will never be attractive enough.

I wonder if age, weight, or beauty didn't make us feel insecure, would there be something else? Insecurity seems to be free-floating, attaching itself to any explanation that happens to be helpful.

Looking Good

AUGUST 2002

Women today are under tremendous pressure to look and be sexy. Sinuous, sexual images flow as freely as water, and they are a source of visual pleasure. With boobs, butts, and lips oozing from every media portal—commercials, music videos, movies, and magazines—it is no surprise that women are obsessed with their looks and frantic about their sex appeal. Some spend their lives keeping up with trends, fashions, and conventional values. Regrettably, with their constant comparisons, innocuous grumbling, and faultfinding, they are constantly falling short.

The Right to be Ordinary

Something terrible happens when ordinary women compare themselves to waif-like models with striking faces hoarding the spotlight on sleek magazine covers, big screens, and runways. Many tend to feel a tad bitter that their looks are not being adored. In offices, cafés, and salons across the nation, women are deriding celebrities and talking about sagging tushes, flattened breasts, and crow's feet. And with extra cash in their pockets and the image of recent celebrity makeovers imprinted in their minds, women are seeking the aid of cosmetic surgeons by the millions.

Hardly a day goes by when someone on staff is not talking about cosmetic surgery, so this day was like every other day. After grabbing lunch from the Catauga Power's company café, my colleagues and I gathered in the lobby at a table for six and immediately began our roundtable discussion for the day.

"Having plastic surgery for medical reasons is passé," I said, throwing raw meat to the sharks.

"I'd say," Anais said, catching the bait. "Now it's purely elective and very cosmetic."

"Magazines are flooded with ads on how we can improve our appearance," I added, lifting a spoonful of clam chowder.

"With our worth gauged by an appearance meter, it's no wonder that no one thinks they look okay anymore," Karen smirked.

"And things are so competitive now," Anais shot back.

"Correct," I chimed in, taking a swig of water. I'd smelled the desperation in offices and at parties.

"As a society, we have become so self-obsessed that we can scarcely see beyond our permanently-lined eyes and bleached teeth," Anais said.

"That explains why we're all nervous wrecks," Joanie interjected before taking a bite of her sandwich.

"This society just won't let us love ourselves the way we are," Karen said.

"I agree," Anais rattled on. "Women are forced to change to be considered attractive."

Nearly coming out her chair, Karen said, "We're all chasing someone else's idea of beauty."

"Let's not forget the standards," Anais threw in, "which are so ridiculously high that they're laughable."

"Oh, stop crying," Gayle said with excitement. "Cosmetic surgery is great! Now we can all be young and beautiful."

Men are always griping about the time women spend applying makeup, buying clothes, and exercising. Beyond question, good looks generate psychological returns. It seems as if the scales may be tipping, however. Plastic surgery today is what cosmetics and braces were ten years ago—something we once lived happily without but which we have bumped up to a necessity. Many are feeling the seductive pull of the scalpel, which is why waiting rooms at the best centers in town are overflowing.

Hoping to get another rile from Anais, Karen said, "Some women pull into the surgeon's office for work as if they're going in for a routine oil change."

Gayle laughed, "Yeah, the ones whose bodies and faces change with the latest fashion trends."

Trends that change so fast that they're caught in a whirlwind, I thought. With so many drastically altering their appearance, what's considered normal and abnormal is starting to blur. Many women seem to prefer beauty stereotypes to their own faces and bodies.

"Sure, they may have tight faces, but their necks and hands are speckled with age," Anais snapped with an air of condescension.

"Oh, please. Everybody is getting work done," offered Gayle with her face brightening.

"I'd like fuller lips and a rounder tush," Joanie announced. "Move over, Beyonce'!"

"People who want surgery are unhappy with themselves," Anais said, raising her voice two octaves. "It's an act of desperation."

"Oh, let it go," Joanie said, looking at Anais as if she could scratch her eyes out.

Karen said casually, "There's nothing wrong with wanting to improve yourself."

We live in a society that values women more for their looks than their intelligence or talent, which partly explains why so many women are obsessed with their appearance. But it's risky when one's looks are pinnacle to one's self-worth. From creams and diet pills to cosmetics and plastic surgery, companies are fervently peddling panaceas to women, pandering to their quest for their ideal selves. Many women are being used and owned by these beauty aids instead of enjoying their benefits. Liberation turns into an enslavement to glamour.

"As soon as I get $4,000, it's lift city for me," Gayle replied defensively.

Recently divorced, Gayle was entering the single's world again. She was hoping to catch the eye of a handsome guy and be rescued from obscurity.

"Oh, damn!" Anais screeched. "No one wants to look like themselves anymore."

Gayle asked candidly, "What's the big deal?"

Leaping at the chance to offer her opinion, Anais fired back, "It's disgusting that so many women are willing to cut up their bodies to be plucked from the crowd and placed on a beauty pedestal."

Though Anais' words were spiked, she did have a have a point—a hard point, I might add.

Unquestionably, cosmetic surgery has raised the beauty bar and now everyone wants to be noticed. "Look at me! Look at me!" Millions seem to be suffering with a kind of media-managed neurosis. Some women are so unsure of their own worth that they are wholly dependent on others to tell them who they are—if they are pretty or valuable or smart. They may as well wear a sign that reads, "How do you want me?" Accordingly, a lack of attention, like a dose of cyanide, practically destroys them. But Nadya did not seem to have this condition; she was a rarity.

"I like myself fine—fat ass, double chin, big belly, and all. If people don't like it, tough," Nadya said, speaking like a true individual who wasn't a trend-follower or crowd-pleaser.

Raising her cup of coffee for a celebratory toast, Anais announced, "The thought of someone putting me to sleep with a knife in their hands is terrifying."

"You could wake up looking like the Bride of Frankenstein," said Nadya, lifting her cup.

"I plan to grow fat, wrinkled, and old in peace," Anais said. "To hell with it all!"

Everyone laughed, which was a welcomed relief after thirty minutes of acrid venting.

"You two should do a commercial for *Oxygen*," said Gayle in an incredulous voice.

The bitter truth is that most people just don't feel good about themselves. Everyone in this group was dissatisfied with some aspect of her face and/or body, even Anais. I had been looking in a full-length mirror lately, imagining myself with a slender, twenty-four-inch waist reminiscent of the one I had in college. It was certainly more appealing than the current waist that had been puffed up by medication.

This conversation continued for an hour with a nonstop discussion of flaws that we would like to have corrected and of others who'd gone under the knife and looked fabulous. Surprisingly, there was talk of how plastic surgery had somehow upset the natural order of life. Most agreed that many women over thirty-five who were aging naturally now looked horrible compared to the select population of surgically enhanced beauties who'd been lifted, tucked, and sculpted to a state of near perfection. By twelve thirty p.m., I felt like I had been in a war zone. If my insecurities weren't apparent before, they were jumping up and down now. Lunch ended, and we returned to our cubicles. I was drained and needed a nap.

The Media Authority

Our culture has woven a set of tight-knit rules to which women's bodies and faces are subjected every single day. Women, regardless of age, race, or income, are somehow bound by these rules. When it comes to judging their own bodies, many women consider the media authoritative. The media shapes and sells the view that everyone has to have a particular set of traits to be beautiful. We now look to models, actresses, and other celebrities to define how we should look.

It is nearly impossible to not be influenced by the beautiful women whirling around on prime time TV and spread out across the pages of trendy magazines. We notice the fabulous clothes they wear and the opulent life they represent. Their voices speak to us saying, "I am beautiful and you don't look anything like me." The images they project grip our imagination, flood our senses, and seep into every aspect of our lives. Few seem to be aware that the camera has transformed these images we "ooh" and "ahh" over. The photographs we see are shot by professional photographers, scrupulously selected, and computer enhanced. They are not one hundred percent truth; we just consider them to be truth.

Not only does the media nurture images of the perfect body, it also hones what many of us have come to deem as normal. We now believe that thinner is better, younger is better, bigger breasts are better, fuller lips are better, and round rears are better. Today, more and more women, particularly younger women, want to look like this stereotypical ideal. Pressure to possess a perfect face and body comes in many forms: lovers, spouses, neighbors, and peers.

Repeated exposure to advertisements aimed at women tends to make them more self-conscious about their bodies and obsessive over their appearance. Consequently, women with perfectly normal figures harbor the delusion that their bodies are abnormal and flawed. More, they believe that the only cure for their problems is plastic surgery. Alas, this preoccupation with appearance has not helped women to see themselves more clearly. Instead of offering insight, it seems to breed discontent and fuel the relentless drive for women to continuously improve their looks. Self-doubt and depression are predictable realities for those aspiring to unrealistic standards.

Although most intelligent women can rationalize the absurdity of one partial definition of beauty—the tall, sexy, thin, beauty with a chiseled face and ample breasts—some still succumb to the belief that those veering from these standards are unlovable, unacceptable, and invisible.

An Epidemic of Self-Loathing

Our culture has gone wacko about physical beauty. There is an epidemic of self-loathing in our critical society, the kind that emerges with nearly imperceptible feelings of doubt and self-contempt. Whether justifiable or not, women and men are being systematically programmed to be unhappy with the way they look. Having a gnawing dissatisfaction with one's appearance is so rampant in this culture that it is considered by most to be normal. Albert and Riley fit neatly in this trend.

Lacking the ability to see themselves with realistic confidence, women and men are being molded by concepts and beliefs imposed on them by others. When the predictable feeling of dislike raids their lives, they look for a culprit, something to blame: "I'm too thin," "I'm too fat," or "I'm too old." Beneath this feeling of self-doubt is fear: a fear of not being loved, of being pronounced ugly by someone else, or of being judged to be unworthy of attention. And so it was with Layne.

Layne Barrett and I attended the same church. She lived fifteen minutes from the Fresh Market in an area where streets were named after trees, like Oak and Plum. After a quick trip to the market, I pulled up in front of Layne's duplex. My timing was perfect. Layne was busying herself in the yard. Her lawn was neatly manicured and an old Pinto was parked in the drive.

Layne's dark hair was twisted up and held in place with a plastic clip. She was wearing denim shorts, a bleached-out yellow shirt, and mud-spattered sneakers. She looked across the yard, smiled, and invited me in for a glass of lemonade.

"Come on in," Layne said.

"Sure," I told her.

"It's so nice of you to stop by," she said as we walked inside the duplex.

I followed Layne through the living room to the kitchen.

"Have a seat," Layne told me. "Would you like some ice?" Layne asked, plainly happy to have some company.

"Please," I answered. "I love the décor; sunflowers are my favorite."

"Ah, thanks," she said. "Flowers make the kitchen look happy."

"Yes, they do."

Layne poured two glasses of lemonade. "It's rather warm out today," she said, placing two glasses and the pitcher of lemonade on her wooden dinette table.

We chatted a few minutes about church and the people there, and then the conversation changed. Layne was beating up on herself about her looks and the unfairness of life. She had once been a local beauty queen and calendar girl for Hank's Harleys. Now she worked part-time as a customer service representative at Magic Mart, and her husband managed a small automotive paint shop. In Layne's opinion, they were one paycheck away from poverty.

"I used to have a killer body," Layne said, tooting her own horn. "Guys would get whip lash giving me double takes."

Now, according to Layne, she was just an aging wife and mother of three. "Where did I go wrong?" she asked, shaking her head.

My guess is that many women have had this conversation.

"When I make the grave error of viewing my body in a full-length mirror, my self-worth takes a dive," Layne griped, and then slowly sipped her lemonade.

"Oh, c'mon," I said.

"That's the problem with having been dazzling. Once you're not gorgeous anymore, you're nothing," said Layne, looking at me with large, luminous eyes. With an aquiline nose and a full mouth, traces of beauty remained on her slightly lined face.

"You're a scream, Layne."

"Since the kids were born, my body looks like a Slinky with skin on it," she explained.

"Not good."

"You should see the condition of my tits after I breastfed my third baby," confided Layne.

"I'll take your word."

"My boobs have no cleavage and have lost all hopes of jiggling. Can you say, 'low-hanging fruit'?"

"No, no, no."

"I'd kill to have self-supporting breasts again."

Layne Barrett's inner critic was on overdrive. She hated the way she looked and there was nothing anyone could say to sway her otherwise.

"Why not do something about it?"

"Wish I could," Layne snapped. "My husband doesn't even find me sexy."

"How do you know?"

"He hasn't touched me in months and who can blame him?" she explained. "In fact he doesn't even recognize me in bed."

Layne was so ashamed of her body that on those occasions when she and her husband had sex, she wore a T-shirt and kept the lights off.

"I'm so horribly dried-up that I'm no longer *hot* to a man who was once obsessed with me. I nearly cringe whenever his groping hands touch my body," she said.

It didn't help matters any that her husband drooled over the latest pop princesses.

"It's all in your head, Layne," I reassured her.

It was in her head. Layne desperately wanted her husband to love her, but she didn't think that she was pretty enough.

"Are you nuts? When I ask him about my looks, he offers me the standard, 'Honey, I think you're beautiful.'" Layne said. She wasn't convinced.

"Ask yourself, 'Is my husband making love to my body or is he making love to me?'" I said.

"I don't know anymore."

"Think about it," I said, tapping my fingers on the table.

Layne continued to rant about the injustices of life and she was sure of one thing: The beautiful women get the prizes!

"Rich women have it all: the rich husband, the fine home, the compliments, and all of the attention."

"Yes, they do."

"I'm definitely not in their league. I drive a Pinto—a dumpster on wheels—live in a duplex, and my husband doesn't know that I'm alive. Life is so lopsided," Layne surmised.

"Sure looks that way sometimes."

She inhaled deeply. "I envy rich women like Phillipa Sloan. Her job is staying beautiful for her husband."

"Oh, yeah," I concurred. "Most women only dream of living that kind of posh life."

Phillipa worked out daily, played tennis, had a glamorous face, and visited the salon four days a week for hair and body treatments. When that failed to produce the desired results, she'd eagerly go under the knife to maintain her flawless appearance.

"Oh, the clothes, cars, shopping, trips abroad," Layne said, exhaling. "She's so pretty, she can forget about her looks."

"What a life!" I said. "Maybe Phillipa jogs in the rain because her life depends on it."

"Oh yeah?" questioned Layne, leaning forward on her elbows.

"It could be fear," I said, hoping to bolster Layne's confidence.

Eyeing me with suspicion, she asked, "Fear of what?"

"Fear that her husband will leave her for a newer, younger model," I answered, completely at ease. "It's a practice in many affluent circles."

"You're kidding?" Layne responded, seemingly grateful that the conversation had shifted from her.

"Celebrity breakups are all over the media. How'd you miss them?"

"I've been swathed in my own misery."

Layne, walking near the opened window, said, "The other day I noticed a stunning girl in her early twenties while walking downtown. My immediate thoughts were, 'You'll never look like that again. You're thirty-nine and getting older.'"

We chatted a while longer about aging bodies and marriage. It had been a long day, and I was ready to head home.

"It's been great," I said before springing to my feet.

"I enjoyed it," she said. "Come again."

Layne walked me to the door and stood outside on her porch as I drove away.

Bodies fall apart, and after thirty maintaining a good body is a full-time job. Like many women, Layne believed that her desirability and lovability hinged on physical perfection. She had a fear of not being good enough to be loved and she would always find a flaw to sanction that fear. Layne no longer appreciated anything about herself; if she did that, fear would fade with time. But focusing on one's self accurately, crisply, and clearly takes time and practice; it does not happen overnight.

Consequently, this conversation seems to happen to the millions of women whose self-perception is shattered when they fall outside the socially constructed standard for what is considered beautiful in women. I hear about it daily—the growing rift between couples. Physical changes, which are a natural part of the aging process, can chip away at one's self image and make one feel less sexy. Though advertisers add to the quality of our lives, they also stimulate our fears of getting older and losing our sex appeal.

Both men and women often feel that their partners no longer seem to be happy with the way they look. It seems that few can comfortably say, "This is who I am." Undressing, for some, involves dazzling feats of daring and huge leaps of faith. When couples are behind closed doors facing each other as they really are—no makeup, teeth out, toupees off, corsets removed—only seeing each other with eyes of young love will keep them from fantasizing of fresh-faced beauty or a young hunk.

One could reason that if one looks better then one feels better—and this is likely true when one's self-worth is largely linked to appearance.

Men Overboard

The male physique is also under attack. Countless advertisements, preying on men's fears, read: "Got a scrawny chest? Beer belly? Chicken legs? Love handles? We can help ..." or "Wouldn't it be wonderful if you had defined shoulders, bulging biceps, and awesome abs? Our workout videos guarantee success." The media has started to exploit men by showing images of the new ideal male body, which is an extremely muscular, lean frame. Underwear giants were among the first to capitalize on this image by selling their products showing barely clad models in their briefs. Call it equality or turning of the tables; nonetheless, the results are the same. The ads heighten our collective anxieties and drive us to seek remedies for minor imperfections, product by product.

We have entered the age of the modern-day Adonis with washboard abs, bulging biceps, sculpted chest, and muscular legs. Today, masculinity is displayed and qualities that symbolize manhood—confidence, tenacity, and strength—are being packaged and sold to men. According to the advertisements, which intend to salve the male ego, whatever distresses men can be cured with a gym membership, a new head of hair, or a bottle of Viagra. Some men feel dehumanized when they are judged by their incomes, biceps, or careers, just as women feel when they are judged by their attractiveness, bra size, or weight.

Though once the strict domain of women, being attractive is fast becoming an obsession for men. Blame it on age discrimination or on trying to get an edge on the competition, but men have been drawn into the cosmetic world like moths to the vanity flame. No more gulping down chili dogs, pizza, fries, and beers with sheer abandonment. Those glory days have ended and men are flocking to the gym in droves. Chip Rogers, in his early fifties and jovial, and I belonged to the same health club, Olympiad. We were talking about America's obsession with good looks while taking a thirty-minute walk around the indoor track. It turned out that he had also received a knockout punch.

"Never really cared about my appearance much before now," Chip said.

"You're not the only one," I replied.

"Who can ignore the infomercials that remind a guy that he's balding and shaped like a human blob?" he continued.

"Most can't," I told him in a robot-like cadence. "It's like we're all brainwashed androids."

"You can say that again," he laughed.

Those timeless before and after shots—with the before photo looking like Chip and the after photo like Brad Pitt—nearly tempted him to order a year's supply of Trim and Slim. But, he decided to exercise instead.

"Still hitting the weights?" I asked.

"Trying," he said, "but I'm in bad shape."

"It'll get easier," I said.

"Hope so," he said. "I tried to bench 200 and nearly ripped a tendon."

"You're hilarious," I said, and we both laughed.

"The show-offs ragged my ass for a week," he continued.

"The buffed twenty-year-olds with the bulging biceps?"

"Yeah," he said, somewhat deflated. "I could work out for forty hours a week and never look like that."

No wonder he felt nervy. Chip couldn't help noticing the miniature Arnolds.

"Beautiful babes drool over guys like that and turn their noses up at me," Chip announced. "This kind of scene can damage a guy's ego for sure," he added.

Men are becoming more conscious of their physiques as advertisements objectify the male body. With the duress of trying to achieve model-like bodies, many in the male population have become unsatisfied with their bodies. Just go to your local health club and you're sure to find tons of guys lifting, pressing, squatting, and crunching in an effort to reach the ideal that seems achievable with hard work.

Masculinity is often measured by how much attention a man gets. Many men feel the pressure to capture the limelight much the same as women feel and have felt for centuries. As ideals of manhood shift, body image neurosis is becoming more prevalent among men. Dieting, steroid abuse, and compulsive exercising—five to seven days a week for hours—are definite clues to this dilemma. Men are also acquiring eating disorders, diet pill addictions, and low self-esteem strongly associated with women.

Damien Kennard, Chip's workout partner, was walking on a treadmill nearby. His anxieties were also on high alert. According to Damien, when he looked in the mirror, all of his imperfections stared back at him. Chip and I completed our walk and then talked to Damien for a bit.

"My hair is as thin as November ice and I have a gut the size of Brooklyn," Damien told us jokingly. "Portly men like me are tremendously disadvantaged in climbing the ladder of success. We always seem to be beat out by taller, more handsome men."

I guess that was part of the reason why Damien was going in for liposuction and a hair transplant.

"I need to be the best that I can be," Damien smiled.

"So do I," Chip threw in.

Several weeks after Damien visited the surgeon, I saw him exuding self-assurance and walking with an air of one born to take charge.

"I'm just trying to stay in the game," Damien told me.

Right or wrong, our confidence often rises from our physical attributes, even if it's only a game of pretense.

Oh, Aging

JULY 2004

Talking about aging is like having an impacted tooth pulled without anesthesia—excruciating, ghastly. It's like having flesh ripped from the bone. The open socket and dull pain that remain are reminders of what we've lost. We have all been affected by our appearance-conscious culture, which has convinced us that it is disgraceful to be anything other than young and beautiful. People over forty are likely nearing the stage where they are vulnerable about aging. Out of the blue, wrinkles appear, double chins form, and gray hairs sprout. These telltale signs of aging are seen as an affliction that must be nipped, dyed, and drenched, but never welcomed.

In a society riveted by what we can control, growing old has become a lifestyle choice that cannot wholly be avoided, but certainly delayed. We are passionate in our mission to stop the hands of time and every effort is made to stay young. With improved health care and cosmetic surgery, one need not grow old until he/she is ready. Forty is what fifty used to be. Many faces in this generation confirm the peculiar fact that human skin can be pulled as tight as a drum. We can now have wrinkle-free faces from birth to the grave.

Anything that threatens our illusions of immortality—the chronically infirm, the dying, the elderly, the deceased—are segregated in nursing homes or swept briskly away to hospices to die out of view. The dead are quickly buried or cremated. Death, it seems, is no longer a part of life but a mere interruption. So we hold on to the delusion that we can eat healthy, exercise, lower our cholesterol, take vitamins, and cheat death forever. We have an arsenal of age-fighting weaponry: there is Alpha Hydroxy for the sagging skin, Rogaine for thinning hair, Meridia for the expanding body, and Viagra for the … you fill in the blank.

I felt like a fish out of water, surrounded by middle-aged men and women who were aging and hating every minute of it. While I was savoring in my youth and making party plans for the upcoming weekend, these guys were lamenting about receding hairlines, aching joints, poor eyesight, Social Security, and retirement homes. Before long, my own fears about aging, which were never apparent before now, began to emerge. One need not be over-the-hill to know how tough it is to watch yourself age and to lose the immediate value that youth bestows. As our faces change, we begin to sense that our ability to be loved and valued will soon fade. Clearly, growing old defeats anyone who is not profiting from the multi-billion-dollar cosmetics industry.

I had never given aging much thought. Maybe I believed that I'd lived in a perpetual state of youth as if my face was frozen in time. But after a co-worker announced to the staff that I had two gray hairs, the reality of aging hit me like a swift snowball to the head. *You're getting old, Kay!* I thought. I realized that at some point I would be one of them, and what a horrifying thought!

Aging, in this society that fears death, is seen as a failure, a humiliating embarrassment, something that people dare not do in public. Most approach aging beset by a dull sense of dread and swayed that old age will be a time of depression, infirmity, and loneliness, which is why few of us look forward to it. I'd been privy to countless age-related conversations from the over-fifty crowd, particularly those on staff at Catauga Power Company.

Ross, a self-proclaimed genius with salt-and-pepper hair, was at it again, bitching and moaning about the lack of recognition he received from the company and its preference for younger employees. "I've worked like hell for Catauga Power for twenty-five years, and what did they do? They filled all of the upper management positions with new recruits who are all under thirty, hired for their image, not their expertise."

"So I've heard," I whispered.

"This new dream team is driven and energetic," he went on. "Quite frankly, most of the older employees kind of feel inferior to them."

"Well …" I said.

"No one gives a damn about a fifty-year-old employee anymore," lamented Ross.

"The company wants us out like yesterday," Nick, his partner in crime, added.

Close to retirement, Ross was certain that his goals with this company were never going to materialize. He lived with a fear of never achieving greatness. Though he had considered getting another job, he was convinced that a fifty-year-old employee didn't have a chance in a job market with an affinity for twenty-year-olds. Ross promised himself daily that as soon as his son graduated from college, he'd retire.

"After fifty, life only gets worse," Ross continued. "No one thinks you know anything."

"Sure you do," I assured him, hoping the fuming would end.

Ross had a point: The job market for the over-fifty crowd was somewhat strained. Employers were looking to hire young computer whizzes who could perform similar tasks for half the salary of a "seasoned" employee. These new hires had connections in the industry and were years away from retirement.

Ross was visibly upset. He hadn't made a million dollars and hadn't done a damn thing worth public recognition. Isn't it odd? Sometimes we don't know who we're angry with or why. I was tempted to ask him, "Will a billboard with your face on it suffice?" Ross needed reassurance that he was contributing to something big and making a difference in the world.

"Tell me, where the hell is Easy Street?" Ross asked jokingly.

"I don't have a clue," I laughed. "But I sure hope you can find it."

Ross was questioning what all of his struggle and sacrifices were for. His home life offered him little reprieve because there his darling wife spent her days pacifying her mother—*the Anti Christ*—a permanent guest in their house whose very presence had given Ross violent stomach ulcers. He'd given up on an empty nest.

Then in walked willowy Polly, fifty-two and holding, refreshed from her morning workout, carrying an oversized Prada handbag. She had flowing bleached hair and her makeup was done to her idea of perfection. Tanning salon bronze, she made a star-like entrance, sucking up all of the air in the office. Beneath this outward show of confidence, Polly was consumed with a fear of aging and had already had several nips and tucks. This fear would probably kill her long before natural causes.

As soon as Jim entered the office, he had a joke for the day, as usual.

"Hey, Kay, did you hear the one about the senior driver?"

"No, and please spare me," I replied.

It would be just another trite joke on aging and I'd just about heard them all; we all had.

No doubt aging is made more difficult by an anti-aging disease spread by social delusions, which is fast approaching epidemic mass hysteria. People are on edge about aging thanks in part to the media, which offers a barrage of advertisements about loss of bladder control, electric wheelchairs, hearing aids, baldness, age spots, Alzheimer's, job loss, and preplanned funeral arrangements. Naturally many of us have come to associate old age with frailty, sickness, and ugliness. We're all haunted by the grim specter of jobless-ness and lovelessness that accompany the loss of youth and beauty. Most of us are frantically trying to avoid both fates.

As we age, we lose some of the things that we have been taught to value, like health and good looks. Time strikes a rough bargain, and our faces wrin-kle, our eyes get puffy and lined, and our features shift and sink, changing the natural contours of our faces. More, our bodies soften and our bones get brit-tle. For many (people like me), the thought of this happening to them is absolutely frightening. I've heard people comment that they've glanced at a reflection of an aging face in the mirror and then slowly realized that it was their own images. Scary stuff!

An Obsession with Youth

Youth is a national fixation and looking younger is more often highly regarded by the masses than a Nobel Prize. Even twenty-year-olds are con-cerned with looking younger. Take my cousin, Lela, for instance. She is turn-ing twenty-five and she is already watching the clock. Sitting around the kitchen table at my mother's home late one Saturday evening, we snacked on popcorn and sipped our sodas.

"Are you planning to celebrate your twenty-fifth birthday?" I asked.

"I'll be twenty-five, but I won't be celebrating," Lela answered swiftly. "I can't believe that I'm five years from thirty. I'm getting old."

"You're hardly old."

"Sure," she giggled. "At least I don't look my age."

Lucky her. For a long stretch I had also enjoyed the perks of looking younger, which engendered the divine fantasy that I was younger. I'll admit it was quite flattering for me to be called "Miss" in public at my age with the weight of gravity slowly pulling me down. I kind of liked it.

The message in our culture is clear: Once you're older, you're out of the game. So Americans want to stay young looking to beat the clock, so to speak. Not only do we not want to look old, we don't want anything old. Our reason-able desire to not look old has ushered in a deliberate propagation of adult immaturity as a cultural norm. In prior generations, people may have tried to defy time and appear younger, but we've gone a step further. Today's current fascination with childlike things—games, toys, movies, and dress—among adults seems to be indicative of grave insecurities about aging.

Forty years ago, society was concerned about what was age-appropriate and women over thirty typically steered clear of jeans. Today, fifty-year-old women, lusting after the latest must-have look, shop at the GAP and Abercrombie & Fitch for the same fashions that their daughters wear. While many adults are wearing miniskirts, hip-huggers, ponytails, and barrettes, children are increasingly dressing and behaving more like undersized adults. Something is definitely haywire when major retailers are selling sheer lingerie and padded bras in the children's department while adults are lounging in pajamas with Mickey Mouse logos. Adults have definitely hijacked the kids' world.

Few things are more embarrassing than an adult desperately trying to look younger by wearing teen fashions and making other weak attempts. Rather than looking younger, most tend to look ridiculous. Their efforts are transparent and what people really see is a picture of insecurity and fear. Tell me: When did we become a nation of teens?

Holding Back the Years

Back at Catauga Power Company, Polly was trying hard to stave off the ravages of time before any permanent damage was done. After being away for a few weeks, she appeared at the office on a bright Monday morning with a new face and dressed in a fuchsia miniskirt, a low-cut fitted shirt, and platform sandals. As soon as she entered the office, you could hear giggles from members of the staff.

"What the hell is she wearing?" said one guy, laughing like a hyena.

"No clue," another answered.

Another offered, "That skirt probably would have been cuter on her about thirty years ago."

"Is she blind or desperate?" another chimed in.

"She's never going to be twenty-one again," said one.

"And where'd she leave her face?" laughed another.

"Yeah, the new one is tighter than Dick's hat band!"

They all laughed and quickly resumed their talk.

"If women are so insecure that they'll spend a mint to get noticed, they deserved to be fleeced," the first guy added.

"Nature always wins," replied another.

"You guys are being way too harsh," barked another.

Another said, "My wife has had work done and she looks fantastic."

"Right, get with the program," another guy tossed across a cubicle wall. "By the way, men are having work done too."

"Is there a sucker in the house?" yelled another.

All of the guys laughed heartily, dispelling the strain in the office.

A few of the women on the staff complimented Polly for looking so young and striking.

"Wow! What an adorable ensemble," said one.

"Makes you look ten years younger," another said gaily while gesturing towards Polly.

Polly responded, "Thanks! I may not be able to compete with the young girls, but I can still turn a few heads at my age."

Four other women in the office were prompted by Polly's remark to provide their take on the issue of aging.

Chloe was also having a time since she turned fifty-six. "I'm sick of these hot flashes, mood swings, and bouts of vaginal dryness. I haven't been on speaking terms with my vagina in years."

"Aging is hell and certainly not for the vain or the weak at heart," said Henrietta. "The fresh face doesn't last, and those who are enamored by their own youth and beauty will surely be devastated by the loss. They should do themselves a favor and die just before they break."

Youthful looking Annette, age fifty-one, knew that aging was certain, but offered that she was not as uptight about it as most women.

"I live a very active life! I exercise, travel, volunteer in the community, spend time with my grandchildren, and work in my garden. I don't want to give in to fears and stereotypes about aging and lose my zest for life," she said.

"Most of who I am comes from the inside rather than from my outward appearance," said Ellen, who was sixty-one and retiring in another month. "The more secure I am with that image, the less I need to tamper with my face and body."

After Ellen's talk ended, I returned to my desk just long enough to tie up a few projects before my five o'clock alarm sounded. This day was done so I logged off of my computer and headed for the parking garage.

Another Look at Aging

Old age does not have to be a death sentence. It can be rewarding if we remove some of the stereotypes and social barriers that we've created. I know of lots of golden girls and boys who live very full lives and turn the fear of aging on its ears. They maintain a healthy diet, hike, golf, dance, socialize, exercise, travel, play bridge, have sex, and volunteer in the community. These people are not waiting to die. They have chosen to live!

Margaret, a seventy-eight-year-old member of my church, once said, "When you reach your seventies and eighties you don't have to be envious of those with youth because you can say, 'I was young once and had a ball!' I was once twenty-one. People seem to forget that fact."

Norah, another dear friend and a Silver Fox at eighty-five, summed it up this way: "The face tells the story of a person's life. It is the face they have created in many ways. Old age, and whatever comes with it, should be accepted in the same way that we accepted the faces of our youth. Changing the face shows the fear inside people who yearn to be young and lovely again."

My neighbor, Esther, offered another view of aging: "Actually America is the only culture that refuses to age gracefully. Other Western nations and all Eastern ones value age and the elderly. In France, a woman is not considered interesting until she's thirty-five and has had the opportunity to gain experience and the knowledge and wisdom that come with it."

Face it: We are all going to grow older and eventually die. Death is inevitable and a part of the circle of life. The Bible, in Psalm 90:10, promises us the possibility of "three score years and ten," or seventy years. After death, our faces, bodies, or careers will no longer define us. Instead, we will be remembered by how well we loved and were loved by others. Facing the loss of love and life should make both all the more precious because we know that they are fleeting. Wouldn't life be a lot merrier if we could learn to rejoice in the time we've lived and all of the knowledge we've gained? We can only hope one day to create and live in a society that cherishes the elderly so that growing old won't be so dreadful, or better, that we learn to value ourselves as we grow older.

At some point in our lives, we all discover the bittersweet truth of the Biblical admonition, "To everything there is a season." It matters not whether we like our current lives as they are or wish for change; nothing in life remains the same by virtue of its own will. To the extent that we resist change, we will cause our own suffering.

Fantastic Plastic

MAY 2004

Though many sneer at the triviality and superficiality of appearances, in America looks are no dismissible matter. We have created a society with a pervasive emphasis on appearance—and not substance—constructed around image, celebrity, and marketing. Beauty has become a form of status, like being wealthy or otherwise privileged. In a country where trends rule and money flows as easily as Perrier, more than a few have succeeded in creating faces that bespeak the ultimate beauty fantasy.

Physical appearance has become a gauge for identity and happiness. Some people were teased for their imperfections and grew up feeling deprived, shameful, and abnormal. For people like them, cosmetic surgery is a means of escaping this feeling by allowing them to achieve the look that their genes did not. Others with a dreaded fear of aging hope that cosmetic surgery will help them remain in a state of permanence similar to a twenty-year-old. But what makes plastic surgery most appealing to Americans is that it offers us the ability to transform ourselves to mirror cultural ideals of attractiveness.

We now have the opportunity, often by illusion, to be a part of a group with which we so desperately need to identify. We yearn to be included amongst the "beautiful people," those whose lives make the headlines and whom we rapaciously read about in magazines. No doubt, our intense longing for a celebrity lifestyle and comparable admiration rouses today's makeover rage. In our consumer market, it is often hard to tell where good genes end and plastic surgery begins.

Once the secret privilege of wealthy elites, aging movie stars, and center-folds, cosmetic surgery is slowly fanning into mainstream American culture. The process comes complete with in-house financing options and coming out parties. Whether it's a speedy breast enhancement or a lunch break Botox, the plastic surgery craze is gradually becoming the norm. It has become standard media fodder with constant coverage on prime time television, magazine covers, and talk shows. Celebrities continue to reign supreme in the makeover world, and we all marvel at the latest Hollywood alterations. We are enthralled by how many nose jobs the "King of Pop" has had or Pamela Anderson's current cup size or how many face-lifts the "Mouth of Style" has undergone. For those whose fame lies in their faces, trying to stay afloat in an industry that shelves thirty-year-olds is no easy task. We have all seen our share of stars come crashing down when the bright lights faded and the adoration ended.

Looking good is considered a panacea for unhappiness. In a culture fed on quick-fix solutions, cosmetic surgeons are being called "psychologists with a scalpel." They are transforming faces and making people more outgoing. Undergoing surgery is considered a business decision with psychological benefits, such as a boost in self-esteem and a surge in confidence.

With the media persistently advertising the hottest body as an achievable asset, and the beauty industry promoting ugliness as a defect that can only be corrected by going under the knife, cosmetic surgery is no longer a luxury or an option for many; it is a necessity. Modifying and improving the body is now vital to one's sense of worth. A co-worker and I once discussed the issue of undergoing plastic surgery. According to Brooke, "The world simply writes you off if you're not beautiful. It's like, if you're not perfect, you don't exist."

The search for the perfect face and body is in motion, with an emphasis on homogeneity. No longer does nature determine who will be beautiful; now it is the most skillful surgeons and those who can afford them. If we're willing to shell out enough cash, we can change most anything we don't like about ourselves.

We now have the power to design our faces, bodies, and overall look in the same way that we choose our fashions, hair color, or lipsticks. No more sagging faces, shriveled boobs, or hanging bellies; we can all now have something firm and appealing. Life in plastic is fantastic! But with every brow lifted, tummy tucked, and wrinkled smoothed, the list of operations seems to grow and grow without limits.

One has to wonder why so many men and women want to change what they were born with in such a dramatic way. It seems that having a measure of control over our appearance has actually diminished our ability to live with the traits with which we were born. There seems to always be something else that needs to be nipped or tucked. Slaves to a myth that our value is based solely on our appearance, we strive to achieve the perfect body and judge ourselves according to how well we measure up. In the views of many women, a minor blemish (what am I saying—there is no such thing as a minor blemish today!), an extra pound, slightly sagging skin, thinning hair, and small breasts all have the power to undermine our social confidence and self-esteem in ways that other things do not. Gretchen, another thirty-something-year-old colleague, was on board and looking good. She was part of a growing army of women who were prepared to spend big bucks and take big risks to improve their appearance.

"I've always loved body-hugging dresses and skimpy bikinis, but didn't have the body for either," Gretchen related. "After I'd gotten tummy liposuction and a breast lift, I decided to remove the puffy bags from under my eyes. A few bruises and weeks in isolation were a minor price to pay. I'm so pleased with the outcome that I'm planning more nips."

Our appearance has some consequences that we cannot deny. Sure there are other equally important parts of ourselves, but beauty seems to carry the most weight. Clearly, beauty is rewarding. Not only does it increase the longed-for admiration from others, but it also offers a route to intimacy, power, and riches. People are more prone to want to please good-looking people without any expectation of reward or reciprocity. Good looks often offer perks like more job opportunities, a wealth of sexual suitors, and a host of other privileges. A striking face can generate success as freely as competence in the workplace and socially.

Other co-workers shared with me their opinions and experiences regarding their decisions to undergo plastic surgery. At thirty-seven, Blaise, a contractor with Catauga Power Company, seemed like a premature candidate for a face-lift. However, she fitted neatly into a pattern of increasing numbers of women hoping to hold off the ravages of time before the big damage occurs. In a few weeks, she'd be going in for her lift.

"I know that drooping jowls and cheek folds are minor complaints, but I have to fight against the inescapable effects of gravity," Blaise told me while repairing my computer. "I don't want to lose my competitive edge in the workplace."

Another colleague, Catherine, had always been told that she was beautiful, but when she turned forty-five things began to droop a little and so did her identity. So she embarked on a plastic surgery binge that made the Hollywood greats pale by comparison. Still, nothing could hide the fact that Catherine continued to age, and because her entire identity was wrapped up in her looks, her self-esteem was obliterated.

Further driving this makeover mania are prime-time shows like *The Swan* and *Extreme Makeover* that highlight a kind of magical physical transformation. As the shows participants' personal flaws go under the knife, their looks, lives, and destinies are forever altered with new faces and bodies. In each episode, self-declared ugly women offer themselves up like human sacrifices to an array of cosmetic surgeons and dentists. These experts rearrange their faces, bond their teeth, reshape their noses, siphon their fat, lift their boobs, and lead them down the path to newfound self-esteem, which is reflected in the mirror.

Each seems convinced that with a tweak to the nose, fleshier lips, a bit more chin, and a tighter tummy, life will be one sweet, happy song. It's obviously engaging to watch women with mutilated self-esteems and towering insecurities change their lives by changing their looks.

In one episode, Wendy was a contestant on *The Swan*. Most of her life, Wendy considered herself disgusting-looking and worthless. Believing that no one would love her, she hoped that the surgical procedures would magically fix her face, body, and life. After numerous procedures, Wendy emerged from a chrysalis of bandages and bruises. Cheered on by an excited audience, she made her entrance and was hailed one the beautiful people. Wendy was no longer ashamed of being seen in public. She summed up her experiences by stating, "I feel so much better about myself. I'm no longer the brunt of jokes, and getting a few glances from the opposite sex is nice. My surgeon was truly a godsend."

Brimming over with confidence and a radiating smile, pleased at having achieved the ideal of physical perfection, Wendy, like other contestants, attested to the hype of the makeover creed. It appeared that years of crushed self-esteem could be fixed by undergoing a laundry list of surgical procedures.

Arguably, these shows have helped to manufacture a new brand of dissatisfaction among people, especially those who can't afford a new face and body makeover. They may have also helped to elevate beauty to a need and made people more obsessed with how they look. We have to realize that not looking like celebrities or the current super models doesn't mean that we look bad or need altering. If prime time TV had its way, we would all be inculcated with the constant preoccupation of altering rather than simply being.

These shows gloss over reality by failing to offer the flipside of the coin. That's entertainment—that's Hollywood. The reality is that after the lights dim, all of these stories of ugly ducklings turned beautiful swans don't have such a happy ending. Their partners may be threatened by their new look (particularly if they felt more secure in the relationship with their old face), or their friends may envy their new image, or their relatives don't recognize them. Even worse, some of these emotionally delicate women return to their dreary lives to find new things to hate about themselves.

Bigger Things

Boob jobs seem to be the hottest gifts for sixteenth birthdays and graduations, surpassing new sports cars. Teens engulfed in a sea of images swimming with young pop idols—like Jessica, Britney, Lindsay, and others who are very thin with improbably large breasts—are feeling the squeeze to meet those same standards. Though these girls cannot order highballs, they can order bigger boobs. For vulnerable teens whose self-worth is judged by the attention they get, breast implants are an alluring self-esteem quick fix. They all want to experience that loving, exhilarating, and constantly happy life that a curvaceous body seems to guarantee.

Ignoring the health risks, teens are marching in droves into the surgeon's office in search of this sensual look. Some want fuller breasts to make their boyfriends happy: "My boyfriend totally loves girls with big breasts." They probably never consider that there are guys who'll like them the way they are. A few are encouraged by parents who believe bigger breasts are essential to their daughters' well-being. Such were Emma and Hailey's parents.

Emma and Hailey, my neighbor's daughters, received breast enhancement surgery courtesy of their parents for their high school graduation gifts. The parents certainly didn't want their girls to fall behind aesthetically. At one of our monthly neighborhood meetings, Emma told me with excitement, "All of the guys fantasize and ogle over girls with big breasts." Hailey threw in, "We want to look as good as the other girls!" They would soon be feminine symbols of desirability.

Breasts are considered gauges for sexuality, which partly explains the skyrocketing demand for breast implants, some as big as a human head. This fad also accounted for why my formerly obscure cohort, Lauren, who'd recently gotten a new bosom had suddenly blossomed socially. I had once considered boosting my bra size up a notch as a way of speeding up my search for Mr. Right. But that thought was deflated like a popped balloon when a friend reminded me that bigger breasts could make me look like an inverted pear with legs.

Lauren, age thirty-one, wife and mother of four, had her breasts done.

"Small boobs were poisoning my life. I was ashamed of the way I looked in a bikini," Lauren recalled. "Compared to other full-breasted women, I was so unsexy."

Since Lauren enhanced her breasts from a 34 A to a curvy 34 D, she felt more confident.

"The scars are minor and my body looks better than ever," Lauren added. "When men see me now, they are like, 'Wow!' I feel fabulous!"

Cosmetic surgery is often treated like a competitive sport and the winner gets the prize. The race is on and may the vainest woman (or man) win. This viewpoint alone keeps us nipping and tucking without feeling any happier. In fact, we are more miserable because someone else has nipped more. There is virtually no limit to what surgeons can do to reshape our faces and bodies, so where is the cut-off point?

There is certainly nothing wrong with wanting to look your best. If something bothers you, you fix it. What's the problem? Movie stars and models do it all the time. Right? Of course. Certainly people feel more secure after changing something they've been unhappy with for a while. But are people capable of changing their appearance once and then calling it quits, or are they creating problems for themselves in the long run? Self-improvement is good, but sometimes the line between looking better and psychosis gets blurred.

Impressive results pave the way for even higher expectations and more surgery. If our expectations are unattainable, they will only lead to disappointment and a sense of being "less than." Trying to achieve perfection is a vicious trap which you can't be released from by changing your body.

This is definitely the year of the man-made woman. Is it possible that in obsessing about our bodies, we've lost our minds? Possibly. If you believe the media hype, scores of women want to emulate the look of famous stars. At the top of most wish lists are lips like Angelina Jolie's, breasts like Pamela Anderson's, a derriere like Beyonce Knowles', a nose like Gwyneth Paltrow's, eyes like Salma Hayek's, and cheek bones like Halle Berry's. We're fast approaching the age of homogeneous beauty. A few surgeons already seem to be helping to create a society of people who all look eerily alike. I see it in countless familiar ways: The world still idolizes Barbie and consequently sets the intellectual standards suitably low so that women can fit in without doing anything special.

Conventional beauty is artificial beauty. With women adding and modifying parts as if they were machinery, there will soon be an assembly line of Penthouse-like, female robots with pointed noses, pendulous breasts, pouty lips, jutting cheekbones, and permanently surprised expressions.

Who's Getting a Makeover?

People can talk about surgery—"I just want to feel better" or "I'm doing it for myself"—until they're blue in the face (as if simply reshaping their outer selves will automatically brighten their inner selves); but even Stevie Wonder is aware of what society deems attractive and desirable. We should take into account that few people would likely think of getting a tighter face, fuller breasts, or a flatter tummy if it weren't for cultural ideals that reward those who possess them and ignore those who don't. Even the beautiful people are riding the wave of discontent and are just a few operations shy of the face and body they really crave.

Any number of reasons motivate people toward change: other people's expectations, competition among the sexes, rebounding from a divorce, seeking attention, emulating celebrities, trying to advance in a competitive job market, and romantic hopes all contribute to a person's decision to surgically alter his/her appearance. The newsstands offer more than a few stories of recently jilted wives desiring to upstage their husband's new companion.

Many people are deluded into thinking that changing their appearance will change their lives. It may not, particularly if the root of their unhappiness is more than skin deep. It's a slippery slope to rely on a surgeon to solve your self-esteem problems, because in the end they will not be resolved with a scalpel. The surgery may not turn out the way you expected or change your life the way you hoped.

Without question plastic surgery can make you look better, especially if you're thinking, "If I had a gorgeous face or bigger breasts, people would love me." Then you have the surgery and you don't feel any more worthy; instead you feel just as inadequate as before. So you go back and have more cosmetic surgery and yet you don't feel any better about yourself. Enough is never enough. Continually improving one's self on the outside will not automatically make one feel worthy on the inside—though some surgeons are willing to oblige one's fantasies.

A sensual appearance cannot guarantee that you will get more attention from the opposite sex, climb the corporate ladder, or be the star attraction. People who believe that a cosmetic change is going to fix all that is wrong in their lives risk emotional aftershock. They may wind up depressed and suicidal when they realize they are still the same person with the same life. Zoe, my Pilates instructor, had Botox, breast implants, and lip enhancement surgery in hopes of adding spice to her life.

"After the surgery, I thought that my life would be perfect," Zoe lamented.

"Please," I said. "Guys are running into walls looking at you."

"Sure, guys notice me more, you know, mostly the fetish types," said Zoe.

"Ahh, yes, that type."

"Honestly, my life really hasn't changed much."

"You can't be serious?"

"Most people don't seem to notice the new me."

"That's interesting."

"Nothing can change your life but your attitude about who you are."

Life is too complicated for a boob job or Brazilian butt lift to make that much difference in one's life. Clearly, we have to create and save our own lives. Looking like somebody else on the outside will not change the internal ache that results from years of torment. Words hurt and the pain is still there until people make peace with it. Forgiveness is the only way. Otherwise, you keep replaying the insults over and over until your own critic takes over and beats you up some more. The inner critic echoes, "You're still ugly … You're too fat … You're too wrinkled …" The critic never runs out of flaws to magnify.

Plus, not everyone will celebrate your new look. Often family, friends, and peers treat you differently after surgery and occasionally resent you for looking and feeling better. Having cosmetic surgery awakens a kind of antagonism; people don't like to think that you're cheating your way out of the competition.

Shifting Perspective

Cosmetic surgeons can create an "improved" you, but not necessarily a twenty-year-old you. So if people are having surgery to put off aging, the result is only temporary. Gravity is pitiless and a person who undergoes surgery cannot defer growing old forever. Although today's enhancements in cosmetic surgery can turn back the hands of time, they can only turn them back so far. The aging process continues and a person who has had a cosmetic procedure could end up looking worse in a few years than if they hadn't tampered with nature. The corrected feature may simply play up other flaws that haven't been tucked or lifted.

Skin loses its elasticity with time and even if the skin is pulled tighter, you cannot recreate the subtle natural contours of a youthful face or replace the dewy skin of youth. You are fighting a losing battle against genes, gravity, and time, which ultimately you can't win—none of us can. Those in search of eternal youth will eventually be disappointed. If some people are not careful, they'll look like a few popular celebrities for whom surgery has become a fashion accessory. Their tight, shiny faces are void of individuality and character, those traits that we profess to prize most. With grisly face-lifts born of warped expectations, they seem to have wandered out of Madame Tussaud's Wax Museum.

To apply broad generalizations to all persons seeking cosmetic enhancement leaves us lacking. Whether a person is motivated by dissatisfaction, dysfunction, or simply the desire to slow the signs of aging or correct minor imperfections, the decision to undergo surgery is an individual choice, deserving neither applause nor denigration, and one with which the person who has cosmetic surgery will have to live. We can all spend a lifetime lifting, tucking, and suctioning, but we will one day have to face the inoperable truth that all the surgery in the world cannot displace our need for self-acceptance.

The best way to be happy is to start liking the bodies that we've been given. It is in altering our mindsets—undoing the negative attitudes and releasing punitive self-judgments—that we find happiness and confidence. This, of course, is easier said than done, particularly in our nip and tuck world. But it is doable.

As our bodies become commodities, physical perfection will be seen as necessary to ensure the quality of life and cosmetic surgery necessary for psychological health. Is this the kind of mad world that we really want? If our culture continues on this path, we will soon be a society of plastic surgery fiends. I have a feeling that this desperate quest for perfection will soon be regarded as a more burning cry for help than anorexia or drug addictions.

Given the opportunity to be handed physical beauty on a platter, few of us would refuse it. Nonetheless, pinning our hopes for happiness on physical perfection sets the stage for a disastrous crash. Beauty will not last forever; call it aging. Few of us can achieve the perfect body, face, or anything else. Perfection is simply a great illusion. As the culture continues to test the limits of good taste, we will never be beautiful enough.

The storage shelves underneath my vanity are overflowing with skin care creams, vitamins, and hair products. Every commercial for wrinkle cream, exercise equipment, and protein conditioner kindles my anxieties and makes me wonder if I'll be left in the dust. Despite all of this, it is apparent that real happiness results not simply from trying to be like everyone else, but from one's own individuality. With each passing day, I am learning to feel more satisfied with the image reflected in my mirror and not the image on the printed page or big screen. Clearly, those who are bound by convention are soon lost in the crowd.

Wouldn't it be great if we could just say, "I'm okay the way I am," and then sit back and admire the beauty of our untransformed selves? For the masses, it seems there is no fable or appeal in that resolve.

4 Love

Rescue Me

JANUARY 1999

Most people speak of love; it is the center of our lives. We thrive on intimate relationships. Romantic relationships make us feel attractive and seductive; we smile more and seem to get more enjoyment out of life. We are elated when we have romantic relationships and miserable when we lose them. For many of us, when we are not in a relationship, we can think of nothing we want more, which explains why dating services and personal advertisements have sprouted up at every turn. In twenty words or less, we secretly hope to find love lurking in the ads—that special someone who will add romance to our lives. But most of all, we hope to meet someone who will end our loneliness and make us blissfully happy.

The initial attraction is the ability of an individual to bring us joy, solve our problems, and offer us solace. We fall in love with their sculpted bodies, beautiful faces, incredible talents, alluring smiles, and swollen bank accounts. If we are lucky, we fall in love with who they really are. However, as the maxim goes, "All good things soon come to an end." So we channel surf through relationships, switching the station as soon as it fails to deliver its promise, which occurs as soon as we begin to see these idealized images of our affection as only human. The minute they fail to satisfy what we crave, the euphoria wears off and we continue our search for that perfect someone. We want excitement, stimulation, and release. Our wants are self-indulgent and insatiable.

In the fall of 1998, I met someone who I thought could deliver me from my lackluster existence in the valley. Kohl Moreland was good-natured, generous, and easy on the eyes. We met downtown one day and struck up a conversation about new restaurants in the city, which lasted for nearly twenty minutes. A few weeks later, we ran into each other again and decided to meet for lunch. Numbers were exchanged and after a few lunch dates, dinner dates, walks in the park, and trips to the movies, a budding romance began. Initially we had an uncanny sense of familiarity; we just clicked. His presence was intoxicating. Kohl and I dated for almost a year and life was good. I felt happy and laughed more. Suddenly, life was exciting and fun again—at least for a while.

Over time, it was evident that our values and dreams were not in sync. Success was not on his agenda. Kohl wanted a modest life in the country, which I translated to a total lack of ambition. Despite my best efforts, I could not picture my life with Kohl for the long haul; marriage was not in the cards. Feelings are good, but we also have to use our brains.

Nearly a year later, I started dating Blake Sinclair. Still caught up in the false advertising of romantic love, I believed that if I met a special someone, he would be everything to me. It didn't take long to discover that he was not.

Blake reeled me in with his charm, attentiveness, daily phone calls, and flowers. He seemed to be smitten with me, and before long I was hooked. I may have been a bit in love with Blake, but there was something about him that baffled me, like the way he could be perfectly delightful one minute and raging just under the surface the next. I didn't live in the fantasy world of perpetual bliss, so I dismissed it for a while. This time I was certain that I'd hit the jackpot and finally found Mr. Right.

Highly image conscious, Blake packaged himself as a model of success. He was smart, handsome, ambitious, and engaging. A perfect gentleman, Blake opened doors and pulled out chairs with ease. Dating him every day was like a holiday until that one day, about five months into the relationship, when I commented on him arriving two hours late. Then everything changed and every ounce of Blake's hidden self-criticism, resentment, and humiliation transformed into a firestorm of outrage. This was some real life Dr. Jekyll and Mr. Hyde stuff. "Damn! Everyone wants to use me! I can't please anyone! End the relationship! You never loved me anyway … no one does!" *Whoa*, I thought. Whenever Blake wanted an emotional connection, he would find a way to feel victimized. For him, pity was a manifestation of love. I decided not to counter, not wanting the volcanic activity to erupt a second time. Then I remembered that on occasions when I was extremely nice to him, he still had a problem.

Talking about real truths was not Blake's strong point. Easily offended, his eggshell ego could shatter at the slightest criticism. Somewhere in the deep recesses of his being, he simply could not tolerate a view about himself that differed from his own. Underneath his confident façade, Blake knew his fallibilities were worse than any naked truths that I could offer. This explained why he responded with such mad theatrics, kicking and screaming. Talk about a blood-curdling event.

Making a good impression was critical to his sense of self-worth. Unencumbered by the decorum that kept others in check, Blake shamelessly fished for applause and flattery. Much like a chameleon in his ability to adapt to the expectations of others, he was constantly changing his colors. He nearly lost touch with reality. Blake, like Bailey, didn't seem to realize that behaving in ways to gain other people's approval is calculating.

Whenever Blake didn't get the praise, I wouldn't hear from him for a few days. Feelings of unworthiness would overwhelm him and he needed time alone to mitigate any criticism or sense of failure. After he'd had time to figure things out, we would resume our talks.

This was new terrain for me. It was apparent that there was more underlying Blake's actions than I realized. Blake was constantly projecting his negative thoughts onto me. Never mind that I did not see, feel, think, or judge the same as he. Filled with contradictions, he wanted to be loved but then rejected love when it was offered because he didn't believe that it was genuine. Blake was always certain there was a hidden agenda: "What do you want from me?" No matter what I said or did, I could only make a small dent in his unhappiness. He simply dismissed most positive intent.

Initially, I thought he was just having a series of bad days; but as I connected the dots a clearer picture began to emerge. I recalled him telling me about his parents who were classic control freaks who knew how to lay on the guilt. Blake frequently groused about how critical his parents had been of him growing up, belittling him for the slightest infraction, and how that had damaged his feelings of worth by making him feel that he wasn't good enough. They would tell him, "You're an idiot! You never do anything right," "You're useless!" "Shut up, you stupid piece of shit." Blake was not allowed to say, "You hurt me" or "I need you." Emotionally enmeshed, their words continued to have a stranglehold on his life.

Alas, Blake never bounced a sense of self off of his parents, so every word punctured his view of himself. He had denied his needs for so long and put up a barricade that didn't allow him to be loved for who he was because that would violate his parents' edict that he was flawed and unlovable.

It was clear now that Blake did not love himself, so he could not fathom that anyone else could love him. Sadly enough, he could date one hundred women but things were not going to improve for him until he surrendered his victim status and his emotional dependency on his parents and their judgments. To break free, Blake would have to accept responsibility for his feelings and then take steps to unlearn the damaging script that he'd been handed. It is odd that adults sometimes cannot tell the difference between when someone is disapproving of something they have done and when someone is disapproving of their entire being. There were other things that were interfering with our relationship.

Blake had also internalized the conventional wisdom that really good relationships were conflict free—"I'll make you feel good, and you make me feel good"—which made the possibility of ironing out the rough spots in the relationship impossible. Everything that we needed to discuss was threatening for Blake, and every word was considered a personal attack. His defense mechanisms were always in full gear and he was incapable of truly opening up to me. My matrimonial dreams, with Blake at least, went up in smoke. Working through problems together leads to deeper intimacy and trust. Sharing the most private parts of ourselves, parts that we rarely reveal, is a significant element in all meaningful human relationships. When we open up to the truth of who we are, we find real love. But love, it seems, is often deaf as well as blind.

Going Deeper

I needed insight into the male psyche, so I called my friend Cooper to see if he could help. Though Cooper's dating record was anything but stellar, his counsel was generally good. Failure is often a better teacher than success.

Now, Cooper Neubecht, thirty-seven and single with movie star good looks, was the consummate bachelor and workaholic. He hit the gym twice a day, trying to create an image of perfection in hopes of attracting another image of perfection. Cooper had been searching for Mrs. Right for fifteen years. Before his relationships got off the ground, Cooper started zooming in on faults: "I've seen prettier women," "She's a bit flabby," or "She's not affectionate enough." In the end he always concluded, "She's not the one." With all of his unrealistic expectations and protective barriers, Cooper made the possibility of real love impossible. Focusing on looks instead of love, it was no surprise than Cooper only saw flaws.

"Hello, Cooper," I said.

"What's shaking, baby?" he laughed.

"Same old relationship stuff," I said. "Who's your new hottie for the week?"

"Ahh no," he sung. "Let's not talk about that."

"Still looking for the perfect woman?"

"Only the very best is good enough for me."

Cooper wanted a woman who didn't complain, who let him have a night out with the guys, and who didn't harp on how fat her butt and thighs were. Now that's original. He also wanted a woman who was accepting and accommodating. A few years ago, Cooper was sure that he had met the one.

"I met a beautiful girl once that I felt very comfortable with. And the reason that I felt comfortable with her is because she wasn't too bright." Cooper laughed, humored by his remarks.

"How nice, Cooper," I said.

"Seriously. I mean her head was so empty that if you looked in one of her ears, you could see daylight. I never worried about satisfying her or what she thought about me."

"So you were having sex with a blow-up doll with no feelings and no thoughts," I ragged. "Easy sex made to order—no seduction, no real connection."

He'd been hurt, so he hedged his bets in his relationships to minimize his losses and protect his manhood. In sparing himself from pain of not being loved back, Cooper was living a loveless existence.

"Aren't you the stand up comic?" he countered.

"Ha!" We both laughed.

"I was in full control," Cooper continued. "I could carry out my sexual fantasies with her and hide my true self. She never challenged me or demanded anything."

"I see," I said with my voice trailing off.

"That she was totally uninhibited made sex with her the ultimate fantasy," Cooper said, giddy with lust. "I banged her until my eyes popped out."

"You're the man."

"The way she moaned when I sucked her nipples and stroked her ass made me feel like a king!"

"How nice for you," I said, laughing.

Sexual performance is, of course, a badge of masculinity. Cooper loved the thrill of the conquest.

"She really made me feel the way I wanted to feel," he said.

"Special?" I asked breezily.

"Yeah, special," he whispered. "She did everything to please me. I had no fear of being judged, only pure pleasure."

Cooper wanted to feel comfortable with himself, but in order to achieve a level of comfort he had to be perfect. So Cooper was dating women who were so mentally dull that if he wanted to discuss politics, world events, or anything that required intellect, he'd have better luck talking to a fence post.

Cooper offered with nervous laughter, "I could be an actor and play any role I wanted."

"Super Stud!"

You could have mind-blowing sex with a smart woman if you made her feel safe and significant, and if you felt safe, I thought. The truth is, men are highly vulnerable in the early stages of a relationship, much the same as women. But I hadn't given that much thought until now.

I laughed softly, "Sometimes it looks like we're always ducking and dodging hoping to prevent people from seeing us as we really are, which is draining."

"That's human nature," he told me with certainty.

"I'm not sure about that," I countered, ruffling his feathers. "When we trust that we're okay, we no longer have to hide or mold ourselves to satisfy other people's expectations."

"So we accept ourselves and then what?"

"Our insecurities fade," I said. "And the fear of being judged is minimal."

"That sounds like a bunch of psychobabble." Cooper managed a strained laugh.

"Being who we are is essential to our happiness."

Trusting that we are okay takes effort when the world is constantly trying to reassure us that we are not. But it is achievable. We know that we are whole when we can reveal our weaknesses and still feel valuable. I was beginning to see that the more comfortable we are with ourselves, the better our relationships are with others. Then the conversation shifted gears and continued for thirty minutes more.

Cooper, hoping to maintain his image, said, "I'm not the only one with relationship anxiety."

"Of course you're not."

"Anyway, I've matured and now my mind leads my body more than my body leads my mind."

"That's good," I chuckled. "It's really quite energizing when we can be ourselves."

There was a long pause. "You're right," he conceded. "Still, the fear of having my inner self exposed remains."

"We have to think enough of ourselves to be ourselves."

Though Cooper had always found bachelorhood appealing, lately he'd been feeling unexpectedly empty. Thoughts of marriage surfaced. Cooper's expectations for Mrs. Right were not grand.

"I want a woman who is at ease being my wife, not some high-powered control freak who makes more money than me."

"You're a regular riot, Cooper."

Right. To hell with college; girls only need to prepare gourmet meals and give fabulous massages. I'll confess that I have some difficulty with domestic goddess stereotypes, no matter how often I hear that women with no career and no desire for independence are ideal wives. Maybe Cooper had hang-ups about successful women and found them intimidating. Or maybe those ambitious women, with lots of loot, were really impregnated with power and unbearable. Just when I thought that he'd come to the end of his wish list, he added more.

"A compliment here or there, rather than never-ending criticism, probably wouldn't hurt either," said Cooper.

"Fair enough," I agreed.

"Men want love, affection, and attention, too," Cooper blurted out. "Being the leader, the stoic, the protector, and the provider gets tiring. Sometimes we just want to be human."

Finally we were approaching neutral territory and there was a general relaxing on both sides.

"Kay," Cooper continued, "you're not a model of dating perfection either."

"Well, I'm not terribly unreasonable," I said.

"Are you serious?" Cooper laughed. "You're picky, picky, picky, which explains your dating record."

"I have standards."

"Of course you do."

We talked a bit more about Cooper's ideal woman and my Mr. Right until my ears felt a bit numb.

"Coop, I really hate to end this wonderful conversation, but it's getting late," I said. "I have to get up early in the morning."

"I understand."

"It's been great talking to you."

"Yeah, you bet."

"Have a good night."

"You too, babes," he said and hung up the phone.

What I really wanted was a guy who was comfortable in his own skin. Okay, and a few other things. I was like millions of other women. Either the guy was too tall or not tall enough; overly ambitious or not ambitious enough;

too eager or bordering on lethargic. Plus, relationships today, to some degree, seem to have an artificial quality, a kind of socially approved inauthenticity. It hardly seems worth the effort anymore. Like a veteran meteorologist, I can detect bullshit and games with my radar, and as soon as I do it's over. Believe it or not, I still believe in love, and I think most people do. But sometimes we have to wait to find it.

Finally, after my discussion with Cooper, I could see a terrible pattern emerging. I shared some of Cooper's bad traits. I realized that as soon as a person failed to meet my expectations—a lousy date, disagreement, or lack of ambition, the fairy-tale romance ended.

However, I wasn't the only one with this mindset. Both Blake and I were in search of the perfect relationship, the answer to our well-being, so the disillusionment was shared. We were both looking at each other through a rose-colored haze. Over time, the illusion of the perfect relationship began to dissipate. Imperfections were revealed. They were always there, but the love haze obscured them. As the haze lifted, these shortcomings were made clear. I was still bored and Blake still felt unloved. Blake could no more help me overcome my feelings than Rocky the squirrel. This had to end.

Both of us expected the relationship to be the solution to our problems and the source of our happiness. The danger of this falsehood was that when we could not find the lasting happiness that we expected, we each blamed the other for failing to do what was right. In reality, we were the only ones who could solve our problems and create lasting happiness in our lives. What we were searching for in others we would have to first find in ourselves. I had been looking for my savior, but I was slowly learning that I was my own salvation.

My experiences with Kohl and Blake revealed to me that our partners are often barometers of our own feelings of self-love or self-loathing. Learning to understand Blake and Kohl better helped me to better understand myself. Relationships can be hugely instructive. What we each thought was love was just a good facsimile. Thankfully, I am now developing a more realistic outlook on what relationships are all about. I no longer need a guy who meets all of the requirements on my checklist, one who fits comfortably into my world and does everything just right. There are peaks and valleys in all relationships, and what is needed to sustain them is a love and commitment that can endure through the valleys. My dating wish list would have to be revised.

The Sexual Frenzy

OCTOBER 2002

Contemporary sexuality, with its fantasies and fetishes, has left an indelible mark on the quality of sexual relationships. In this sexual cornucopia, sex can have more to do with fear than sexual desire. There are times when it is easier to bare one's body in the company of people you will never rendezvous with again than to bare one's soul. It is just hard to open up in an emotional way. But in such pairings, based on chemistry and void of attachment and meaning, a sense of separateness remains.

Perhaps we've all heard about or maybe even experienced the pure primal joy of sex with a stranger. Taylor Raine, my former co-worker and chum, surely had. Insanely euphoric and then dreadfully depressed, she had a searing reputation for being sexually rapacious and loose. She'd try anything once. In Taylor's view, the *good life* was strictly a life of pleasure. Sex for her was a palpable manifestation of happiness measured by the frequency of orgasms, which gave her a kind of ecstasy that one can get from a pipe or a bottle. Taylor worked hard to convince herself that this clichéd illusion was fact. She was not in search of a permanent relationship, just a temporary release. Sex had become a surrogate for love.

My contemporaries were urging me towards a myriad of sexual exploits, convinced that "all work and no play" was making me a very dull girl. They'd tell me, "You need a few friends with benefits. Live it up now; you can have a relationship later." Never mind romance; satisfy the libido and leave the heart out of it.

I met Taylor at Cell Tech in 1990 when we were both working as marketing representatives. Long-legged with big dark eyes, black tousled hair, and a fleshy mouth, Taylor was so gorgeous that the guys on staff clamored over her and declared she should be escorted by armed bodyguards.

A top graduate of a middling college, Taylor was a self-proclaimed whiz kid who courted attention and paraded in front of her admiring fans. Taylor's aim was to have that winning combination of brains and sex appeal. That intoxicating mix of flattery and ambition was hard to resist. Tagged the "Spandex Queen" and "VD Champion," she delighted the men on staff by wearing tight pants, short skirts, and low necklines that showed lots of cleavage. Restraining her sexual impulses was not on her to-do list. "What good is a beautiful body if you don't enjoy it?" she'd told me. Men flocked to Taylor like beach bums to a bikini contest. Office rumor had it that her legs were opened so often that she could pick up sound waves for local stations.

With a promising career, great looks, and a few close friends, thirty-something Taylor appeared to have it all together. When I visited her in Florida, she filled me in on a few surprising family details.

A closed-faced and solemn Taylor told me, "I haven't felt like a whole person since my dad died." Taylor's miserable rapport with her mom was another story. "You know, we've never had a close relationship," Taylor said, speaking through tears and near-psychotic laughter. "My mom has just never understood me."

Taylor was having emotional spasms; something was missing from her life. Deep down she felt unlovable and inadequate, and the pressures of trying to be perfect and meet everyone's needs were overwhelming her. The only time Taylor felt good was when she was indulging her erotic fantasies with a man— most any man. While Taylor was marinating in feel-good chemicals, her troubles dissolved. Each partner would fill her empty life and make her feel good enough. Although Taylor knew these relationships were meaningless, getting laid provided her with a temporary sense of being valued, safe, and loved. Taylor loved raw sex for the sake of sex; her appetite was insatiable.

"I hate to face my real feelings so I wash away my fears, disappointments, and failures in a sea of hot, sweaty sex. With every stroke and every moan, my body convulses in delight. I feel so alive! We drift in and out of consciousness as smoothly as we slide in and out of each other. There's nothing like manipulating a man's mind and controlling his sexual experience. It totally turns me on. Mmm, pussy control!" Taylor said, flaunting her sexual prowess.

On a never-ending search for sexual pleasure, Taylor ripped through men like a tornado in a trailer park. Scantily clad, she cruised malls, private parties, bars, and restaurants, and picked up strangers for wild romps in her love nest. Why wait around for Mr. Right when Mr. Right Now was waiting for her at the nearest mall or the hottest club? She had slept with her boss and with half of her company's jet-setting clients. It has never been clear to me how or why she had sex with countless no-name men—"Camel Herders," "Super Men," and "Cowboys"—but I was convinced that she was simply a slut on wheels with no self-control. When she picked up the bouncer at a club in Miami, I told her, "You'll screw anything on two legs. Gossip, self-respect, and AIDS be damned!" We both laughed. Seeing guys through beer goggles, she picked some real winners. I often wondered if she needed her head examined.

Tragedy blended with a series of failed relationships left Taylor feeling like love was too painful to embrace fully, so she didn't. Instead, she retreated behind a wall and interacted through lenses of insecurity and fear. Taylor had spent most of her life running from genuine intimacy. "Everyone leaves ... I'm always getting hurt," she told me. "So it's better to just hook up with a guy for a moment and leave my emotions out of it."

Taylor's life easily reads like an episode from the fabulously successful and sensual *Sex in the City*. The series shows women in search of men, enjoying free sex while yearning for deep, fulfilling, and lasting relationships. Like the characters on episodes of *Sex in the City*, Taylor often candidly discussed her sexual escapades. Though she frequently talked about how thrilling it was to be free to experience the diversity of multiple sexual partners, one has to wonder if Taylor was telling the truth with her endless procession of casual lovers and usual heartbreaks. With all of the unhappiness in her life, Taylor seemed hardly content with the "just sex and no commitment" relationships. It was pretty clear that Taylor would much rather love and be loved than string together a series of meaningless sexual conquests. What an awakening for me: abundant sex—divorced from tenderness, intimacy, and respect—is as unsatisfying as no sex. Clearly, liberated sex fails to consider desire and falling in love, which are deeply satisfying.

Shades of Delight

Quite recently I met Paige McAllister, a tenant at my apartment complex in Catauga. We both liked to sunbathe by the pool on Saturday mornings during the summer. Paige, age twenty with All-American cheerleader good looks, was hooked on the limelight and hotter than a Rolex in Time Square. She loved the free-spirited life. Paige relished discussing what—or, better yet, whom—she'd done the prior weekend. To Paige and her friends, bedding a ton of guys was a badge of honor and merited recognition parallel to famous celebrities. It meant that they had it all—"Hot Girls" personified. I also knew of guys who played a similar game of chance where each sexual conquest earned a point and high scores made them winners.

Paige had been a defiant child who detested her mother and craved the attention of her father, who she described as cold and distant. Her parents were real Holy Rollers who spurned the devil's snares like drinking, dating, and dancing. It was their way of maintaining an illusion of righteousness and purity. Serving a rigid, demanding, and punishing God, they cemented their extreme parental authority. I'm sure her parents thought the devil had gotten into Paige as she entered the world lacking self-discipline and a sense of worth.

Spurred on by biological urges and peer pressure, Paige, rebellious and attention starved, easily slipped into the culture of casual sex. Possibly her sense of rebellion was the result of her not being permitted to voice her feelings or even to feel. Paige had been the ultimate party girl before she had a revelation. Basking in the fall sunshine, we talked to pass the time.

"Where are the guys?" Paige giggled.

"Probably still in bed," I said.

"Alone?" Paige asked with a big grin.

"Who knows," I said. "A group of them went out last night. I heard them banging up against the walls and yelling down the hallway like raving lunatics at the crack of dawn."

"Sounds like they were completely trashed," Paige said.

"The usual," I laughed.

"Guess I missed out," she said. "Oh, my god, you should have been with us last weekend. We, like, totally turned the club out."

"Table-top dancing again?"

"Don't hate me because I have a fun life!" she ragged.

"You're lucky you don't get arrested," I teased. We both laughed.

Popular on the night circuit, Paige partied at City Lights and Margaritaville, where she'd drink Tequila shooters all night, flash her breasts for the crowd, and dance like a Las Vegas stripper. Paige loved being the center of attraction.

Flashing a wide grin, Paige said, "Guys were throwing tips and yelling at me, 'You're so hot!' 'I want you!' 'I'm in love!' 'Can I have you tonight?' I felt so cool. All of the guys wanted me."

Was she swinging around a pole? I thought. It seemed to take so little to make Paige happy, just a few screaming men and all eyes on her. Like Taylor, Paige's self-worth was quantified by exposure. Caught up in the moment, Paige would swap tongue baths with guys at the bar that she'd never met. When things really got heated, she'd have sex in the bathroom or leave the club with guys she didn't know.

Paige laughed. "We used to party all night. The morning after partying I'd ask my roommate, 'Who was I with again?' Talk about wild," Paige recounted, dizzy with delight. "I felt like a beautiful star in a porn video. I still have flashes of those delicious marathon sex sessions. My inhibitions disappeared along with my ability to say no."

"It's easy to confuse great sex with love," I said.

"Like, whatever," Paige shrugged.

"Guys who are not really into you can be great in bed, thanks to good chemistry."

"I see," Paige said with regret. "After the sex was over they all disappeared. I was all freaked out."

"How tragic!"

"I mean ... I'd pleasure them and make them happy, but still none of them wanted me for keeps."

"Ingrates," I smiled, trying to lighten things up.

"Most of them couldn't remember my name."

Apparently sex alone failed to strengthen the connection between Paige and her casual lovers. Like Taylor, Paige was looking for closeness where it could not be found. Deeper pleasures require commitment, love, and a meaningful emotional connection. Paige needed someone else to constantly reassure her that she was pretty and valuable.

"If guys wanted to rock my world, I felt desirable," she told me.

Paige now saw her years of below-the-belt exploration differently.

"Being wanted was probably more important to me than having sex," Paige said candidly. "Sex, even mechanical sex, was the affirmation I needed."

"Everyone wants to be loved," I said.

"Yeah, right," Paige continued. "Sometimes after sex I'd feel bummed out again. All that I had left were clammy sheets, guilt, and loneliness. I didn't feel loved."

"That's not good," I nodded with understanding. Loveless, empty, manipulative sex—no wonder she felt more alone.

"Like, none of them cared about me," she sighed, rubbing on sunscreen. "They made me feel trashy and dirty."

"I'm sorry," I said. "You deserve better treatment."

"I hated myself and my self-esteem bottomed out," Paige said, glancing up at me.

Depersonalized sex had eclipsed her happiness. Her treasure hunt yielded a booby prize. Over time, being with so many guys got to be complicated for Paige. Though she tried to have sex without feelings, she couldn't entirely. Plus, there was always jealousy, and things never worked out.

"We were just using each other to feel good, to feel like we had worth. It was just mutual stimulation," Paige confessed with a coy grin.

Though often sexually fulfilling, the sex had no connection to the rest of Paige's life. Soon the pleasure disappeared, along with her reputation. Paige's mutually exploitative relationships had left her scarred and mistrustful of guys. Clearly, what we do with our bodies deeply affects who we are. Paige was slowly realizing that with all of her attempts at loving freely, she was neither free nor happy. She wanted more than hollow orgasms; she could feel better than that.

"You know, I envy people who live their lives with some limits," Paige said. "They are actually freer than I, and for sure they love themselves more."

Gradually, Paige's life began to change. She had recently started volunteering at a community center.

"Playing games and making crafts with the children is a total blast. I have more fun than the kids!"

Paige had the feeling that she was doing something worthwhile, which gave her the confidence to stop having sex with anyone who wanted to have her.

"I never thought I was good for anything other than sex," Paige explained.

With a renewed sense of worth, Paige wanted to be treated like a person and valued for who she was.

"I can't believe that I went to such great lengths to be liked," Paige remarked. "I wanted to resist those guys ..."

"Hey, we live and learn," I said.

"Everything I did was for male approval. How sad is that?" Paige asked.

"You tell me," I said.

"But aren't all women ..." she stopped mid-sentence.

We had been sitting outside near a drained pool for more than an hour, and we were both ready to go inside.

Quickly ending our talk Paige said, "I'm starved."

"So am I," I said. "Let's blow this popsicle stand."

We collapsed our portable chairs and walked toward the complex.

Paige had hit the nail on the head. Women have been socialized to see men as the final authority and to rely on their constant approval. Though men also have a similar need for approval, it seems to be worse for women. With girls being conditioned from childhood to meet the needs of parents, teachers, friends, and family in order to be liked, it's often terrifying for them to establish an identity that may not satisfy other people's expectations. In doing so, they may find themselves unacceptable and alone. Instead, they lose themselves by detaching from their feelings, values, talents, and dreams, giving up their freedom.

Getting approval is tricky and conditional. It is chancy to allow other people to determine who we are. We have to always be what others want us to be, which is impossible. More, the approval high fades rather quickly and we have to search for approval all over again to ward off feelings of self-doubt and insecurity. Eventually we feel betrayed and alone.

Compliments are nice; everyone loves them. Praise and recognition make us feel happy and alive. We love to be adored by our lovers and told that we are beautiful, sexy, and hot. But relying on praise is a double-edged sword that can render us dependent and powerless. When we are comfortable with ourselves, our appetite for approval shrinks and compliments become the icing on the cake and not the cake itself.

Seeing the Light

Our sense of freedom can easily get distorted in a culture that promotes free sex as the ultimate freedom. After meeting Paige, I recalled how critical I had been of Taylor's lifestyle. Who knows, maybe my judgments were tinged with envy; she certainly seemed to be having more fun than me. Looking back, I could now view Taylor's life through more empathetic lenses. I could see that Taylor and Paige were starving for love. They longed to be cherished and connected, yet had sex with men who didn't know their names. I wonder if Taylor had ever considered what she really wanted from sex. Clearly, sex with strangers can be wildly exciting, but even when the most mind-blowing sex is over, then what? Pleasure is a good thing, but the sensation starts to fade once the pleasurable act ends.

Having been privy to the sexual frolics of my friends and others helped me to recognize some real truths about sexual relationships. Women who are sexually adventurous rarely seem to find happiness or lasting love. Their lives often look like little rats on a spinning wheel, racing after some elusive pleasure with the song "I Can't Get No Satisfaction" playing in the background. Casual sex promises to be great, but in that arena no one will ever be really satisfied. The excitement is superficial and the emptiness underneath remains.

Free sex seems no less than a recipe for broken hearts, bad nights, and crushed souls.

It seemed that neither Taylor nor Paige gave much thought to their encounters, their own sense of integrity and self-worth, or what they actually lost by sacrificing both for a night of pleasure with a stranger. This is a dream that ends when you start to see yourself with new eyes—as someone deserving and worthy of love.

When you think about it, exploiting others for our own purposes doesn't really make us popular, lovable, or mature. Maturity is being able to exercise a measure of self-control over our bodies rather than letting our sexual appetites control them. Real love means liking ourselves enough so that we are not dependent on other people's approval to feel valuable and lovable. Maybe one day these messages will ring as loudly as the "If it feels good, do it" slogans.

Clinging to Love

MARCH 1999

Women are supposed to be married. That is the way it goes, according to tradition that has been perpetuated from generation to generation. Marriage is a well-established social institution in American life. If women are not married, they are thought to be aberrant—typically bitter old maids with dried up ovaries, bad breath, false teeth, and boobs sagging down to their stomachs, and filled with avarice. The only way to avoid this dire predicament is to land a man. Unfortunately, this incredibly belittling message seems to appeal to mass audiences. Although there are millions of single women, popular culture still glories in portraying single women as social outcasts.

I was living in a world of dates, numerous bridesmaids' dresses, wedding invitations, baby showers, and daily grilling from peers, co-workers, and relatives. Everyone was asking me the same million dollar question: "When are you going to get married?" Not to mention those well intentioned (sure they are) remarks offered by married women: "I just can't imagine being single at your age; it must be horrible for you. Well, don't worry, you'll meet the perfect guy some day and get married. God has somebody for you too." A few even offered prayers to help me steer through the waters of loneliness and regret.

All of this was sending me teetering close to the precipice of madness. I used to secretly say, "If I have to go to another wedding, I'm going to shoot myself!" Sound familiar? At least they were still asking me about marriage, so they hadn't written me off—not yet.

According to my cousin, Jarren, I hadn't given it my best. "Kay, you're not applying yourself." Maybe he was right. Who knows? To me, there was no reason to apply myself. I hadn't met anyone lately who fit the bill, and I wasn't desperate enough to settle to appear more valuable to others.

When I met Jillian Bloom, I was all too familiar with the immense social pressures that were staring her in the face. Whenever I would see her, she'd tell me about her latest love interest.

Jillian and I worked out at the same health club. Her go-getter parents had given her gifts instead of love. As an adult, being her own emotional caretaker and being responsible for her own happiness were not on her agenda. Jillian knew that marriage was a highly valued and romanticized ideal. To ensure her marital success, she had subscriptions to dozens of bridal magazines and stacks of books with titles like *How to Rouse His Pleasure Receptors,* and *What a Man Craves*—all of which stirred her insecurities. Predictably, Jillian was fast becoming an emotional cripple in search of relief.

Just as it appeared in her favorite movies, Jillian wanted to abandon the legions of desperate single women on a perpetual manhunt and be magically transformed into a happily married woman. Burning with bridal fever, she would have settled for an engagement ring and the automatic bragging rights that accompanied it. "I don't deserve to die an Old Maid," she'd told me. "Surely, I'm good enough to be somebody's wife." Being dubbed an "Old Maid," "Spinster," or "left on the shelf" were all labels implying that she was unwanted and unloved. So Jillian used an array of self-promoting ploys, love games, and seduction rituals to reel in the men. After many romantic catastrophes and close calls, which set off a maelstrom of emotions, Jillian had yet to land a man or to get a grip on what a healthy, happy relationship entailed.

Jillian, age twenty-nine, was academically bright, though some would argue emotionally scalable, striking, and hopelessly dependent. For years, she had been swept up in a huge tidal wave, searching for love and identity outside of herself. Jillian needed a man in her life to keep her from vaporizing. As long as she had someone, she existed. It didn't matter who it was as long as someone was available to give her a sense of self. Jillian wholly believed the watery platitudes about finding lasting happiness with the perfect man. But people like Jillian are their own unhappy endings.

With optimistic delusion, Jillian progressed through a tear-jerking stream of relationships with men who were below her in terms of status, ability, and intellect. She dated petty criminals and high school dropouts, convinced that she could make the relationship work. "I know he has problems, but love changes everything," she once said. It never worked because Jillian had a habit of choosing undesirables that she would cling to and demand more and more proof of love from. She hoped to love her partners enough that they would love her in return. Her love was partial and tinged with manipulation. Jillian hadn't embraced this truth: We cannot make another person love us.

Each of Jillian's breakups was traumatic and left her more emotionally burned. "Sometimes I really feel loved. But if one thing goes wrong, I cry, I rage, I totally lose it," she'd once told me.

It didn't take much for her to feel unloved, which sent her feelings straight down the tubes. After a series of lovers, Corey entered her life. He was everything that she'd been searching for, that one person who would make her whole. Shortly afterwards, we'd met in the gym. Jillian, shapely and fit, bounced in with her long ponytail swinging.

"Hey, where's your boyfriend?" Jillian asked.

"That's over," I offered coolly. "I'm flying solo for now." I was tired of dealing with other people's neuroses; I needed to clear my own head.

"What happened?" Jillian asked in a cool Southern drawl.

"The thrill was gone," I sang off key in my best B. B. King rendition.

"Bummer," she laughed. "I don't know how you do it. Really, without a boyfriend, I zero out."

"I'm tired of dating for dating's sake," I said. *Enough of the dating treadmill,* I thought.

"When I'm alone, it feels like a part of me is missing," she said, curling a ten-pound weight. "I get so lonely and horny."

I shook my head and smiled.

Changing the tone, Jillian said with excitement, "I'm dating again!"

"No way," I said, appearing to be surprised.

"I'm in love!" she said. "I've found my soul mate, the one that I've been searching for all of my life."

"Oh, my."

"Corey is perfect. He's handsome, smart, and fun. We've been out every single night since we met—dinner, movies, you name it."

"That's fantastic!"

"Kay, he's the best. He treats me like a princess and makes me feel good about myself. He buys me things, sends flowers and balloons, and tells me I'm beautiful! I've never felt anything like this."

"Talk about perfection," I smiled.

"The thought of him turns me on."

"I'm impressed."

"It's unreal that someone like Corey wants to be with me," she beamed. "I mean he really loves me!"

After hearing this spiel, I wondered if Jillian realized what she was saying to me: that she really didn't love Corey; she was simply using him to help her love herself. Apparently, she must have been thinking, "If he loves me, I must be lovable."

"I hope things work out for you," I said.

"So do I," Jillian said, blushing. "The sex is to die for. Corey makes my body quiver with pleasure. Normally, I'm not the type to holler, but …"

"But what?"

"But he knows just what I like," she said, glowing. "I can almost taste him."

"Sounds like paradise," I said with an impish grin.

"Oh, it is!" she said, her hazel eyes sparkling. "I'm so incredibly happy right now, so complete."

"I can see that!"

"If he leaves me, I'll die."

Nothing mattered to Jillian anymore except being with Corey. He was her whole life. She knew his favorite foods, favorite sports, and favorite sexual pleasures. She knew how to make him happy, but not herself.

"Let's hope he sticks around for a while," I added.

Shifting her tone, she said uneasily, "He is flirty, but that'll change."

I offered bland reassurances that I hardly recognized leaving my mouth. "Of course it will."

"You're nothing until someone loves you," Jillian said with a wide smile.

"Yeah."

"It's the best."

Grabbing my towel and gym bag, I said, "Gotta go."

"Later."

Jillian's gushing sense of feeling complete resulted because, with Corey, she no longer felt deficient on the inside. While rapt in spine-tingling passion and romantic agitation, Jillian bartered sex for the promise of security and commitment. She was willing to do just about anything to keep a man in her life. True giving is an act of love with no expectation of reward or even a thank you, but maybe that wasn't clear to Jillian. Corey and Jillian's relationship started off with a bang, all happiness and fun. However, the more time they spent together, the more she began to depend on him to make her happy. Before long, Corey started to feel the pressure to be with her instead of the desire. Fear has a way of sabotaging romantic affairs.

Jillian's adhesive personality and FBI-style interrogations were more than Corey could bear. He felt trapped and smothered, and he hated it. Jillian told me about their latest talk. "Jill, I need some space; I can't take anymore!" Corey told her. Desperate to hold on, she'd pleaded, "You do love me, don't you? Please don't leave me!"

Jillian was in the fast lane going one hundred mph and Corey wanted her to put on the brakes. She didn't, and Corey got out of the race. I saw Jillian at the gym shortly after the breakup, and we talked during our routine thirty-minute walk on the treadmill.

"How's it going, Jill?" I asked.

"We broke up," Jillian told me with tears forming in her eyes. "He told me he loved me."

"I'm sorry."

"How could he leave me?"

"I don't know," I answered. "Sometimes feelings fade."

"I can't live without him," Jillian lamented. "I'm all alone."

"You have yourself."

"That's not enough," she moaned. "If he would just tell me what I did wrong, I would change. I need him."

Jillian needed to feel the love that she felt with Corey. She needed him to remind her that she was sexy and special. Jillian's period of mourning was always short-lived. She would soon find a new man to love her and make her whole again. But love curdles through neediness and strain.

"Love can be so painful and so cruel," Jillian murmured.

"You're right," I agreed.

Jillian wrapped up the conversation. "I'll see you on Wednesday; same time," she said, turning off the machine.

"Sure thing," I smiled.

Jillian flashed the peace sign and was gone.

Looking at Jillian's life, it was plain to see that expecting someone else to make us happy sets the stage for endless disappointment. No one can fulfill all of our needs. When we don't love ourselves, others cannot love us enough. It is as if we have a gaping hole begging to be filled, but it can never be completely filled. Those who fail to realize the importance of loving themselves generally keep going from person to person, trying to find happiness and wholeness. Sometimes I wonder: How many people get enough love?

Solely focused on the men in her life, Jillian gave up her own views, interests, and hobbies in order to please them until she nearly lacked individuality. A close friend helped to steer Jillian to the spring of self-sufficiency, and she had gotten her feet wet. When I saw Jillian a year later, I saw a new Jillian, one who was filled with ability and self-respect, and was fully engaged in the world. She had completed her degree in sociology and made new friends. Life was good. Now that Jillian had created a life of her own and learned to appreciate her own humor and intelligence, she no longer needed to manipulate her partners into being with her. More, she had learned to tolerate being alone. The drama had ended.

"I have a new guy," she told me with enthusiasm. "Drew's so caring and supportive. We share everything: thoughts, feelings, dreams, interests, fears, hopes, delicious meals, and lots of laughter." Jillian smiled. "We spend all night on the phone."

"Oh, that's great," I said.

"I love kissing him and cuddling with him," Jillian said, beaming.

No more tug-of-war or screaming matches. The cycle of desperation was broken and Jillian had stopped dancing the dance of fantasy and need.

Scores of guys are at the mercy of clingy women like Jillian—the insecure types who are self-doubting and helpless. It's not normal for people to want to spend every moment of their lives with you, particularly when you have just met them. Die-hard romantics might misinterpret this need as an adoring sign of love and affection. "That's so cute. She wants to spend twenty-four hours a day with me. I'm so special." Desperate attachment may be flattering initially, but it leads people to be calculating and unloving. Most healthy people appear to be attracted to confidence and happiness, not neediness.

Needing someone else for our emotional survival makes us somewhat of an addict, and we live with an unending craving and the danger of withdrawal. We would probably be better off addicted to painkillers. At least, as long as we had an adequate supply, it would always make us happy. When we see ourselves as helpless beings with our self-worth wholly dependent on how another person treats us, love is tainted.

I was gaining other insights. If we are so overly sensitive that we can be destroyed by the slightest hint of disapproval, we may need to work on ourselves before inviting another person into our world. Likewise, if being without a partner makes us feel inferior or deficient; we might be better equipped to handle life if we remained single until we are at ease being independent and alone. While we're waiting, we will find that we can meet some of our own needs, even if we would rather not. We may even have the time and energy to extend ourselves to others.

There are enough people in the world to interact with in order to lead a happy life. Love is plentiful. Bonding with friends, neighbors, and relatives calms our anxieties and cravings. Even so, we cannot truly love others until we love ourselves. Once we love ourselves, entering into a relationship becomes a choice, not a need.

A Panoramic View

Remember high school crushes, kissing in the locker room, dating a star jock or bombshell cheerleader, and trying to catch the most attractive guy's/girl's eye? Our boyfriends and girlfriends were used to evaluate our worth and attractiveness. Though teen years are frequently romanticized as a time of innocent love, most adolescent crushes have nothing to do with real love. Teens, wrapped up in themselves, often use each other for pleasure and status, then discard each other like broken toys when they've used each other. "I love you if you do this for me; if not then it's over." With their young libidos in overdrive, neither is likely concerned with being caring or loving.

In subtle ways we never overcome this viewpoint on life, basing our worth, desirability, and attractiveness on the partner(s) that we are able to attract. In a culture steeped in consumerism, sex easily becomes a marketable commodity, with relationships measured by their cash value.

Men, following the lead of red-carpet icons off-screen, often seek trophy girlfriends and wives not for their individuality, but because of the admiration they receive from the public for winning such eye-candy. Women often compete for the honor of being seen with, and possibly marrying, a good-looking or wealthy man, the kind that other women will envy her for having. Partners are approached like prizes, not people to be known. In most cases, what we are admitting is that we really don't love them at all; we only love the feeling we get from being with them.

Society seems to have evolved in such a way that we rely heavily on others to get our emotional needs met. Ironically, our inner deficiencies and appetites habitually drive us to search for satisfiers, and people become the principal source of our happiness and our misery.

Matrimonial Bliss

OCTOBER 2003

Long gone are the days of blissful simplicity when women pretended that being married, cooking, cleaning, and providing comfort for others were always satisfying endeavors. Though the troubles of the singles have always been in the public domain, little is known about the secret lives of married women. If anyone had told me eight years ago that married women felt lonely, bored, or depressed, I would have been both disconcerted and incredulous, particularly with so many pushing me down the matrimonial aisle.

Lately, I have been hearing more and more complaints about married women and their hectic, joyless lives. Quite recently, a friend in Catauga was discussing the heartache of her troubled marriage. Kate was mired in an unhappy marriage and having a time. The pressures of everyday life—the kids, the untidy house, the guilt, and the erosion of intimacy—left Kate feeling distant and out of sync with her husband. Kate invited me over for tea and girl talk. I pulled into her driveway just after noon.

"Hi," Kate said as she opened the front door. "Thanks for coming over."

"Thanks for the invite," I said.

"Come on in and have a seat."

I followed Kate into a spacious family room accented with heavy molding and expensive furnishings.

Kate Landers was thirty-something with straight chestnut hair and a curvy, svelte figure. She had high expectations for her husband, Wyatt, a successful real estate developer. Kate imagined a happy marriage that would satisfy her deepest needs for love, intimacy, and children.

"My husband will have admiration for everything that I do. He will adore me, kiss me softly, and lavish me with diamonds," she'd once said.

Kate also envisioned that the marriage would offer financial security, a fine home, and a posh lifestyle. For a time, she'd achieved her goals, but Wyatt had needs of his own.

While they managed polite greetings, one too many chilly remarks had been exchanged across the breakfast table. Kate believed that her husband had lost interest in her, and she was considering a divorce or at least a fling with her son's soccer coach, Aidan. She needed assurance that she was still attractive and desirable.

"Kay, my marriage is slipping away right before my eyes," Kate said blithely, lifting her arms in the air.

"That's nothing to joke about, Kate," I said.

"I'm serious," Kate said. "Wyatt doesn't have time for me anymore, so I've found someone who does."

"Say what?" I teased.

"I've been flirting with Aidan, Ben's soccer coach," she said. "I have the biggest crush on him."

"Careful," I said, raising my voice three octaves, "you're playing with fire."

Kate was feeling lonely.

"I love the way Aidan looks at me. It's like I'm all that he sees," she confided. "He makes me feel beautiful, like a woman."

Shortly after their honeymoon, Wyatt started devoting all of his energies to making money and not to their marriage. Sex was rare, minimally allaying Kate's incessant boredom. Worse, the passion and intense attraction had started to fade.

"Sex has become rather routine and impersonal, just a physical release for Wyatt," she said. "Sometimes I have to fake an orgasm because I'm not aroused enough to enjoy the sex and I want it to end quickly," she continued.

"Faking it reduces your chances of getting what you really want in bed," I explained.

"Oh, what the hell," Kate said dully.

"Have you had this talk with Wyatt?"

"Not really," she exhaled emphatically. "Maybe I should engage in some self-pleasuring."

Kate slumped back in her chair and stared at the ceiling. At her core, she worried about her marriage and wondered if it could be saved. Kate couldn't bear the thought of living without Wyatt; she still loved him.

"Things weren't always so stale in the bedroom," Kate recalled. "Wyatt used to drive me wild with his lips and the flicker of his tongue. The thought of making love to him used to make me shiver with ecstasy. I remember the tenderness, the feeling of his bare skin against my own. Every curve and every movement brought me waves of pleasure. It used to feel like heaven."

"Try something new in bed or ask for what you really want," I suggested.

"I shouldn't have to ask," Kate said under her breath.

Obviously she expected Wyatt to intuit her needs. "Is Wyatt telepathic?" I asked, wondering if she were aware of her expectations.

"Well ..." Kate stopped talking mid-sentence. "This is supposed to be the happiest time of my life. What's wrong with me?"

It seemed that Kate was trying to recapture the mind-blowing sex that she had during the honeymoon and the early years of her marriage, and maybe that was a high expectation. She had not realized that sex, like one's weight and career, ebbs and flows. Much had changed. Wyatt was overworked and stressed. Kate was burned out and needed help with bathing the children and cooking dinner. A nice body rub would probably help her feel energized without the expectation of sex afterwards. But they weren't on the best speaking terms.

Happy Together—Until Now

Kate and Wyatt were living in two different zones. According to Kate, Wyatt had a challenging career that took up all of his time, leaving no time for the children or her. Focused on her unmet expectations, Kate felt dispirited. It seemed that her goals and desires were not and would never be fulfilled with Wyatt. But Kate wasn't exactly Wyatt's idea of a perfect spouse either. Wyatt had given Kate diamonds, furs, a fine house, and exotic vacations—anything she wanted. Now he wondered if the marriage ever meant anything to her. Wyatt had overheard the tail end of the conversation, I gathered, and he immediately rushed in to defend himself. A long conversation ensued. At six feet tall with dark bronzed skin and an athletic build, Wyatt was the archetype of tall, dark, and handsome.

"Kate was supposed to make me happy," Wyatt offered edgily. "That's what wives do."

Kate, obviously on a roll, redirected the conversation to me. "He works all week and on weekends he plays golf with his buddies, leaving me all alone."

Cut off from an extended family, Kate had hoped to create a microcosm in her marriage. But that hadn't materialized.

Wyatt, angered by the accusations, countered, "Someone has to pay the bills."

"Sure," Kate snapped.

"I don't get you, Kate. You married me because I was successful; now you want to bitch because I can't spend twenty-four hours a day with you."

"Wyatt, please," Kate said.

"You sure as hell don't complain about the rewards that I provide; you just can't handle the sacrifices that I have to make to get them. Make up your mind," he continued.

"That's not fair," she said.

"I work my ass off for this family, and now I'm a shoddy father and husband. Go figure."

"You work for yourself," Kate fired back, "and this marriage takes a back seat."

"Oh, thanks," Wyatt said. "It's great to know how you really feel." Wyatt's face was tense.

Kate stared at Wyatt and didn't comment. I felt like running for the door.

"I'd better go," I said quietly, getting up from my seat.

"Oh, please stay," pleaded Kate. "I'm sure he'll be leaving soon."

Wyatt shot Kate a piercing look.

"Fine," I said, sitting back down.

"He's so full of it," Kate mouthed silently, looking directly at me.

The conversation continued.

"I work long hours and I need an outlet!" Wyatt said.

"I know," Kate said.

Wyatt had other outlets, like spending hours manicuring the lawn, going on biweekly drives to the market, and taking extended business trips. He would rather sandpaper a tiger's ass in a jail cell than to listen to Kate's non-stop whining.

The room was suddenly quiet. Then Kate said, "When you're home, which is rare, you're emotionally absent and hardly involved with the kids."

"Oh, for God's sake, Kate. Give it a rest." Irritation flickered in his gray eyes.

"I cook, I clean, I take care of the kids, even on bad days," she said, her face glowing with satisfaction.

Wyatt said caustically, "Of course."

"I rarely ask him to help. When I do, he accuses me of nagging," she continued, speaking directly to me as if Wyatt were suddenly hollow.

"You're an ideal mother and wife," Wyatt scoffed.

My head was beginning to spin.

"I try to keep things hot and sexy in the bedroom," Kate flared as her cheeks flushed.

"Yeah, sure," he mumbled, ruffling his dark, wavy hair.

Utterly frustrated, Kate said, "It doesn't matter what I do. You never show me any signs of appreciation!"

"I'm doing the best I can," Wyatt shot back. "What do you want from me, Kate?"

Wyatt retreated into an injured silence after hearing Kate's accusations. This new ideology of the egalitarian couple was light years away from their reality. Clearly, both were failing to fulfill their roles and to meet their partner's expectations. Kate felt overwhelmed, living in a tightly spun web of laundry, fatigue, and angst, tightened by constantly caring for the children. Her intimate connection with Wyatt had been lost between the midnight feedings and diaper changes. More than anything, Kate wanted the husband who'd loved her and who'd loved having sex with her before the stork arrived. Now Wyatt was just one of a dozen irritations that made up her day.

"I thought he'd always be there for me," Kate said, on the brink of tears.

Kate was looking directly at me and speaking as if Wyatt had left the room. Wyatt was pacing back and forth like a caged animal. Things were getting heated and I was ready to go. Slowly, I was beginning to understand those little things that gradually erode the foundation of marriage. Kate was questioning her love for Wyatt.

Wyatt tightened his angular jaw and waited.

Kate wanted a marriage that was as perfect as those depicted in the movies where men adored their wives and put them first. In her opinion, that never happened for her. Wyatt wanted the same from his wife. Fortunately, there was a break in the conversation as Kate poured three cups of hot tea and served biscotti. By now, I was feeling like a divorce attorney.

Wyatt's Side of the Story

Speaking slowly, Wyatt said, "In the beginning, things were awesome. We were in love. I'd married an incredibly beautiful woman who was an excellent cook and a great lover."

"How romantic," I said.

"Kate was so sweet, so appreciative, and so perfect. She never took me for granted."

"You'd met your dream girl!"

"For sure," he said. "Kate used to think I was the most magnificent man on the planet, and she made all of my needs first in her life."

Slowly stirring my tea, I said, "Sounds ideal."

"I felt like the luckiest guy in the world," Wyatt said amiably. "And the guys thought she was hot, which made me feel good."

"I'll say," I leered.

"Kate really tried to make me happy," said Wyatt, his voice anxious and Boston accent blaring.

"So what happened?" I asked, reaching for my tea.

Wyatt narrowed his eyes and spilled. "She gave it her best, but she couldn't—at least not for long."

Wyatt had always hoped that Kate would eventually learn to understand him and make him feel like a man. In Wyatt's view, Kate never understood his ambition, his drive for success. So she was always jealous of the time he spent away from her. After competing against his cohorts for land acquisitions, successful deals, and commissions, Wyatt wanted a refuge from the rat race. Now that refuge no longer provided comfort. Wyatt was completely fed up with Kate's anger and competitiveness.

"I see," I said, seeing a pattern of mutual blame emerging. No understanding, no compromise—a recipe for catastrophe.

"Sex nearly disappeared from our marriage after the babies came," Wyatt said with his voice dropping to a husky whisper. "Now Kate is forever waving her 'no sex tonight' flag."

Kate was using an old trick of the trade. At that moment, I recalled that my friend Cooper once told me a tale of a night of begging until he damn near fainted. Withholding sex in a penalizing way is a classic female power move and men hate it. Sex is always a formidable weapon in any kind of power play.

"Exhaustion tends to kill the mood," Kate threw in and offered a strained laugh.

Wyatt wasn't amused, but managed a bitter laugh. "My sex kitten has turned into a frigid ice maiden."

Okay, they could really spare me the bedroom details. I looked over at Kate with a smirk, but Kate seemed mentally withdrawn from the conversation. Wyatt was slowly giving up. From Wyatt's view, Kate was always wearing her all-about-me blinders and it was driving him insane.

"Nothing I do for her is enough. All she does is criticize me," Wyatt muttered.

The conversation grew more intense and then stopped. Wyatt was now pacing the floor. I threw in a few jokes to cut the tension. They laughed, but soon returned to their talk. The venomous fight raged for another five minutes. Wyatt was stomping around and Kate was flailing her arms. They each seemed to derive pleasure by being right as if it were a private victory.

"You don't make me happy," Kate fumed.

"You nag all the time," Wyatt answered swiftly.

"You never listen."

"Well, you never apologize."

"Oh, give me a break," Kate hissed. "You don't have an emotional marble in your head!"

"And you have too many."

"I hate you!"

"You used to believe in me," Wyatt said to Kate, peering directly at her.

The skirmish was on, and Kate felt like Wyatt was withholding that which would make her happy; Wyatt had similar thoughts about Kate. Grabbing for what they each wanted, they were entirely blind to the other partner's needs. Instead, each perceived the other's behavior as a failure to love. Forgiveness, a true act of love, was out of the question. Neither seemed to be willing to accept the other's flaws without bitterness and resentment. Once we understand that there are no perfect people, we no longer expect perfection.

It was difficult to listen to them accuse and blame each other. They were killing my dream of a picturesque marriage. The key question was: Was anybody listening other than me? Listening is an expression of love. But it seemed that neither Kate nor Wyatt had any regard for what the other had to say. They simply wanted to be heard. This was definitely not like TV where marriages are blissfully happy, all kisses, hugs, and flattery. Within an hour the tension faded and I decided to go home. After witnessing this drama, I finished my tea, said my good-byes, and walked towards the door. The day was passing and I was tired, but I had learned something valuable about marriage. It was now apparent that marriages are not automatically fulfilling relationships, despite what the culture promotes.

A once charming romance had become increasingly caustic, destructive, and constricted. In the midst of those outbursts of temper and flashes of selfishness lay a tangled net of denial and defensiveness, and an unwillingness to express regret and to change behavior. Each was looking out for his/her own interests, and the relationship was failing in the sense that it was no longer producing what they each wanted. Denying all that was good and inflating what was bad, they created more space in their relationship. Their sizzling marital affair had now become a cold contract—to hell with mutual love, mutual care, mutual respect, and mutual fulfillment.

Just six years earlier, I watched them exchange vows filled with the hope of an eternally happy and fulfilling marriage. I recall Kate telling me on her wedding day, "I've waited for this moment all of my life. Today my life is perfect." No doubt they expected this perfect day to continue for the rest of their lives. Now that their marriage no longer conformed to the fairy tale, they were both disenchanted and contemplating a divorce. Their unwillingness to understand resulted in the fun, the tenderness, and the affinity to all slowly evaporate into thin air. Somewhere they seemed to have lost the deep sensitivity to each other, a feeling of belonging that they once shared. Or perhaps they expected their marriage to maintain itself based on promises and goodwill. If we truly love someone, we demonstrate it through our actions. Clearly, love doesn't always cure loneliness; being understood does.

Influenced by the fairy-tale illusion that someone else was responsible for their happiness, each was convinced that happiness should come from their partner. Apparently, they had not considered that the mix of children, work, hormonal swings, and money concerns would wreak havoc on their sex lives. It was more than they'd bargained for.

From the looks of things, neither Kate nor Wyatt was willing to adapt to accommodate the necessary changes. Instead, the unspoken message for both was "I'm suffering, baby. Make me feel good." But, at this point, neither of them could meet the other's need as they were both emotionally empty and in need of relief. Often what people need or want from us is that of which we are most starved. What an eye-opener!

The seeds of Kate and Wyatt's marital troubles were apparently sown long before they were capable of verbalizing them. Underlying their love were the hidden expectations that each would fill the other's voids and make the other person feel valued, admired, and loved. Kate and Wyatt also expected their spouse to boost their self-esteem and quell their anxieties, which was more than each could realistically deliver. I'm sure neither Kate nor Wyatt ever considered that the love they felt initially was merely a response to need fulfillment.

Now that Kate and Wyatt's needs were no longer being met, disappointment set in. Each blamed the other for not being who each needed the other to be. Neither could look beyond personal needs to the needs of the other spouse. The real problem was not all of the trivial complaints, but that neither of them felt loved, cherished, or respected. Neither had the spine to say, "I want to be loved and appreciated." They were both reacting to the mounting need for reassurance that they were accepted. Minor irritations drop out of view when people feel loved by their partners, particularly when they already love themselves.

By loosening the unrelenting focus on yourself, feeling loved from within takes the extreme neediness out of romantic love. It frees you from keeping score in a relationship by sizing up what you are owed and guarding against giving too much (and having nothing left for yourself). Rather than shielding your own back, you can face the person you most want to be loved by.

Since their illusions of perfection had faded, Kate and Wyatt could learn to appreciate and celebrate each other's distinctions. They were, after all, separate beings. With real love, we learn to accept our partner's flaws and limitations—and they accept ours, hopefully—without keeping score, becoming resentful, or slipping into martyrdom.

Till Unhappiness Do Us Part

We all have needs and what most of us see in another is a way to get our needs met. Though we are not willing to say that at the altar, on an underlying level, that's we mean. So we strike a deal: "If you give me this, I'll give you that." As soon as one fails to keep one's end of the bargain, the love fades, disillusionment seeps in, and they're ready to end it all.

Scores of marriages today are overburdened with expectations that the unions cannot fill, and they crumble underneath this emotional weight. Few marriages are able to provide a lifetime of love, friendship, romance, sexual intimacy, fulfillment, and happiness. The feeling of being swept up in rapture doesn't seem to last, nor does the illusion of perfection in the other partner. Many people spend their lives in a state of infuriated self-pity when it does not happen for them. The concept of framing one's desires without needing to control other people's actions is apparently difficult for many people to grasp.

When we rely solely on the actions of another to make us happy, we also give them the power to make us unhappy. As long as we lean on our partners for our happiness, our feelings will be based on their moods and whims. Undeniably, the precondition for the best adult relationship is a clear understanding of who we are—emotionally, physically, and spiritually. Maybe a truly loving and sensual relationship is possible when we fully recognize that our partners are no more or less deserving of love, acceptance, and forgiveness than we are.

Love's Myths and Illusions

FEBRUARY 2004

Once upon a time our parents delighted us with poignant tales of love and happiness found in many fairy tales. As children we relished in fantasies of meeting our prince or princess and riding off blissfully into the sunset. Jillian, Kate, and Wyatt were seduced by such tales. In our adult lives, the culture continues to feed this myth of meeting that perfect companion who will create happiness for us for the rest of our lives. Glimpses of romance are sold to us through steamy love scenes and sleek photos of beautiful couples sharing intimate touches. Advertisements for breath mints, bath gels, and shampoo all feed into the fairy tale. Loving someone can be thrilling.

Relationships, however, are not the same for all people. A lot of disappointment stems from confusing facts with myths. Believing in the proverbial myths about romantic love, needy strangers become smitten with each other and marry, clueless about who the other is before they exchange I do's. United in *love*, they feel that all problems can be overcome. "Together, we can conquer the world!" When reality intrudes, the outcome is often predictable: These pairings, filled with unmet expectations, ultimately flounder.

It's All about Love

Humans have a basic need to be loved, to have our feelings taken seriously, and to be validated as people who matter. All of us are looking to be pampered, to be bathed in the loving warmth of a mother's tenderness or comforted in a daddy's sturdy arms. We seem to crave the kind of security, attention, and care that our parents once provided, which offered us a sunglow feeling that we were special. Some view themselves as powerless and want to be cared for like small children. Others want someone who thinks that they're interesting and charming. This craving for attention is endemic. I had noted it in Jillian, Taylor, Ellis, and others.

Once the intimacies of childhood are broken, we immediately seek to establish them elsewhere, as if our survival depended on it. We start looking for someone else who will cherish us in an exclusive and intimate way, someone on whom we can depend. When we find this loving relationship with a person who provides us with what we need and reveals our unseen qualities, we completely merge with that person who melts our self-doubt and makes us feel whole. Naturally, when the romance ends, we end up feeling like we've been rejected and abandoned, like a lost puppy.

Most of us have been conditioned to believe that finding the right person will cure our feelings of loneliness and that romantic love is the key to happiness. Perhaps the greatest myth is that marriages/relationships should always be ecstatically happy and that all of life's fulfillment should come from our partners.

Relationships surely have their joys and rewards, but they can also be risky affairs. Nonetheless, each year millions—all with assorted intentions and delusions—leap into marital calamity. One of the reasons people take the nuptial leap is because they are awash in a culture that is nearly obsessed with the good sex promised by marriage. Clutching their fantasies, many people rush into marriage lacking a clear picture of the realities, which are veiled by the myths about the institution. The motive behind the marriage is simply immediate and ongoing pleasure, with no thought of what is required to make the marriage work. People joining for purely sexual reasons are more apt to relate to each other as objects rather than as people. When sexual communions are without mutual respect, care, and compassion, they are somewhat akin to a high-minded form of prostitution.

We've Got High Hopes

"Till death do us part" is still a lifelong vow for millions of couples all hopeful of reaping the benefits of a happy marriage. Such couples honor their covenant agreement, rear their children well, find that clever blend of giving and receiving, and embrace the issues of life together. But increasingly, couples who have been married for decades are forfeiting their marital security in pursuit of happiness.

Relationships in the new millennium are mobile and sinuous, with each partner looking out for his/her own interests. Marriages are transitory, forming and dissolving at alarming rates. Brittle relationships are the norm. Greed is hotter than gratitude, and competition is spicier than compromise. Compared with our parents' era, this "sex without strings" generation is marrying later, marrying less, and divorcing sooner and more often. This is only part of the picture. People seem to connect out of convenience or usefulness, and frequently lack the commitment necessary to make relationships work.

As pop culture continues to bleed into the mainstream, encouraging us to regard others as objects for consumption and not as humans deserving love and respect, those hoping for real intimacy and lasting relationships are not likely to find either.

Calling it Quits

So what's with the high divorce rate? Well, reasons run the gamut. While getting married is still immensely popular in America, the role of marriage in our social lives is changing. Marriage is no longer the only springboard into adulthood. It no longer has the monopoly in providing status, intimacy, and significance in life. Further, the economic considerations are not pivotal as women are fully integrated into the workforce. Once taught to grow up and marry lawyers and doctors, women now grow up to become lawyers and doctors, with their six-figure salaries in tow. The changing social climate has also affected men, who no longer feel compelled to marry for political gain or to make it in the corporate world.

Unquestionably, America's high divorce rate springs from high hopes. People are marrying less for economic reasons and more for love and emotional fulfillment. In this era, people join with higher expectations than prior generations. They believe that their spouses will meet their needs for affection, companionship, and erotic pleasure. To make certain that this perfect relationship happens, they (particularly women) buy stacks of books and tapes that offer expert guidance on how to improve communication, resolve conflicts, and have magnificent sex. Jillian surely believed in these tools. Regrettably, as our expectations for marital bliss and satisfaction increase, so does the potential for deep disappointment.

When each partner pays attention only to those aspects of the marriage that affect his or her own happiness, marriages are readily dissolved when they no longer serve their purpose. If they married to find happiness, why stick around if they're not? Right? So, once the feel-good aspect leaves the relationship, it's Splitsville. Amid the clamber for endless fulfillment, commitment flies out of the window.

There are people who march down the aisle with one partner after another, each time hoping that the new partner will succeed where the last one failed. Each hopes to find that one perfect, understanding, sacrificing soul mate who will create lasting happiness for them. But they rarely find that person. Rather, their unhappiness seems to intensify with each new relationship. Then they repeat the cycle all over again because they haven't done the work of understanding themselves. More, they seem to constantly overlook one vivid reality: They are looking to imperfect people in hopes of finding ongoing happiness.

It is risky to rely on another person to satisfy all of our emotional needs. Our demands are probably a bit unrealistic. We are expecting a person with his or her own needs, fears, goals, and insecurities to give us what they are unable to give. When this person no longer fits the model image we have of them, frustration, anger, and disappointment inevitably build. Surely, loving someone brings joy and comfort, but our misconceptions about love often cause us to be disheartened.

Happiness begins with self, but most do not seem to realize this fact; so they jump from person to person, only to leave again when things go sour. Ironically, unhappy people who split up are often no happier than those who remain in their relationships. Running from our difficulties and responsibilities will never lead to happiness. Real love is about maintaining responsibility in an ongoing relationship, through ups and downs with people who depend on us and on whom we can depend. Healthy marriages require mutual contributions of time, effort, and attention. Such marriages exist to nurture and support each partner individually.

Now I could see that the key to finding fulfillment in life is not finding perfection but being in a loving relationship with another human being. When all is said and done, we cannot feel another loving us. Love is a personal experience; we can only feel ourselves loving others.

So much of what we need—love, validation, life satisfaction—we convert to sex. Sex, for some, is a merging of passion, ambivalence, and desperation. This was surely the case with Jillian, Paige, and Taylor. We want our sexual relationships to make up for everything that is lacking or painful in our lives. Our lovers are expected to fill our lonely lives with fun and intimacy, and make our lives exciting even if we are grouchy or dull. In the presence of our lovers we yearn to be ourselves, even if we do not know who we are and are not willing to find out. Most of all, we insist that our lovers love us unconditionally just as our mothers did, even when we do not love ourselves unconditionally and our lovers are just as famished as we are. With time, the discovery is made that we have needs that cannot be met through sex.

Seeing Love Through New Eyes

We have all been fed fairy-tale promises of a magical romance with our dream lover. We expect a partner who will soothe our woes, lavish us with attention, shower us with love and affection, parry our anger, and give us an identity. More, we imagine that person will intuitively fill all of our needs, like an idealized parent, and make us whole. Although many of us have come to expect that this fantasy is real, I have discovered that this love story unfolds more like a gripping novel than an enchanting fairy tale. The narrative is brimming with subtle and startling intricacies, a mixture of joy and sadness. At least, that is the way it appeared to me. I'd had my own experiences and was privy to other relationships, which sharpened my awareness of how this fabled romance can make us miserable rather than euphoric. It can also make us fractured rather than whole. Now that I know how potentially ruinous these myths and idealized romantic tales can be, unraveling myself from the web of delusions about love and romance is the wisest choice.

Hollywood productions encourage the idea that a wedding is the crowning achievement of love. I too carried an image of a white wedding gown, delicate flowers, and a dream of enduring true love—but I now see marriage differently. After the vows have been exchanged, the rice has been thrown, and the grand celebration ends, I will be prepared for a different reality. Marriage requires a huge leap of faith, devotion, naked honesty, and spirit. Clearly, the scripts that we've been handed for marriage are limited. Those who lack the courage and ingenuity to find new ways of relating to their partners will likely be snared.

It would be unfair to omit the fact that there are marriages, mutually fulfilling partnerships, that work. Fortunate or insightful men and women have found the kind of partners they want, who share values and interests, successfully nurture their families, and meet the other's needs. These lasting marriages tend to have genuine love, friendship, passionate sex, commitment, and reasonable expectations. However, such marriages are not the trend.

All over, marriages seem to be crumbling. Nearly half of all marriages in the country end in divorce. Failure is lurking just on the other side of a "toilet seat down" debate, careless action, financial crisis, scorched meal, wounding remark, or change in plans. We are accustomed to seeing the fractured marriages of everyday people plastered on magazine covers and television by way of Judge Judy, Judge Mathis, and the like. In fact, feasting on these bad marriages has become a weekly staple for avid magazine purchasers and televisions viewers.

Many would agree that these divorces are preferable to hollow marriages that are held together for decades by a bond of fear, emotional dependency, lethargy, financial security, and mutual helplessness. These couples instinctively know that the honeymoon is over, but they attempt to make their reality conform to a romantic myth. "We're still in love," they'll say. In such marriages, each partner feels trapped by the one they are supposed to be loved by.

5 Roles
and Traditions

Switching Roles

MARCH 2000

In this society, some gender roles are exclusive to men, and others are solely for women. These roles give us a sense of identity and direct much of how we live our lives—our preferences, relationships, speech, dress, desires, pursuits, and views. The roles are generally clear: Men are expected to be competitive, strong, and successful, while women are expected to be dependent, nurturing, and sexually appealing. Though some rebel against these stereotypes, most people readily conform to societal standards for how men and women should be. Cheered on by fans, both men and women are starring in their own movies playing roles that make them feel admired, valued, and envied.

At one point, Kirk Aldridge's role had been carved out; he worked sixty hours a week and brought home the money. Then an unfortunate accident muddled conventional boundaries and Kirk lost his compass in the world. In the prime of his career as a construction engineer, Kirk was paralyzed from the waist down after a tragic industrial accident, and his American Dream dissipated right before his eyes. Kirk's life had been cut off midstream—at least that was the way he felt. He could no longer fulfill the stereotypical role of an independent man, and his anxieties soared.

When I met Kirk, I had already experienced my bout with depression and that experience opened my heart to the suffering of others. Many people have suffered hard times and been dealt incredibly hard blows in life. Some are changed by their experiences while others wallow in pity and remain bitter and depressed. Kirk had chosen the pity route and his courage curdled into rage and gloom.

I met Kirk at the physical therapy clinic in Catauga, where I was being treated for tendonitis of the knee. When I entered the clinic, he was conversing with his therapist and I could hear the entire conversation. The arrangement of the beds in the office offered no privacy. Beds were placed one next to the other in one huge room, and patients regularly held conversations with other patients in beds near them.

Kirk shifted the conversation to me.

"One minute I was normal, and the next I was being transported away from the job site on a gurney," Kirk groaned.

"I'm very sorry to hear about your accident," I said.

"It was a horrible nightmare," he said.

Ruggedly handsome, muscular, and darkly tanned, Kirk had lost the identity that being the king of his castle offered, and his sense of worth had tumbled.

Myopic Sight

Talking to anyone who would listen, Kirk continued, "I'm nothing now but a cripple."

Kirk's wonderful life ended in twenty-four hours. He had everything—a great job, wonderful wife and kids. Now he couldn't work, which was a hard pill to swallow.

"I'm sure that's difficult," I said.

"You're telling me," he said. "My wife is the breadwinner and I'm a stay-at-home dad. I feel totally emasculated."

Kirk's memories were a poignant reminder of what he'd lost. He and his wife had reversed roles and making the transition was tough for both. A woman was playing the role of breadwinner, a symbol of masculinity and the sole domain of men, like being head of household. Now Kirk would have to explore a new self-identity to define his manhood, possibly one without public validation and surely one not listed in the gender rulebook.

Kirk was no longer living according to tradition. In fact, to Kirk it was downright gender reversal that his wife was now the breadwinner. Certainly, a working wife is no longer an aberration. Yet we are all products of hundreds of years of enculturation that espouses that the man's job is to support his family while the woman's post is in the home, being cared for and protected.

Regardless of how much the world has changed, most of us have retained this mindset.

"Kirk, for a time you fully supported your family," I said.

"I know," he said. "But I'm trekking down a nontraditional path, one where my purpose is lost. I hate it!"

"I understand," I told him.

"I shouldn't have to do dishes and change diapers all day long; that's not what men do," he said, filled with distress.

"Kirk, you're feeling bad, but constantly beating up on yourself about something you didn't cause is not healthy. You had an accident and now you're doing your best to recover," the therapist offered gingerly before leaving the room.

Noticing another guy in the room, Kirk continued the conversation.

"My doctor says that I'll never regain my sexual function. I'm a eunuch, for God's sake," he lamented.

"Damn. I would just die if my guys quit on me," the other gentleman commented.

"I'm no good at anything," Kirk said.

Kirk's self-confidence was completely disintegrated. He was dying under the weight of his circumstances.

"What good am I if I can't please my wife sexually?" Kirk continued, nearly hysterical. "I should be happy to be alive, but sometimes I wish that I hadn't survived the accident," he said.

"But you're alive!" I said.

Kirk wasn't being lifted by this conversation. There was nothing that we could offer that would relieve his emotional pain. He felt useless and was terrified that his wife would leave him for someone better. Kirk would have to learn to explore his options.

"My wife and I may as well be divorced," Kirk said. "I can't walk, can't work, can't have sex; hell, I can't do anything!"

I did not comment and neither did the other guy. But we were both attentive and maybe that was enough for Kirk. Anyway, Kirk appeared inconsolable, and his spirits would never lift as long as he focused on what he had lost.

As if Kirk's load wasn't heavy enough, his wife was freaking out about turning thirty and badgering him about buying a bigger house.

"I sure as hell can't buy it now. Our budget is already stretched to the limit," Kirk lamented.

Then his mood started to shift.

"My four-year-old has gone mad and thinks he's Peter Parker ... Spider Man. He's practically destroyed our home hopping on and off of the furniture."

"How cute," I said. "I'm sure he's a joy."

"Oh, he's a great kid," Kirk said with pride in his eyes. "When the doctor recommended that we start him on Ritalin, my wife burst into tears and wailed for hours, 'I'm a bad mommy. I'm a bad mommy.' I feel like a scuba diver wearing a lead suit."

"Cute analogy," I said, and Kirk managed a slight smile.

"I used to be his hero," Kirk said, changing his tone.

"I'm sure you still are."

"Not anymore," he said. "But what can I do?" he asked, dejected.

Speaking at nearly a whisper, I told Kirk, "Try new things, one day at a time. Activity is better than idleness."

I had the secret hope that I was helping the situation, but no evidence. Kirk, it appeared, could use professional help, but he was riding through the pain alone. He was willing to live with depression when he could have lived without it. With the negative press and stigma surrounding depression and treatment—"Only weak people get depressed," and "Meds are for crazies,"—it was easy to see why he avoided it.

My sixty-minute therapy session ended and I waved good-bye as I left the facility.

Widening the Scope

Life was moving in the wrong direction and Kirk demanded that it change to suit him, but it would not. So he was not sleeping or eating well and his enthusiasm about life was dangling on a thin thread. Kirk fluctuated between believing that he somehow deserved this tragedy and considering it bum luck. Obviously, Kirk was sinking under the weight of his own thoughts—feelings of hopelessness, a preoccupation with his condition, and a lack of appreciation for the good in his life—all of which made him feel powerless. He could surely use a new perspective as well as a renewed sense of power and personal responsibility.

Talking about our problems without attempting to solve them only makes us feel more powerless and depressed. There is no easy solution, no magical path to eliminate all of our personal difficulties. Restoring happiness lies in our ability to see alternative solutions. That approach offers a sense of control over our lives. However, unhappy people generally don't want to put forth much effort, even to improve their own lives. Rather, they want someone else to do the work for them— their partners, bosses, or relatives. But generally nothing changes without effort. As soon as one problem is solved, our energy level seems to rise. The better we feel, the more we are able to come up with creative solutions to solve our own problems.

Life had shown me that self-pity is a destructive emotion and often the motivating factor behind low self-esteem or self-hatred. We sing the pity song, secretly hoping that someone will rescue us from our misery. There are others who have endured equally horrible experiences who were able to go on and live happy and fulfilled lives. Those people have not forgotten the experience, but they have interpreted it in such a way that it is bearable. For instance, they have focused on what they can do instead of what they cannot do. Kirk would have to find the energy, love, and courage within himself to make up for what was lacking in his life.

In Kirk's circumstance, he could not work at the same job, but he could certainly do some things around the house, like load the dishwasher, prepare meals, do the laundry, and lend a hand with the children. All of those tasks would be a significant help to his wife. He could also throw a baseball with his son and listen to his family and friends. There were countless ways for him to be intimate with his wife, from a warm caress on her neck to a sexual embrace. Instead of wallowing in pity, maybe Kirk could imagine new ways of doing things like pleasing his wife sexually. Pure naked bonding and attention would probably be just as pleasurable as those pelvic throbs—not to mention pleasuring her orally. More, sharing innermost thoughts with someone is another way to feel connected.

Kirk simply needed to shift perspective, to view his problem from a different angle and see the possibilities. By constantly focusing on his own failures and inadequacies, he was immobilized by self-pity.

After listening to Kirk, I understood how I must have sounded while I was singing my pity party song. Kirk's pity cocktail was also spiked with anger— anger that resulted from his resistance to a life that was not the way he wanted it to be. His anger barely covered his pain. It is easy to come to this conclusion when we fail to acknowledge, appreciate, and value our own worth, intelligence, gifts, and abilities. I had also experienced this feeling. I'd wished for my unpleasant thoughts to drift away, but still they stuck to my brain like parasites. Anger softens with deeper understanding, but Kirk wasn't there yet. Kirk had options. It was just a matter of whether he chose to utilize them or give up. His solutions had to come from him, and the more he exercised his personal power, the stronger he would become.

It would not take a revolution for Kirk to get rid of his pity and anger; small steps would help free his heart from the pain. For example, he could acknowledge that he had suffered a hard blow and then gradually learn to make peace with his reality. He would have to accept that his life would never return to its former state. Kirk could also consider joining a support group for paraplegics or investigate job opportunities that would allow him to work at home via computer or telephone. With a renewed purpose in life, the memories of his traumatic accident would eventually be overcome.

Pity parties consume us with hurt from unfair circumstances and drain the life out of existence. Worst of all, they allow us to cast away our responsibility, and, in doing so, we cease to solve our problems. The veneer of happiness that envelops this culture makes it nearly unbearable for us to contend with painful realities. Instead, we tend to drown ourselves in pain, repeatedly feeling sorry for ourselves. Although we often feel temporarily consoled by self-pity, the long-term benefits are hardly worth the misery.

We can dwell on the unfairness of life—insults, personal tragedies, job loss, or not getting the best genes—and let these things determine the quality of our lives. On the other hand, we can accept and make peace with what we cannot change and forgive those who have injured our spirits. For some, the tenor of their entire existence is determined by a seemingly uncontrollable obsession with horrid memories and thoughts. Such distasteful experiences recur obsessively like the reruns of reels in old movies. Sometimes the films seem more real than the reality ever was.

Problems inevitably arise in our lives, but problems themselves do not necessarily cause our suffering. If we focus directly on finding solutions, then problems are changed into opportunities for growth. However, when we add an element of "this isn't fair" to the mix, then problems perpetuate suffering. Often our thinking that life should be fair is on a level that oversteps logic and reasoning. The immutable truth is that suffering is an inescapable part of life. It demands the most undiluted kind of courage. Well-adjusted people know how to accept life's hardships and people's shortcomings much the way they accept water as being wet. It just is!

Reproductive Rites

JUNE 1999

Any woman nearing thirty with no children is likely familiar with the insidious biological clock that seems to tick faster and faster with each passing year. Liz had been ringleader in our circle of women who paraded around monthly, chanting slogans and waving banners that read "Save Our Eggs" as our hormones shifted. Each of us held prayer vigils to prolong our fertility and grieved the loss of another precious egg that went unfertilized. Several of our friends had already had babies, and the rest of us were suddenly driven by the primal urge to procreate. Motherhood, after all, is our sacred calling.

Some of my panic-stricken friends went on a dating rampage as soon as they turned thirty, and married Mr. Wrong—or any sperm donor with passable genes—in order to have a baby before their eggs dried up. A few decided to wait and play a chancy game of reproductive roulette with Mother Nature. And she won. They seemed to have forgotten the basic biological fact that fertility declines with age.

Liz Hutton was an attractive woman with a round face framed by dark, short hair. Quite ambitious, she was on her way to achieving the American Dream. She had graduated from college, started her career, gotten married, and purchased a home. The only thing that was missing was the baby. Like most women, Liz had grown up playing with dolls that taught her how to be a mommy. As an adult, she knew that becoming a mother was expected and a

175

natural part of a woman's life. More, she had been besieged by the imagery that told her that having a baby was the most gratifying and joyful experience in the cosmos.

In some ways, Liz and I were in a similar predicament. In my twenties, I had given hardly any thought to marriage or children. I wanted the free and easy life. At this point, I was well aware of the ticking clock and had no real prospects for marriage. Getting closer to the end of my childbearing years, which was rushed by a possible diagnosis of uterine cancer; the pressure was on and I was stressed to death.

I knew Liz from college and had kept in touch with her since we graduated. Liz wanted a child and was feeling left out of the regenerative circle of life and punished by God. During our last conversation, Liz was throwing a small pity party and I was an invited guest.

Liz had been reading *Women's Magazine* and the headline read "Happy New Moms." She started sobbing uncontrollably. These women were all first-time moms flooded with waves of maternal love, enjoying their babies' smile, midnight breast feedings, and bonding with their babies.

"Hi, Kay," Liz said. "Sorry to call you so late, but I really need to talk. I tried calling you earlier, but …"

"Okay," I yawned. "What's going on?"

"Spencer and I have been married for a while," she said. "We're having a hard time conceiving."

"I know of couples who were married for more than five years before they conceived a baby," I said, my voice raspy with sleep. "Anything is possible."

"Well, why hasn't it happened?" she asked.

"I don't know," I replied.

"I'm never going to have a baby," said Liz.

"You haven't exhausted all of your options," I said.

"Sure looks like we have," she said. "There is nothing more painful than not being able to have a baby."

"I know how you're feeling," I said. "Have you considered adoption?"

"We want our own baby," Liz whined. "I just can't handle that I won't have my own family."

I couldn't console her, so I ended the conversation before things got too emotional. This was really not a subject for debate. Though married with a successful career, Liz still branded herself a personal failure. Liz was measuring her success and worth as a human being based on her ability to have children. At least that's the way it seemed. It also occurred to me that people who don't have children rarely consider themselves a success. Madison had this condition too. On the flip side, I had seen a number of teenage mothers who considered their children an achievement that made them feel like a success. No doubt they'd all inhaled an endless parade of happy mom images atomized into the atmosphere by media jets, which insisted that all women needed children to make their lives complete and fulfilled. I'd done the same.

Suddenly, Liz's primary reason for wanting children seemed sort of selfish. She had omitted the real gifts that children offer, like the gift of love and teaching one to be tolerant, patient, flexible, forgiving, generous, and accepting—not to mention a range of emotional rewards children offer, including a new outlook on life.

Liz and Spencer had been married for five years and had hopes of producing a baby biologically, but their loving marriage remained despairingly childless. After years of frustration and infertility, they decided to try invitro fertilization, which can be agonizing and ruinous. Liz's body was receptive to the implantation. At her first prenatal exam, two tiny bodies appeared on the monitor. Immediately Liz started to imagine a life with twins and days filled with feeding, bathing, cuddling, and dressing the babies.

By the thirty-second week of pregnancy, Liz's blood pressure skyrocketed and the twins had to be delivered early. Neither of the infants survived. Liz and Spencer were devastated. "How could a loving God be so cruel? What did we do wrong?" they'd questioned. They were so angry with God that they stopped attending church and cut off contact with other parishioners. "It's hard for us to pray to an indifferent and unsympathetic God who allowed such a terrible tragedy to occur," Liz had said.

Liz imagined God the way many people do and concluded if something good happened to her, it was luck or attributed to her good works. She also felt that when bad things happened, God was to blame. Liz was disillusioned with a God who granted other people's wishes, but denied her own.

Living in a community that valued women according to their ability to bear children, Liz's infertility made her feel like a shunned outcast. At the same time, relatives, friends, and church members were harping on her mom with the famous "Any grandbabies yet?" question while proudly showing off photos of their own grandchildren. Her mother was in a near-flustered state, worried sick about never becoming a grandmother, which to her was the culmination of womanhood. "Not having a grandchild is literally unthinkable," she'd once told us. "I simply couldn't bear the disgrace."

Months later, I got another call from Liz. The phone rang just before midnight, so I expected the worst. A mutual friend of ours had given birth to twins, and the news poured salt on Liz's open wounds. Anger turned to despair, and life seemed to end for both Liz and Spencer. Liz couldn't sleep, eat, or find any happiness in life. Spencer was also numb.

"Did you hear the news?" Liz asked.

"What news?" I asked.

"Rona had twin girls."

"Oh, yeah," I said. "That's really nice."

"She has twins and I have nothing," she moaned. "I want my life to be different." Liz was in pain.

"I know."

"I crave motherhood," she cried. "It's one of life's most priceless experiences and one too precious to sacrifice."

When Liz realized that she could not change her life, she sank deeper into helplessness. Then she started to believe that she deserved this tragedy. Since the death of her twins, the mere sight of baby commercials made Liz cry. Just seeing other pregnant women ruined her day.

"People don't seem to realize that losing a baby can happen to anyone, no matter how healthy you are," Liz told me.

"You're right."

"Everyone blames me."

"Some things in life, like having a baby naturally, are beyond our immediate control," I explained.

"I feel so empty, almost dead inside," she said, raising her voice three octaves.

"I'm sure it's very hard for you."

Liz's body had betrayed her and she was mad as hell. Drenched in shame, Liz sobbed, "Why can't I be normal? What in the hell did I do to deserve this?"

"You didn't do anything."

"I'd better go."

"Okay, feel better."

"I'll try," she moaned.

"We'll talk later," I said to her before hanging up.

Just when Liz and Spencer had given up on having a baby and decided to adopt, a miracle happened. Liz was expecting. On a bright September morning, Liz and Spencer became the proud parents of Matthew Spencer. After his birth, they knew that all things were possible. Liz slowly started to realize that God is not responsible for life's tragedies. God loves us even when we find it difficult to love ourselves.

Some suffering is simply the result of the workings of natural laws, and God does not interfere with that. Also, our prayers are not always answered the way that we'd like. Sometimes God makes a few changes. Is it wise for us to imagine God as a God who has the power to grant our wishes, as if He's holding a magic wand, but who arbitrarily chooses to give or withhold what we pray for? I don't think so. Suffering is a part of life. From some Christian perspectives, suffering can be viewed as nurturing to our spirits, which makes us more compassionate towards others and draws us nearer to God.

So many of us are reluctant to face the truth that death, accidents, and sickness are not punishments from God ("God's will") for our wrongdoing. This kind of an outlook can cause real harm and often borders on heresy. Seeing bad things as divine retribution can lead people to be callous instead of compassionate when things go wrong. For instance, one shrugs at a cancer diagnosis or a fatal accident when sorrow is more appropriate. Further, it implies that if we say the right words with enough zeal, we can make God want to grant our prayers.

To come to the realization that God is not punishing us can be quite liberating. Such awareness frees us from the unrealistic belief that if we can be perfect, we will be immune to life's hardships and tragedies, because they only happen to those who deserve them. And it spares us from utter despair and disillusionment when sickness, aging, and death befall us. Most of all, it keeps us from losing our faith in God and believing that we aren't worthy when God doesn't answer our prayers.

I'm Having a Baby

Before now it really wasn't clear to me that there were psychological—self-esteem—boosts associated with becoming a parent. Suddenly, I recalled the many patronizing remarks that women with children had offered me since I had passed the age of twenty-five. "You don't have children?" "I can't conceive of my life without my children—they are everything to me!" "Your life must be so empty." I now had concrete proof that children were more than gifts from God. It seemed that no area of our lives was off limits for enhancing our egos; offspring were also included. Now when some of my associates raved about their children and grandchildren, I understood why.

It explained why several of my contemporaries—who competed daily for raises, pivotal assignments, and accolades on staff—had three and even four children when they'd pronounced years earlier that they only wanted one child. Naturally, as soon as one colleague broadcasted that she was expecting, the others quickly followed suit, announcing their pregnancies shortly after the pink dot appeared on their at-home tests. Undeniably, for nine months, expecting mothers are movie stars in a world with adoring fans and few critics. Since most of the women on staff were in the childbearing stage, someone had a baby every two to three months. Maternity leaves were taken in succession. After returning to work, the mother's childbirths were ranked: natural deliveries were commended and cesarean deliveries were relegated to the bottom tier.

Several months following the babies' births, the new moms offered stories of how well their children were progressing in their social, physical, and intellectual development.

"Austin can use a sippy cup," said one mom.

"Carlyn is already potty trained," offered another, nearly springing from her seat.

"Austin loves Beethoven and Mozart," continued the first mom.

"I'm enrolling Luke in a Montessori school," one spilled over a cubicle wall.

"Carlyn is learning French," said the second.

"Austin can speak Spanish," said the first.

"Luke can use a computer," the third mom added.

This once pleasant conversation had quickly escalated into a sinister game of parental one-upmanship. It sounded as if these new mothers were each vying for the parent-of-the-month prize. I wondered if they had bumper stickers on their cars that read "Honk if you worship my kid, too!" All of these women were already rivaling for their children's admission into Ivy League colleges and buying laptops for children who were barely out of training pants. With their mode of parenting mirroring product development, they were making these kids so pressurized that they were going to explode before their tenth birthdays. They needed their children to do well to prove that they were good parents. Witnessing this spectacle every day was enough to make me want to get my tubes tied.

Rearing a child is more complicated than perfectly adhering to the product development guidelines, which make no allowances for error. With any luck, these women would learn that children are resilient enough to overcome parental mistakes if they are loved, supported, and relieved of unrealistic parental expectations.

Though there appears to be less pressure for men to be fathers, there is social stress. The men on staff were also applauded for their little ones. Accolades were offered: "You're running with the big dogs now!" and "Way to go, stud!" The new fathers beamed with pride. No doubt their ability to procreate, providing immortality to their DNA, was a source of self-satisfaction. Guys like Rick, who were unable to have children, were chided: "Something wrong with your equipment? Are you shooting blanks?" Rick felt ashamed and humiliated. Unquestionably, fathering a child is considered a way of proving manliness, which is somehow connected to self-identity and worth. Rick told me solemnly, "I've always wanted a son, a miniature me to call me dad."

It all made sense to me now. Much like the story of Hagar and Sarah in the ancient world, women with children have long been lauded over women without children. Children are considered a part of the total success package, which is why comedians and others in the media lampoon outrageously successful women for not having children. Motherhood is why millions of women risk their lives to have children. It also explained why some women and teens, lacking both the maturity and financial resources to adequately care for their children, rush to become mothers. And let's not forget the recent explosion of new sperm banks popping up all over the country as attractive options for women's fertility needs. Sperm without sex—what a concept! Much is done to satisfy our baby lust.

There I was, a tinge piqued that I had spent a fortune on countless baby showers (and bridal showers), but no one had bothered to throw me a party for being single, supporting myself, or accomplishing great things on the job. Okay, maybe I'd gotten an occasional nod at a team meeting or a "Nice job" while passing in the corridors. In this society, celebrations are usually for family-oriented events only. Maybe one day there will be a celebration for "flying solo," "no children," or "happily never married." Sure, when mice bark!

The End of the Circle of Life

Experiencing the death of loved ones is perhaps one of the most painful emotions in life and one with which I am all too familiar. Though our society tries hard to minimize the seriousness of death—often telling others to "get over it" and "everyone dies"—the truth is that grief can last for years. The closer we are to the deceased, the longer the grieving process takes. We never really get over the death of a loved one. However, we do reach a point where the sadness does not overwhelm us and we can carry on with our lives.

We often think that our lives are too difficult or that our circumstances are too painful or that we will never find peace. So we hide our emotions like we are sentries guarding Buckingham Palace. It is not until we allow ourselves to fall apart, to be angry, and to grieve, that we can begin to put our lives back together again. Honest emotions are necessary for real growth and happiness. If we attend closely, death and grief can teach us the value of life and happiness.

Allowing ourselves to experience what we're really feeling is a kind of expiation; a cleansing that allows our souls to breathe. Life is filled with highs and lows, but it is our ability to withstand the lows that determines the quality of our lives.

A Sense of Control

JUNE 2001

Fear and doubt tell some that they are not good enough to have someone who truly loves them, so they settle for someone who does not. This is Dana's story. Frightened dependency kept her in an esteem-eroding relationship absorbing painful insults, wounding disappointments, and surging rages until she was literally gasping for breath. Dana's marriage was, in some ways, a wedding of convenience. She had heard the tale of meeting Prince Charming and living happily ever after, but her fairy tale had a different ending.

The Love of a Lifetime

Dana Smothers had met Chad at a Christmas party, and she was mesmerized by his enormous charisma and good looks. They were married less than three months later. "It was love at first sight. We couldn't keep our hands off of each other," Dana had related to me with a slight smile. "His salary wasn't too bad either. Chad provided me with security, respectability, and enough cash to live the *good life*."

But Dana's enthrallment with her prince soon sentenced her to a marital prison of degradation, unremitting abuse, and the annihilation of her self. Dana's husband Chad was one of far too many men who felt deep inside that women were something to be used and humiliated. Some blame it on violent

182

lyrics and sexually explicit movies, others on lipstick and hot pants. But most know that this mindset is as old as the planet.

Chad was a typical abuser consumed by feelings of omnipotence, a violent sense of entitlement, and paranoia. Employed as a feed plant manager for AgriBus and successful by ordinary standards, Chad was a failure in his own eyes. "Hell, this country has relegated men down to nothing. Women have all of the rights now, and the good jobs!" he'd once remarked. Whenever he was gripped by self-pity, self-hatred, or envy; he would spew his hatred onto Dana, transforming her into the cause of his pain. In truth, his own thoughts created his pain. Somehow he hoped to pacify his own misery at her expense.

In Chad's empire, his wife and children were mere property that did not merit humane treatment or evoke compassion. They were objects devoid of emotions and mere extensions of himself. For ten years, Chad succeeded in converting Dana to his worldview and punished her for being a separate entity with her own feelings, needs, boundaries, preferences, and dreams. Objects, after all, can only be desired; they are not permitted to have desires. Dana had been tethered to her husband for financial and emotional support. Gradually, she realized that her reliance on Chad and their marriage was slowly killing her.

Dana Smothers, self-effacing and polite, was a receptionist at the Day Spa, where I treated myself to monthly pampering. With warm skin and naturally wavy hair, Dana possessed an understated beauty. Though she was always pleasant, there was a deep sadness in her eyes. Initially, I talked with Dana about the weather, museums, or nothing in particular during my ten to thirty-minute wait in the lobby. But over time, she opened up about her marriage and all of her pain poured out, her voice cracking through the hurt.

Dana's Song

"Most women grow up dreaming of a knight in shining armor to rescue them, but I never had that image," Dana stated. "Growing up, I didn't see many women in healthy relationships. The women I knew well were lifeless after years of being beaten down, emotionally and physically, by men. They stayed on for the sake of need masquerading as love. These women were devalued and sought after only for the favors and pleasures their bodies offered. I recall my grandmother telling me when I was a teenager, 'Women don't have any worth without men and you'll learn this well when you're older. Regardless of how things appear on the outside, even reputable married women are sleeping with a man so that he can buy her what she wants.' So when I grew up, I believed that my choices were pretty much limited. My folks were just glad to have me married off," she continued.

On a bright Friday afternoon, I entered the Day Spa and approached the reception desk. Seeing me, Dana smiled and offered the standard greeting. "Welcome to the Day Spa. What can we do for you today?" After I was all checked in, Dana struck up a conversation.

Dana went on to say that from the outside, her family appeared ideal. "We were the family that others wanted to emulate," she told me.

But no one on the outside could have imagined the inside story. After enduring an abusive marriage for nearly ten years, Dana moved from Kentucky to Catauga County to start a new life.

"Communication between us was always strained," Dana said.

"Really?" I asked.

"Yeah," she replied. "Whenever life didn't go his way, he'd begin an emotional tirade, insulting and criticizing me. 'So my drinking bothers you, huh? Well your fat ass bothers me. Get off my back! You don't bitch about my paychecks!'" Dana said heatedly. "It was his way of keeping me in my place."

Dana recalled, "Beating me down energized Chad and made him feel powerful. Chad would get angry about spilled milk or a sock on the floor and rant for hours. He'd tell me, 'You make me so fucking crazy! I don't know why I keep your sorry ass. You can't cook, you're a lousy fuck, you're worthless.'"

Chad could cuss the paint off the walls and his wounding remarks sent Dana's ego reeling from the blows, knocking to her knees. Nothing Dana did was right. And Chad hated Dana for not being what he imagined her to be: picture perfect. It seemed as if Chad tried to cover his own failings with Dana's faults.

Dana's insecurities were not exactly minimized by the relentless jeering from her husband, who tormented her daily about her lack of desirability. Because she accepted Chad's judgments without question, Dana felt powerless. At this point, I was wondering how long I could comfortably sit and listen to this nightmarish account. This marriage, supposedly bound together in love, was void of any recognizable expressions of love.

Dana walked over to get two bottles of water from the refrigerator and then resumed her story. She handed me a bottle and returned to her post behind the receptionist desk.

"The signs were there from the beginning—the mind games, blaming, rages, and intense possessiveness. And I dismissed everything," she said, pouring water into a glass.

"What did he do?" I asked, bracing myself for her reply.

"Chad grew increasingly more violent and started slapping me and choking me until I passed out, no matter how I pleaded with him to stop," Dana went on, her voice dead.

"Oh, Dana," I said, trying to process the words.

"I gave up everything just to keep him," Dana continued.

I wondered if Chad's brains were caught in his zipper or if he'd escaped Green Pastures Home for the Mentally Insane. Now I understood perfectly why women who'd endured years of abuse were wearing orange jumpsuits and waiting for parole.

Living in this nightmare, Dana was scared and never stood up for herself, so Chad accused her of being a martyr. She related that he once told her, "You should be holding a crucifix like other saints." During the lull in the violence, she used to dream that he would love her enough to make up for every time he punched her or chased her with a knife or pistol. According to Dana, he didn't. Dana loved a man who could not love her back; he could not even love himself. So she accommodated herself to a life without love in order to fit in.

A hostage in her own home, Dana wasn't allowed to talk on the phone, have friends, or shop alone. Gifts and extra cash had to be earned. "He made me feel so cheap," she'd said. Over time, Dana perfected the art of absorbing blows to the face. But the beatings became more frequent and the scars harder to hide.

"I became an expert at lying and covering up bruises: 'I'm sick; can't come in today,' or 'My allergies caused my eyes to swell.'" Dana continued, "I just tried to be perfect, hoping that he'd love me and stop hitting me."

"Incredible!"

Glancing nervously at the door, she continued, "I didn't want anyone to know how bad things were; everyone else seemed to have such perfect marriages."

Who could blame her? The dirty laundry aired in Dana's tight-knit community would make *Jerry Springer* look like a tent revival.

"Why did you settle for someone like Chad?" I asked.

"I lost faith in my own attractiveness and worth," she confessed.

Dana believed all of the nasty things Chad said to her, and he had a knack for making her feel useless and used.

"I see."

"I wasn't pretty enough to get another man, so I just kept him," Dana said, looking at the floor. "He was better than nothing."

More, Chad was an excellent provider. He afforded the family with a comfortable home in the suburbs, nice cars, a middle-class standard of living, and a measure of security. Managing and planning a household, much the same as having children, created the delusion of togetherness in Dana's marriage.

Dana said in a broken whisper, "Plus, I was flat broke, and I've never been good at doing things for myself."

With everything gone, it was easy to see why Dana suppressed her needs in order to keep her last shred of love. It's really strange: No matter how lacking a relationship, the loss of personal separateness and the sense of belonging feel good. Somehow Dana had this feeling. She probably would have stayed if Chad hadn't nearly killed her.

Dana recalled with her head lowered, "One morning, I spoke to our neighbor, Ken, and Chad lost it. Chad asked me, 'Are you fucking him too?' Then he threw me up against the wall and beat me for hours until I lost consciousness. There was an incredible cracking sound as my head hit the wall."

"How horrible!"

"My eyes were severely bruised and swollen nearly shut like I'd received the knockout punch in a boxing match," she said.

According to Dana's account, the blows to her face split her lip in two, chipped her tooth, and fractured her nose. There was dried blood caked in her nose and mouth. Her body ached all over. She needed to call 911, but she was too humiliated and degraded.

"I couldn't bear the sound of sirens or a barrage of questions from the police. I wanted to die," she continued.

As usual, Chad apologized and begged Dana to stay. She recalled his pleadings: "I'm sorry. Please stay … it won't happen again. I love you." After midnight, Dana left with her children. Chad had a hard time losing the identity that his family offered him. Though he cared very little for them, he liked that they were all dependent on him. She told me that Chad always said that being needed made him feel like a man. He relished the omnipotence of his role as provider. Now that Chad had lost his wife, cook, maid, lover, cheerleader, and children, he felt alone. More, he was no longer a part of the system that actively defined and supported American manhood. Perhaps he wasn't entirely self-sufficient either.

On more than one occasion, I have been accused of being too independent and too decisive, as if these were negative traits. In fact, for several years my male colleagues have been trying to coerce me into a vulnerable and passive role; possibly because it was more palatable for these God-fearing, head-of-household men who'd transferred their beliefs from the home to the office. These were men who found it amusing that women had career goals. I'll agree that some degree of dependence is good, particularly in a relationship. However, Dana's life showed me that being overly reliant on another person (one's spouse/partner/colleague) to the degree that one refuses to take responsibility for managing one's own life is potentially deadly.

A Vivid Look

Dana was born into a religious background where divorce wasn't an option. Traditions still had a stronghold on her Bible Belt community. "As a good wife, it was my duty to stay married no matter how bad things got. I'd made a covenant with God," she'd later recalled. Living in a place where doctrinal conformity was given a higher priority than love, it's no small wonder that Dana remained in an appalling marriage. Inch by inch, Chad had whittled away everything that made Dana human. Once she started to gain more self-worth, Dana refused to tolerate a marriage that stifled her freedom and maimed her personality.

"I am my own person now, with my own identity," Dana declared. "I won't accept bad treatment ever again."

"I'm glad to hear that, Dana," I told her. "We can't mourn our mistakes forever; we have to go on living."

"You're right."

With surprising resilience and the help of Come By Here, a shelter for battered women, Dana was able to transition into her new life. Dana did not think that she could handle the recriminations from the community or support herself financially, but she managed to do both.

With her voice softening slightly, she added, "Letting go hurt, but I had to stay alive for my children."

"Good for you," I said.

"I'm not so scared anymore."

Though Dana had escaped her abusive marriage, visible and invisible scars from years of abusive treatment still affected how she viewed herself. Thankfully, Dana was regaining some control over her life and a new perspective.

Dana told me, "I know now that abuse is not part of God's plan for marriage. I deserve better."

"Yes, you do," I agreed. "Your life has value just the way it is. You're valuable because you're human."

"Thanks," she said with a smile. "I appreciate your saying that."

"You're welcome."

The room was silent for a minute.

"The therapist is ready for your session now," Dana said. "First room on the left. Enjoy!"

"I always do," I said. "See you the next time." I opened the double doors and entered the salon.

It was evident that the culture also had Chad in a grip. Prevailing stereotypes about men offer that they are supposed to be powerful, rich, and domineering. Chad had failed to meet his goals and he compensated by exerting his supremacy over Dana. Apparently, this sense of having too much expected of you as a man, while being expected to conform and being monitored by an invisible force, is overwhelming for some men. Like Chad, most men don't seem to realize how they are influenced by the culture, or they prefer to ignore it. In fact, we all have a fear that what we have based our lives on may not be true. Ironically, when men and women are fixated on the other's perfidy and convinced of their own righteousness, neither notices the common source of their angst.

The Power of Choice

The happiest people make their own choices. Having a sense of being in control of one's own life makes one feel competent, independent, and valued. We know that we're in command of our lives when we make conscious choices and are not afraid of the consequences. The real suffering begins when we feel that we have no viable options. Although this lesson took a circuitous route, Dana's experiences helped me to realize the power of choice. It was now clear to me that once we have a strong sense of who we are, our choices will no longer be based on neediness and our self-confidence will help us to survive disapproval.

Changing the way we see ourselves is also a choice. People who have been abused don't have to spend another second focusing on the abuse or other painful memories of what their spouses/lovers did to them. Yes, they deserve to be loved, but it's up to them to love themselves and move forward. They only need to look inside; the loving starts with them. Whether we have been abused or not, if our thoughts about ourselves are that we're not good enough or valuable enough or perfect enough to be loved, there's nothing that friends, family, or partners can do or say that'll sway us otherwise.

A Cycle of Redemption

Forgiving others is difficult, and many of us are reluctant to forgive. Quite simply, this notion of forgiving offends and contradicts our rational thinking. When people hurt us, it triggers our deepest fears that we may be inadequate, unworthy, or unlovable people. We believe that they don't really care about our feelings or us. As we replay this message over and over again, we constantly reaffirm negative beliefs about ourselves. Like one of those old-fashioned turntables with a missing arm, the record keeps going around and around until someone or something stops it.

Any form of abuse, even self-inflicted, is particularly difficult to pardon. It is nearly impossible to resolve terrifying memories of abuse. There is simply no quick-fix solution to such unutterable experiences, which can leave us bitter, angry, untrusting, and depressed forever. If someone has mistreated us, hurt us, or offended us, we are entitled to get upset. There is no reason why we should deny our pain, no reason to understand another's actions. Likewise, there is no incentive to let go of the offense, no reason why, in our anguish, we should find empathy for our offender. So with good reason, Dana was struggling to forgive Chad.

"I used to dream of killing Chad. But being angry at Chad didn't harm him; it nearly destroyed me," Dana had told me with her lips trembling.

Forgiving does not mean that we accept poor treatment, reconcile, excuse, or become a doormat oblivious to the cruelty of others. It simply means that we chose to heal ourselves and break an unending cycle of pain. Letting go is uplifting and healing; it allows happiness to enter our lives again. Otherwise, we may feel negatively tied to our offender for life and see ourselves as victims. Sometimes, we may have to learn to forgive ourselves first.

Our worst memories do not fade or get better; they stay with us for as long as we live. The good news is that linear streams of happy thoughts and sad thoughts flow through our minds like a river, but we decide which thoughts to hold.

Life Interrupted

APRIL 2003

The trouble with marrying young before you're ready is that when things go wrong, all of your family's warnings come back to haunt you. Mary Jane Dunlap's life had been flipped upside-down and she was trying hard to navigate through that phase of her life alone. Her husband of nearly thirty years squandered their life's savings on pleasure and fled, in the midst of a midlife crisis, with a topless dancer. Now she was reentering the single's world, a world that she had happily abandoned many moons ago. Once embedded in a close-knit community, Mary Jane now existed on the periphery. No more bridge parties, garden club meetings, or Junior League.

I met Mary Jane at a Princess House party hosted by one of my neighbors. Mary Jane was a soft-spoken, trendily-dressed woman in her early fifties who'd been reared in a small town where many women were living life according to a script that had been handed down for decades. She wore her faintly highlighted hair tied back in a stylish clip and spoke with a pronounced Southern accent. When I arrived, a few women were sitting in a semi-circle sampling homemade desserts and drinking sparkling cider. Mary Jane was warm and struck up a conversation immediately.

"What a lovely party," Mary Jane said as her eyes scanned the room. "And the food is delicious."

"It's quite festive," I said.

"Are you married?" she asked, out of the blue.

"No," I said, a bit stunned.

"You're probably better off," she smirked. "My husband, the serial adulterer, has spent a mint carrying on with every floozy in the Champagne Room at Hot Lips," Mary Jane announced.

Everyone within an earshot laughed, and she continued. "He's sown so many wild oats that he qualifies for Farm Aid," she said, laughing like a drowning pig.

"Farm Aid?" I asked while trying to stifle an urge to laugh.

Mary Jane held the floor for at least thirty minutes while the rest of us listened to her comical stories. Her hubby had busted up their wonderful marriage for a younger, so-called trophy babe who was nearly their son's age.

"He told me that his new doll made him feel like a twenty-one-year-old stud again—a god, to be more exact," Mary Jane continued in a sing-song voice. "Talk about an economy-sized fool."

Her colorful narrative was quite amusing.

"He sounds like an interesting character," I smiled.

Suddenly changing her tone, she said sullenly, "He's taken my life. What am I going to do now?"

Her sense of loss was profound. After being out of the workforce for more than twenty years, trying to enter the workforce at full speed was harder than Mary Jane had imagined. With a scarce job market for even qualified candidates, few employers were seeking candidates with huge gaps in their resumes. More than that, the age of technology was in full force and Mary Jane was out of touch.

"I've got no degree, no technical skills, no real work experience, and no money," she told me, distressed by her state.

There was nothing in the *Catauga County Book of Rules for Living* to guide her through this phase of her life as a middle-aged divorcee with no job skills.

"In my community, women defined themselves by their relationships and men by their professions," said Mary Jane.

"Sounds familiar," I remarked genially.

"We were expected to graduate high school, marry, and have children—in that order," she told me. "We're raised that way."

"Okay," I said.

"God knows I didn't want to be left out," she beamed. "All well-bred, respectable Southern girls got married."

"I understand," I replied, and Mary Jane shot me a grateful look.

You bet I understood. In this town, singles were treated like moral outcasts who needed to be sequestered in leper colonies for having such a tragic malady. I had always believed that the church was a refuge with no barriers or hierarchies where everyone stood equal before God. That belief was shaken in

Catauga. There, I was singled out for a specific ministry, a lower tier for unmarried women, rather than included in a holistic ministry of the church. The conventional wisdom in Catauga was that marital success was the result of one's superiority and/or one's favor in the eyes of God. While seeking comfort in faith, it is all too tempting to fabricate God's will to suit our personal desires. Trapped in a matrix of Christian design, accented by single women's meetings that separated them from the married congregation, women in Catauga were dodging the dreaded unmarried status like a bullet, to avoid being labeled as failures.

"All of my role models were stay-at-home moms, like my own mother," said Mary Jane, smiling brilliantly.

"My grandmothers were also homemakers," I said.

"Where I grew up, there was no talk of professional goals for women or of earning money to support one's self," Mary Jane continued.

"That's interesting," I said.

"Women just didn't do that sort of thing," she told me. "We were taught to look for security." Mary Jane managed a grin and continued, "I wanted to be a good wife, and I was devoted to pleasing my husband and rearing my children."

"That's all worthwhile," I said.

"I think so," she said.

"After graduating from high school, I went to college; it was automatic. I was taught to be independent and to think for myself," I said.

"Oh, please. College was not on the agenda," she explained. "We weren't encouraged to create a life that was entirely our own."

The collision of our comments illustrated a changing way of American life. I grew up believing that women had aspirations that were not essentially different from men's, though the culture claimed that women were fulfilled by exclusively pursuing traditional feminine roles. In Mary Jane's era, most women were conditioned to believe that once they were married and had children, their own personal lives were supposed to end there as their families took precedence. Mary Jane and her husband had been perfect sweethearts and her spectacular wedding was the talk of the town.

"Looking back, it was one of the happiest days of my life," Mary Jane said, quickly flashing a pleasant smile.

Though she was excited about getting married it wasn't just about marrying her husband but following tradition.

"I was supposed to be married like other women in my family and town had been for generations," Mary Jane said proudly.

Up to this point, Mary Jane's life had proceeded according to plan. She had achieved the American Dream and had what most would consider a desirable life. "We were the ideal family," she said. Mary Jane had been happily married to a successful physician and the mother of two gorgeous sons, Carson and Matt. Now her sons were adults with families of their own. Without her husband and children to care for, Mary Jane needed an activity, like work, to demonstrate her competence and to make a difference in the world. She needed to know that her life still had value. It's a human need.

Narrow Vision

Although Mary Jane felt a temporary flow of orgasmic relief after the divorce, she was disgusted by her inability to show her ex-husband how sensational her life was without him.

"Damn! Damn! Damn!" she said. "I've spent my life cleaning and cooking, which was enough to make my brain rot," Mary Jane said as she plunged into a sea of hopelessness.

If it were possible, Mary Jane would be on a missing person's poster for women who'd lost themselves in their husbands and children. In Mary Jane's view, she had misspent her life for "two ungrateful asses" and a "lily-livered bastard," none of whom cared if she were alive.

Mary Jane recalled, "I should never have let my husband convince me to stay home. He'd always tell me, 'No wife of mine is going to ever work outside of the home.'"

At the time Mary Jane didn't protest, as her husband assured her that self-sacrifice was the way a woman proved her love to her husband and children. Perhaps more tragic, she blamed herself for not being the kind of wife he needed her to be.

"I was expected to give everything. Actually, I felt obligated to give. But maybe I didn't give enough," she said with a pang of guilt.

During her marriage, Mary Jane worshipped her husband and spent her life deferring to his wishes. According to Mary Jane, her husband was as necessary to her as air. Now Mary Jane was regretting some of her choices, choices that she believed would keep her husband in her life forever.

"He was supposed to love me until death," Mary Jane said with a gloomy expression on her face. "When he failed to love me, I couldn't bear it. I fell apart. I thought he needed me and couldn't live without me. Obviously, these were my pipe dreams and not a shared reality," Mary Jane explained. "Looking back, our perfect marriage was an illusion. I never really knew him."

The first few months following the divorce were painful for Mary Jane, who once believed that being a nurturer and husband-pleaser ensured a lasting and happy marriage. Now she was gradually amending those beliefs. She could no longer be the listener (and never the talker), or the giver (and never the receiver). Since her divorce, Mary Jane felt rejected, and social interactions were terrifying.

She recalled in a faint voice, "It's humiliating for me to see people who knew me when I was married," Mary Jane explained. "Talk about a failure; in this culture, divorce signifies a failure to make the American Dream work. Suddenly, I don't know who I am."

Mary Jane had cried for so long that her tear ducts dried up. She missed the feeling of safety and comfort that her marriage once provided. Every day, thoughts of her current life sent her plummeting close to an encroaching point of no return.

"I feel so stupid, useless, and old. I'm headed to poverty row," she moaned. "I'm just not cut out to be single."

Mary Jane had run out of steam and she didn't think she had the courage to save herself.

"Things have a way of working out," I said.

"I sure hope so," she said.

"It was a pleasure meeting you, Mary Jane," I said.

"Same here, hon," she said.

It was getting dark and I didn't want to overstay my welcome. "Thanks for everything," I told the hostess and opened the front door.

I'd had an enlightening conversation with Mary Jane and I was trying to sort it all out. Suddenly my skull felt tight. As I drove along I-75 heading south, I let my window down so that I could feel the wind in my face. The air was clear, crisp, and invigorating.

Expanding the View

Several months after the divorce, Mary Jane telephoned me. Thoughts of her husband no longer instantly triggered anger or pity. Mary Jane had slowly shifted her perspective and she was learning to be grateful for the good times that she'd shared with her husband and children.

"Being a wife and mother came natural to me," she said cheerily. "Caring for my family was my life. In retrospect, there were some incredibly happy times." She paused and continued, "Maybe he loved me the best he knew how. I just wish that I'd done more for me."

Her husband had been her lover and her partner, a person with whom she had spent most of her life. It took Mary Jane nearly two years to get her new life in order, but she did it. With a flair for baking and decorating spectacular cakes, she opened a small bakery. I stopped by Mary Jane's new business to order one of her cakes and a few other desserts. For years she'd prepared desserts for her husband's office parties, so she was a natural at creating these masterpieces for weddings and other celebrations.

"Running this business is a breeze for me," she'd said.

She had also joined a Christian singles' group and was taking an Intro to Computers course at the local college.

"I think I'll go sky diving in the spring!" Mary Jane said as a feeling of strength and competence rose within her.

A clearer picture had emerged for me. Like many before her, Mary Jane had slipped into her role bit-by-bit, unaware that conformity was her inevitable fate. She was born at the end of an era where women were given to endless services of cooking, cleaning, and nurturing. Like many women, Mary Jane had learned to get her needs met by meeting other people's needs, and defined herself by what she did for others, the same as men define themselves by their careers. The absence of that definition had left Mary Jane disorientated like a carriage horse with its blinders abruptly removed.

Maybe Mary Jane had eased into martyrdom after she had forgotten her ability to freely choose. Possibly giving everything to her children and her husband gave her something to treasure, like a reward or a sense of worth. Maybe she'd inherited this habit from her mother, who couldn't envision a life free of Aqua Net, bras, girdles, aprons, or freedom of choice. Consequently, Mary Jane had scrupulously done the same. This was her silent tribute to her mother. Regardless of her reason, caring for others should fill our souls and never shrivel them.

Societal rules for women, such as "be nice" and "please others," are so embedded that they are natural actions for most women. Happiness becomes a role that many women learn to play. Sometimes our sense of obligation gets confused with our sense of worth, and being nice becomes the center of our being, thereby creating insecurity and self-doubt. Alas, we are rarely nice enough. My experiences and observations have taught me that life consists of accommodating the reasonable demands of others and balancing them against my own needs and desires, which is often tricky. Optimally, we learn to cooperate with life by offering kindness and occasional compromise.

When Relationships Go Sour

Most people beyond the age of eighteen have felt the anguish of being rejected by a lover. When relationships fail, women often feel that they have failed by not being the hottest sexual partner or having a body like a super model. These feelings are often strengthened by magazines and movies that tend to suggest that women are responsible for making the relationship go smoothly. Some women even think of themselves as failures after relationships end—that they were not good enough, attractive enough, or adequate enough. We fail to realize that infidelity for both sexes is often rooted in fear: fear of getting old, fear of being unloved, fear of being undesirable, fear of intimacy, fear of being inadequate, and a host of other fears that the members of Cheaters Anonymous fail to talk about.

People handle separations in a variety of ways. Some get a new look, new clothes, or a new career. Others are so wounded that they'll make love with anybody just to prove they are attractive to the opposite sex. A few people decide to never date again. But with any luck, one can emerge from the ordeal wiser, stronger, and more confident. One develops new friends and new plans and is ready to move on to something better. Although some believe that they cannot find anyone as good as the one who left, there is an inexhaustible supply of people to love in the world. It is a cruel mind prank to feel that there is only one person in the whole world for you to love.

I could see that our reaction to a breakup or divorce depends largely on how we look at it and our sense of worth. Believing that no one loves us or we'll never fall in love again is likely to lead to despair. But if we focus on the good times and realize that needs change, we might feel some regret, but it will not last for long. Mary Jane's feelings held the answer. If she had genuinely loved her husband (and wanted him to be happy) and not simply wanted or needed him, she could have better consoled herself about his leaving and moved on without acrimony. On the other hand ...

Following the Pack

As human beings weave themselves into society, a fascinating paradox is revealed. We have both an instinctive need to belong to a group and an equally opposing need to be independent and special. Our efforts to embrace this paradox often lead to conformity of a slavish and peculiar sort.

Cultural norms expressed through television, radio, books, and movies speak with a single voice and hold us emotionally hostage. Perhaps we're all cultural suck-ups to some extent, as evidenced by how similarly we dress, style our hair, speak, interact, and live our daily lives. Conformity is usually rewarded over individuality. We all want to be embedded in a social matrix.

A degree of conformity is expected, and independent thinking is hardly extolled; although we do offer that it is an admirable trait, that is lip service only. People tend to fear differences, not celebrate them. Those who refuse to be like other people are considered strange or threatening and are frequently rejected. The level of mockery and animosity aimed at those who stray is often overpowering. Social pressures can be so immense that we eventually give in and become clones. After all, it's easier to go along with the crowd like human automatons without planning our own lives. Mirroring the masses, we dare not veer in thought, deed, or feeling. In this way our needs for inclusion, acceptance, and a sense of identity are guaranteed; though utter feelings of loneliness often remain. Most people never question if traditions and norms are suitable to their own lives. Somewhere in the midst of following the crowd, one's true sense of self often gets diluted and hazy.

As people develop their own sense of self, they become aware of social scripts and deeply-rooted lifestyles that are, in many ways, incompatible with their life goals. For instance, marrying before one is ready, being a stay-at-home mom when one prefers to work, or having children when one wants to wait to satisfy parental and social expectations are all acts of conformity. The purest forms of love are free choices. It's great to live in an era where strict limits on how women live their lives are no longer imposed. Women are no longer tied to a 1960s timid style of conformism; they can get married or remain single, work or stay-at-home, have children or not. Clearly, societal attitudes and traditions are not static. Dynamic influences foster acceptance of new ideas and new ways of thinking.

For more than twenty years, Mary Jane had been a good wife and mother. Nonetheless, some of her choices were based on fear without thought to the long-term effects on her self-esteem or her life.

"I did all of the right things, things I thought I should," she'd told me.

Later, Mary Jane began to see more clearly who she was and what she wanted. "I'm going to make better choices the second time around, ones that support my life and my goals," she finally concluded.

Moving in a direction of self-reliance and independence is tough. It requires backbone and an ability to tolerate opposing views. However, in the long run, you will feel more secure in being your own person.

Another Look at the Dream

This year I met two remarkable people, Anne Marie and Gene Blanchard, who made the decision to chart their own course in life and to reject the compromises of their parents' generation—a generation that wanted only to weave a safety net. They lived in a scattered woodland community, near a lake, so that they could enjoy fishing, hunting, sailing, and snowmobiling, and hear the call of the loons. It was a life that allowed them to fulfill their deepest passions. Their days were filled with that perfect blend of challenge, excitement, and enjoyment!

During my visit to scenic New Hampshire, Anne Marie, a top-selling author, told me, "I'm doing something that I'm wildly passionate about: writing suspense novels." No makeup. No wrinkles. At fifty-two years old, she was quite vibrant. And Gene, her husband, rejected the traditional search for a career and purchased a lawn and garden company, which offered him the freedom to do the things that he enjoyed. Casually clad in faded jeans and an Eddie Bauer T-shirt, Gene said, smiling, "There have been some alarming times when money was low and I had a family to care for, but we survived. We're so happy! Sometimes I wonder if we deserve such a wonderful life." Both Gene and Anne Marie were earning a living doing things that they enjoyed, not simply to pay their mortgage and children's tuition. Life for them was about growing in grace, love, and self-acceptance. "We are coming to know who we are as individuals," Gene continued.

Rather than going with the flow (seeking money, prestige, and success), Gene and Anne Marie opted to follow their personal truths and withstood forfeit. Conventional wisdom says that conformity makes life better and certainly easier for everyone. I'm not sure if that's entirely true, though from a national perspective conformity certainly has political and economic benefits. Even so, I am beginning to play my own song and to say no to the American buzz that resonates the key to a happy life. What we want for ourselves is often not what others want for us. Leading a life directed by other people often leads to nowhere. Knowing our significant strengths and using them for something that is larger than we are—in our work, our romance, our leisure, our families—is where fulfillment lies.

Looking through new eyes, I am now freeing myself from the culturally constructed web of delusions in which I was caught. I can now see how it had shaped my views of myself and others, and how its images had distorted who I am. Rather than accept cultural attitudes without question, I will now challenge a few of them. My life belongs to me, and your life to you; and no matter how tempting, our lives should not be ceded to anyone. A fulfilling life can be lived in many different ways.

Epilogue

Seeing the World
As We Are

DECEMBER 2004

The wisdom of seeing requires an adjustment of the mind, just as clear vision often requires an adjustment of the eyes. Sight can often be misleading unless we are aware of the concrete realities of what we are seeing. The realities become clearly evident only by critically examining core assumptions and beliefs that affect how we interpret our life experiences.

William James said it best: "The greatest revolution of our generation is the discovery that human beings, by changing the inner attitudes of their minds, can change the outer aspect of their lives." We each have a unique conglomeration of memories, beliefs, and expectations, which color our experiences. As a result of our selective vision, many of us have developed concepts that are not in harmony with reality. Dismantling our own thought systems is threatening. After all, our sense of self, identity, and worth are all tied to our belief systems. Without our expectations and beliefs, all that gives meaning to our lives and our interpretation of reality would fade into nothingness.

The brain is both extraordinary and weird. It weaves a story in order to feel that it is in complete control. Much as small children create fairies out of butterflies, we invent realities that exist only in our minds. We are often unaware that we are seeing a blurred view of the world and equally unaware that our real world is based on changeable assumptions. There may be another real world that is more fulfilling and happy than the one we are living. Regardless of whether our sight is accurate, we believe it is real. We rarely test our perceptions for logic and facts. Seeing a world free of subjective illusions is terrifying for most people.

Self-deception is one of the most serious harms that a person can inflict on himself/herself. It is among the most difficult hurts to discern. We can easily detect the wrongs perpetuated by others, but we are the last to see the pain that we cause to ourselves. Self-deception is like choosing to walk into a maze and later attempting to escape. Many of the negative conditions and/or experiences that besiege humankind could possibly be avoided if only we would realistically face the visible truths before us. However, instead of taking that approach to life, we tend to opt for the "pie in the sky" ideals.

After wallowing in pity for a time, I, Kay Carrington, realized that some of my own suffering had been caused not simply by the events and circumstances in my life, but by my interpretation of those events. My interpretation had been based on my beliefs. I had been accustomed to seeing life from only one perspective—one narrow and permanent perspective. For instance, I wasn't working at my ideal job, which I attributed to a lack of ambition. From this perspective, I felt like a failure. Looking at my job from another angle, I realized that I was honing my quantitative skills, which could open doors to new job opportunities.

Realizing that there were multiple ways to see my life helped me to better cope with my problems and thereby removed a huge cloud from my life. Rather than needing to fix my life, I simply needed to change my thinking so that the circumstances in my life no longer caused me grief. I felt like singing, "I was blind, but now I see."

I once dated Blake (remember him?), the Prince of Doom. Blake helped me to see some real truths about the power of beliefs. Sold on the illusion that opportunity for success was equally accessible to all, Blake believed that he was supposed to be rich and successful, live in a luxury house, and drive an $80,000 car. He also believed that people should treat him in a prescribed way and that he should never experience difficulties. Sound familiar? Apparently, he'd misinterpreted the right to pursue happiness, which offers a chance to achieve happiness—not happiness itself. These beliefs were killing him. Nothing in his life was right, and he viewed all hurdles as permanent, pervasive, and, most of all, personal. I'd made similar mistakes.

Blake was skilled at focusing on areas of his life where he repeatedly failed or received negative comments, which conjured up feelings that produced low self-esteem. See how it works? Reruns of upsetting and painful events reeled through his mind again and again, and with each showing he magnified the wrongs. Comments that threaten our self-concept are always more vivid and memorable than those that do not. Despite being comparable to other people in proficiencies and qualities, Blake considered himself mediocre. It was often difficult for him to recognize his own achievements and to accept compliments.

With Blake, everything was absolute, and the glass was always half empty. His father did not love him. A sports injury ruined his chances for playing professional football. Old girlfriends had used him and dumped him. Friends had cheated him. Mythical diseases were destroying him. His lamentations were never ending. Apparently, he was not conscious of the fact that he had a choice about his reactions to those events and that he was capable of exercising that choice. Perhaps more ruinous, Blake wore psychological blinders that narrowed his vision and kept him from turning his attention to himself.

Blake considered any form of rejection an insult that had to be repaid with compounded interest, like a mafia debt. He offered no appeal. Withholding forgiveness made him feel powerful, justified, and right. More, it was a way of safeguarding himself from further hurt. Somehow getting even seemed a poor trade-off for his enduring unhappiness. Isn't it strange that we are inclined to act in familiar and patterned ways while under stress, even when they are futile? It takes a while to develop ways of thinking and responding that contribute to our problems. It also takes time to establish new ways of thinking that make us better off.

There was more: Blake wasn't tall enough, rich enough, or popular enough. Everyone he knew was doing better than him: Bronson had a new car, Clay had purchased a rambling house, and Garrett had gotten a huge promotion. Their gain was his loss. That he'd recently landed a marketing position with a great salary was ignored; it wasn't enough for him. "I should be making more," he'd said, igniting with anger. Quite naturally, Blake's self-image was fried. There was no way it could survive his incessant bashing.

His conversations were filled with, "They won't let ..." "They should have ..." "I want ..." "You don't ..." "I'll never ..." "I can't do ..." Oh, boy! Hearing this day in and day out was enough to make my head pop off. His world was colored in black and white. Things were either good or bad. All of his mistakes were seen as permanent and fatal. There was no space for the ill-defined, muddled complexities of gray areas. Everything affected his feelings of worth. There was no reasoning with him. The thought of deviating from this constricted mindset was more than he could tolerate.

God only knows how I kept my sanity; he was such a pitiful victim. I had also been a pitiful victim, but after witnessing his performance, I would not play that role again. Blaming and projecting, Blake had sentenced himself to a lifetime of unhappiness. Other people were in charge of his feelings. Somebody else was always pushing his buttons and making him miserable. A central aspect of emotional maturity is realizing that there is no one to blame. But Blake hadn't reached that pinnacle just yet.

Blake wanted me to validate his feelings, to tell him that he had a right to be devastated and angry about things. However, the real truth was that Blake had a problem. Millions of people suffer disappointments but don't make a big deal of it. Blake's problem was his own perception. He screened out the good and allowed only the bad in. Every time he reacted bitterly to events without using his intellect, he'd give all of his power away. In doing so, he made everyone responsible for how he felt, except himself. What Blake needed was balance, to focus more on what was good in his life—the sweet as well as the bitter. I was learning to do the same.

It was apparent that Blake did not see any link between his thoughts and his feelings. Without this connection, he would likely continue living in a cycle of blame, denial, and misery. It's befuddling how many people readily accept responsibility for the projects, mortgages, families, and careers but refuse to take responsibility for their feelings. They see their feelings as an innate response to something they cannot control. The truth is, just as one can change one's behavior, one can also change one's feelings.

Well, it doesn't take a psychiatrist to see that Blake was the cause of much of his own suffering. He could vacation in Aruba at an exclusive resort and harp on the one day it rained rather than the two weeks of sunshine. With his plethora of unrealistic expectations, it is no mystery why he was miserable. Apparently he'd never really investigated any of his beliefs; he merely accepted them as fact.

There is a basic psychological law at work in all of us: What we think influences how we feel. People largely steal their own joy and make themselves anxious, depressed, self-pitying, and self-hating through their own beliefs. Blake attempted to change his negative feelings by looking outside himself for solutions. It was his own harmful thinking habits— rigid expectations, over-sensitivity to slights, and a blatant sense of entitlement—that choked the life out of his happiness vine.

Once our basic physiological needs—food, clothing, and shelter—are met, and we are in reasonably good health and feel safe, we do not need the perfect body, perfect mate, amiable co-workers, light traffic, a new baby, sunshine, a new job, a bigger house, a pay increase, power, or plaudits to be happy. What we need is control over our thoughts; how we perceive ourselves and life as a whole plays a major role in our happiness.

"Hindsight is 20/20" is often thrown out as an acerbic jibe, particularly after we've slipped up. It is true that our greatest mistakes become clear to us only when we are looking backwards and they are slowly tagging along. Looking back at my own life, I can now clearly see a ton of mistakes that can no longer be remedied. Thankfully, I can now see them from a different perspective. Seasons of suffering are often followed by seasons of insight and joy.

The pieces were starting to fit together, forming a perfect picture. Happiness is not just a goal but also a requirement for a successful and satisfying life. The problem with elevating happiness to the pinnacle of good living is that it produces guilt when we fail to reach the mark and makes unhappiness seem abnormal. During moments of struggle, pain, or gloom, we tend to feel a sense of personal failure— "Something is terribly wrong with me." To the extent that we hold fast to the expectation of ongoing happiness, we will define the *good life* as a life of absolute ease and pleasure. Oddly, in our relentless aspiration for a perfect life, everything becomes a source of stress if it doesn't go our way. So, life is disappointing for many of us because it is not all bliss.

In the full range of tragedy and suffering available, most of us only get the tip of the iceberg. Overall, we do not experience much poverty. We are not dying of starvation or suffering from plagues, and we don't live in a war zone. However, Americans don't want to experience any suffering; we'd rather explain it away or drown it out in a hurry. Everything in life is presumed to be fun and easy, which is a myth that our culture continuously promotes. In this age of prosperity, health, and wealth gospel, suffering is an aberration and clearly not a part of God's grand design.

In truth, the dance of life is not always happy; it often calls for improvisation. Life is calm, jubilant, and heartbreaking. A myriad of events occur in our lives that we cannot predict or control. To believe that we can command life and make it what we want through positive affirmations is a fairy tale. No matter how perfectly we live our lives, we cannot guarantee our own happy Hollywood endings. Believing in that illusion is damaging. If the story has an unhappy ending, we blame ourselves.

Life has shown me that there is a confidence in a person who has failed and does not feel diminished. When we are able to recognize our limitations and capabilities without succumbing to self-pity, we are stronger. If we can come to terms with those moments when we feel that life has betrayed us—during illness, divorce, old age, death, loss, or personal tragedy—we will gain a greater sense of who we are. As our fears become tolerable, we learn to roll with the punches, to appreciate the goodness of life, and to live more fully.

Perhaps the most valuable lesson I have learned is that life has an unpredictable quality to it and things don't always turn out as we'd planned. Life is simply the way it is. Happiness comes not simply from measuring up to dreams or ideas in our heads, but from finding delight in ordinary experiences—appreciating that which we may have previously overlooked. We are then free to live life, moment by moment, without trying to change it, fix it, or fast-forward it to suit us. I am slowly giving up the wish that life is any way other than it is. I am also slowly dispelling the childish fantasy that I can arrange the universe to be the way I want it to be.

With my new eyes, I am learning to take pleasure in life's offerings and small victories and to appreciate the path of my life to and from success. I no longer wait for bursts of intense pleasure to make me happy. I can now see that happiness is the accumulation of small joys and awe-inspiring moments along the way.

Improved Perception

My thoughts about God were once similar to Liz's. She believed that God bestowed blessings—wealth and other forms of success—on the highly favored. Such thoughts compounded my sorrow when my prayers were not answered. For a time, it seemed that I had lost faith in God, and maybe I had. But what I had lost for sure was an elementary understanding of God. After many of the things I once believed in proved to be false, my image of reality and my beliefs about God collided.

My spiritual life had been depleted. It seemed to have faded just as a new way of seeing life was coming into view. It was now apparent that God may not give us all that we want. He may not send us a perfect lover or an ideal spouse, heal our bodies, make us rich, give us youth, or grant us our dream job; but He will guide us through the darkness until we get to the light of day.

I surfaced from the darkness seeing life differently, with a new image of God and a new relationship with God. My illusion of total self-sufficiency had been splintered. Realizing that I could not control all aspects of my life, I was learning to depend on God more—a stretch for an independent person like me. I could not save my own life, relieve my own anxieties, or give myself courage or strength when I'd run out.

Popular religion tries to convince us that we can bribe, flatter, and manipulate God to get favors, gifts, and, most of all, our way. *If we say the right words, a magical prayer, God will give us the desires of our heart.* The often-pernicious corollary is not difficult to infer: One's level of spirituality is reflected in one's bank account or status. Such a claim appeals to our vanity, particularly when we're doing well, since it convinces us that we are somehow better, more special, or more spiritual than others.

Though many find this feel-good gospel emotionally satisfying and compelling, in some ways it is intellectually shallow. It is a way of thinking where failure is attributed to a lack of faith, which can be remedied by sowing monetary seeds into God's kingdom. Simply put, we fail because we are failures. Maybe, in my vulnerable state, I'd been partly suckered by those manmade myths presented as gospel. Now I know for sure that neither religion nor God is that simplistic.

I have since learned that if we get to know God, getting all that we want is no longer a pressing need. Not having a Santa Claus mentality about God changed my focus from what I didn't have to what I did have, and from taking things for granted to having a sense of gratitude. Gratitude produces joy. Indeed, there is more to life than working, marrying, shopping, achieving, and collecting as much of the *good life* as I can grab. What of compassion, hope, courage, forgiveness, love, and generosity? With all of this new wisdom, I am still spiritually incomplete; I am still growing.

Feeling Good

Our feelings about ourselves seem to fluctuate based on our daily experiences. One day we are soaring because we land that dream job, a good-looking guy/girl invites us to a posh affair, or we get the best score in the golf tournament and win $20,000. The next day we are wallowing in sorrow because we didn't get the position, our co-worker got a raise, our lover has rejected us, or our best friend commented that we've gained weight. These fluctuations in our self-esteem make us feel like we're spinning out of control.

Feeling good about ourselves is not a free gift; it has to be cultivated and earned. It cannot be acquired by repeating daily affirmations like "I love me" or "I'm the greatest." Just as people dream of winning the lottery or gaining other types of wealth without effort, they also dream of acquiring effortless self-esteem. Women who perceive themselves as unattractive go to the plastic surgeon with the hope of being transformed into a perfect ten. Alas, the world is full of panderers to this type of craving.

It is our responsibility to nurture and sustain our own self-esteem. No one can give us self-esteem. When we fully grasp this concept, we are truly gaining awareness. An accurate self-appraisal of our abilities—realizing that we cannot save the world or do everything perfectly—is a great esteem stabilizer. Without this knowledge, we continue to search for self-esteem where it cannot be found, based on perfection, success, attractiveness, wealth, and other yardsticks.

Dr. Albert Ellis, a cognitive therapist, offered insights on unconditional self-acceptance that helped to change my perception. Initially, his reasoning seemed a bit mind-boggling because it clashed with what the culture teaches: We are what we achieve and self-worth equals net worth. Still, his arguments were logical and convincing. According to Dr. Ellis, unconditional self-love is the right path to a healthy self-esteem. With unconditional self-love, we do not rate our total self worth; rather, we rate our qualities or performances, acknowledging that we have weaknesses and strengths. We are who we are. Having a sense of competence (intellectual, culinary, musical, scientific, athletic, etc.), confidence, significant accomplishments, and independence are also beneficial. We are happiest when we do our best and live up to our fullest potential. Feeling good about ourselves enables us to overcome difficulties and to bounce back from failures.

With a healthy self-esteem, we don't need to be the richest, prettiest, thinnest, smartest, or youngest, or wear the latest trends to feel good about ourselves. Our feelings of worth come from within, so we aren't dependent on approval from others to feel good or whole. My observations and experiences have taught me that people who feel good about themselves are more loving, less critical, more generous, more forgiving, less defensive about their mistakes, self-motivated, happier, and better able to cope with life's changes and adversities than those who do not. When we like and accept ourselves, we feel good about life in general.

I am slowly rising above the negative programming, the fears, the rejections, and the criticisms, and feeling better about myself again. Each of my experiences has helped me to appreciate the gifts of being loved and being accepted. Most of all, I am learning to be more comfortable with myself as an imperfect human being. With a clear realization that life is not promised, I am more grateful for each day that offers me another day to be fully me.

Most of our lives are mixtures of highs and lows, good and bad, success and failure. Believing that we should coast along some essential baseline of complacency would render our lives pointless. Our feelings make the experience of life worthwhile. If our lives were entirely free of all anxiety and feelings of inadequacy about our worth, we would not have any impetus to make us strive to improve, to live truthfully, or to accomplish goals that we have set. A certain amount of insecurity is necessary to spur us to work harder the next time.

Finding Happiness

Happiness is an ideal. We all want it and go after it. But even the happiest people are not happy all of the time. Perpetual happiness is not reality; it is fantasy that can only be found in magically woven Walt Disney fairy tales.

Clearly America's approach to finding happiness is off-center. Rarely do our choices produce the kind of life-changing euphoria that we hope they will. It seems that we fail to consider our incredible capacity to adapt to major life experiences and a host of other snags. More lasting happiness, the kind that endures even through the rough spots, seems to be more a function of wisdom than of either income or status.

It is equally clear that striving for wealth and material things may not always yield happiness, unless one's idea of happiness is escalating insecurities, eating disorders, addictions, unfulfilled aspirations, heart attacks, working killer hours, traffic jams, high blood pressure, forfeiting time with family and friends, depression, and so on. Faster growth, towering wages, and bigger profits have not produced happier people. The clear-cut definition of the *good life* seems to have little to do with a real and satisfying life. We can convince ourselves that we are happy for a time, but if genuine needs and desires are not met, happiness becomes an illusion.

Quite possibly, the definition of happiness is vague to us because each person's happiness is contingent upon achieving his own goals and hopes, and not some prepackaged idea. Perhaps the greatest tragedy of the American Dream is that it ignores the fact that how we feel is up to us. Without being aware of this fact, we sentence ourselves to a lifetime of endless striving, constantly preoccupied with wealth, attractiveness, and success. We feel euphoric when we succeed and deflated when we fail. Most success is short-lived and quickly replaced by a thirst for more—for bigger, better, and greater things. It leaves us struggling to find meaning in our lives.

What we filter through our lenses and accept as truth matters greatly. Though we cannot simply remove our cultural lenses, we can begin to recognize their hues and luminance—what they reveal and what they conceal. Once we are aware of the distortions, we can begin cleaning and replacing the defective lens. It is clear to me that no one can spare us from the times when we are most lacking and in need. No one can make us happy or give us health or youthful verve. No one can hand us self-worth or shield us from life's whirlwinds. Life requires that we each take risks and mourn the loss of loved ones and lost opportunities. Aging and death will come, and we will face both alone. This is life. In facing all of life's joys, sorrows, disappointments, and perfect moments instead of creating cheap illusions, we discover courage—we discover life. We equip ourselves with the determination and skills needed to escape the web of delusions.

If we are unable or unwilling to accept that how we feel is up to us, then we expend our energies trying to control the external conditions to create a sense of happiness that has always been internal. A life lived with stipulations for happiness—wealth, beauty, and success—guarantees our unhappiness. Life is far too complex for two or three essential elements to make us happy. Even the richest and most successful among us can attest to the fact that wealth alone will not make us happy, though it does offer limitless opportunities for enjoyment. Walking around the blocks of life, I can now plainly see that happiness depends not on simply achieving all of the tenets of the *good life*, but on whether we like ourselves or not at each corner of life.

Author's Reading List

Andelin, Helen. *Fascinating Womanhood*. New York: Bantam Books, 1992.

Borg, Marcus. *Meeting Jesus Again for the First Time: The Historical Jesus & the Heart of Contemporary Faith*. San Francisco: HarperSanFrancisco, 1994.

Ellis, Albert. *The Myth of Self Esteem: How Rational Emotive Behavior Therapy Can Change Your Life Forever*. New York: Prometheus Books, 2005.

Gibran, Kahlil. *The Prophet*. New York: Alfred A. Knopf, 1999.

Josipovici, Gabriel. *Touch*. New Haven: Yale University Press, 1996.

Robins L.N., Regier D.A. (Eds.) *Psychiatric Disorders in America: The Epidemiologic Catchment Area Study, 1990*. New York: The Free Press.

Veblen, Thorstein. *The Theory of the Leisure Class: An Economic Study of Institutions*. New York: Macmillan, 1902.

Wilke, Rainer Maria. *Letters to a Young Poet* (Translation by M. D. Herter Norton.) New York: W. W. Norton & Company, Inc., 1954.

978-0-595-42180-0
0-595-42180-6

Printed in the United States
94693LV00002B/310-375/A